"Eugene came around yesterday and gave me some diamond earrings as a thank you gift for you."

"What? You mean he came to your house yesterday? He's a disturbed man, Benjamin. That's all I can say. I'm going to get a restraining order."

"Andrea, he said that you wanted to be with him. He said you told him to call here and talk to me so I wouldn't get suspicious."

"That's a lie! He's lying!" Moments passed while we both looked at each other.

He broke eye contact first and clicked the tape back on. When he saw what he was looking for, he froze the frame. The person sexing Eugene in the video had a ring on her left hand just like my engagement ring.

BETWEEN TEARS

PAMELA RIDLEY

Genesis Press, Inc.

Indigo Vibe

An imprint of Genesis Press, Inc.
Publishing Company

Genesis Press, Inc.
P.O. Box 101
Columbus, MS 39703

ISBN: 1-58571-179-9
Manufactured in the United States of America

First Edition

Visit us at www.genesis-press.com
or call at 1-888-Indigo-1

DEDICATION

To my mother, and all women like her who uplift and inspire by example.

ACKNOWLEDGMENTS

The journey to publication has been a wonderful odyssey. It began when I wrote a play about the Dred Scott decision in Mrs. Littlejohn's fourth grade class, to this moment, when Angelique Justin and Genesis Press said, "Okay, we'll publish your book."

I want to thank everyone who supported me, from the people at work who were thoughtful enough to ask, "How's the book going?" to the people who provided information and feedback needed to make *Between Tears* entertaining and realistic. These people include Cheryl Darden, Turgenia Knight, Lisa Becka, Lawrence Parks, FranCina Chambers, the critique groups at Writer's Village University, and my sister, Patricia Ward.

Thanks to my sons, Jonathan and Nicholas, for humoring Mom while she does and did her writing thing.

I've appreciated the help from Clues-N-News and The Crimexcenewriter Internet lists.

Finally, a big thanks goes to Deatri King-Bey and Marylee Smithwick for being the first readers to say, "Pam, this is a good book."

PROLOGUE
The Killer

The dusk of winter sunset washed everything in gray, adding more bleakness to an already depressed neighborhood. Brick homes, majestic in their day, were dilapidated shells of what they used to be. That description fit Carolyn to a T.

Every other house on the block was boarded up. Crack users descended on them like maggots on a dead body, burrowing and feeding. Carolyn, a maggot now, would soon switch roles.

There she was, with her black jacket blowing in the wind. I watched her leave the alley and turn right, then I got out of the car, slamming the door to get her attention.

She spun around. "Who's there?"

"Carolyn," I called softly, my pulse remaining steady.

"Who's saying my name?" She scratched her nose and squinted as I emerged from the early evening shadows. "You? Am I seeing straight?"

"Are you? That might be tough to do, coming down from all that crack."

Concern could be detected by her pinched expression, despite the hazy focus of her brown eyes. "What the hell are you doing here?"

"I need to talk to you." Hope sparked in her eyes, and I knew I had her. I caressed the gun inside my coat pocket, thinking this would be easy.

Looking over my shoulder, she asked, "That your car? Let's talk in there. I'm freezing." Tugging her jacket closed, she bumped past me.

"Wait a minute."

Ignoring or not hearing me, she continued toward the car. "It's cold out here. You want me to sign something, right? Something saying I won't press charges? Thank you! God is so good. Whatever you want. I give up. Whatever it takes to see my son again, I'll do."

No, I didn't want her in the car. Needing to act quickly, I pulled the gun out of my pocket just as a souped-up hotrod thundered its way down the otherwise deserted street, distracting me. By the time it passed, Carolyn was in the passenger seat. *Damn,* I berated myself for missing an opportunity to mask the gunfire; although, why should I worry? Gunshots in this neighborhood were like toe-taps at a dance recital.

As I slid behind the steering wheel, her body odor hit me. At the same time, I noticed unkempt hair so short she'd have to roll it with a cigarette.

Her delicate little nose crinkled as she sniffed. "Popcorn. Got any left?" She snatched the bag that sat between us and began stuffing her face.

"Look at you, Carolyn. You smell, and that's the least of your problems." I imagined funk seeping from each of her orifices. If I didn't hurry up and get her out, she'd leave her smell in the car. "Seriously, what child deserves to be cursed with you for a mother?"

Jaw stalled mid-chew, her face dripped malice. "If you're not bringing my son back, fuck you. I'm outta here."

For a crack head, she moved quickly, but I caught up with her after a few strides, grabbed her arm and flung her around.

"Get your hands off me! I want my son!"

"You lost all rights to your son."

"I woke up and Roy was missing! The only thing I'd been smoking was weed." She wiped away a tear and stood taller, as if to stand her ground. "This shit's not fair, and it's gone on long enough!"

"That's exactly what I was thinking. Long enough. I'll take care of everything."

Her gaze traveled from my face to the gun in my hand. "Oh Jesus, no! What are you doing?"

The first bullet made her groan, grab her stomach and bend forward. The other bullets pierced her skull.

"No more whining or pining, Carolyn. It's done."

CHAPTER 1
Andrea

I knelt and pulled the weeds surrounding Carolyn's headstone, while my dripping tears dampened the earth. Four months ago, I'd buried my sister. The death certificate listed gunshot wounds as the cause of death, but the disappearance of her son and the drugs killed her long before the bullets did.

My grief for her and my longing for my missing nephew threatened to overwhelm me, but thankfully, returning to the church had given me some relief from years of anguish. "*Trust in the Lord with all thine heart; and lean not unto thine own understanding. In all thy ways acknowledge Him, and He shall direct thy paths.*"

Believing and reciting scripture comforted me, but didn't totally erase the heartache I lived with everyday. Was Roy safe? Who held him when he cried? Was he happy?

Carolyn's boyfriend, Benjamin Dunn, had kidnapped his son, my then ten-month-old nephew, over two years ago.

Tracking them proved to be impossible. Age-progression pictures gave us a glimpse of what Roy might look like, but Benjamin had the ability to disappear into any crowd.

Articulate and skilled, Benjamin could be a carpenter or a cabdriver, a dental hygienist or a ditch-digger. In other words, he had become as invisible or as hyper-visible as all black men in America. Neither extreme had helped our cause, and we had given up the search.

My fingers grazed across Carolyn's engraved name. As I stood to leave, the unpleasant sensation of being stared at tickled the nape of my neck. Looking over my shoulder, I glimpsed a person standing on a hill. The sun's glare prevented me from seeing clearly, even after I had put on my sunglasses. I turned back around, took two steps and that's when my heart nearly stopped. Snatching off my sunglasses, I stood frozen, convinced I was hallucinating.

Oh my God! A tall, dark-skinned, bald man and a small child headed in my direction. *Could it be? No, you're losing it, Andrea. First the weird feeling and now you're seeing things.*

"Is this hers?" the child asked, pointing toward a grave marker.

"We're close," the man said. "I'm trying to figure it out on this map they gave us."

They continued to walk toward me. Shaking my head in disbelief, I stared harder. My heartbeat that had almost ceased went into overdrive. They seemed real, but they couldn't be, could they? He'd gained some muscle and shaved his head, but it was him! I'd know Benjamin anywhere.

I wanted to stretch my arms to the little boy holding the big bunch of yellow and white daisies, Carolyn's favorite flower. Unconsciously, I must have done so because he looked up at me with his mother's eyes, and then clung closer to his father's side.

Finding my voice, I whispered, "Benjamin?"

He lowered the map, scanned the area as if unsure he'd heard his name, then his eyes found me. "Andrea?"

He's real. They're real and coming straight toward me.

"I can't believe you're here. I was going to call you tonight," Benjamin said.

Pressing my hand to my lips, I closed my eyes and uttered a silent prayer of thanks. The little boy I'd thought I'd never see again stood right in front of me. I smiled down at him through tear-blurred vision, and then looked at his father. Suddenly, feelings of gratitude faded.

"You were going to call me later?" If I could have laughed, I would have. "My God! Benjamin, do you know how ludicrous that sounds? What's so special about tonight? What about the hundreds of other nights I've been waiting, and waiting, and waiting to hear from you?"

As if stung, Benjamin stepped back from my words, and Roy stepped back with him. Realizing I had scared my nephew sent a jolt of pain to my soul. Covering my chest with both hands to calm my rapidly beating heart, I tried to recover Roy's trust by smiling again. "This is Roy."

Benjamin hesitated before repeating, "This is Roy."

"Then introduce us please."

Benjamin and I stooped to Roy's eye level. "Roy, this is your mother's sister. Say hello to your Aunt Andi."

Big, alert brown eyes and a show-stopping smile, like the one Carolyn and I often received compliments on, greeted me. Short, soft, crinkly hair that matched my long hair's texture delighted my fingers. I gently cradled him in my arms. As Carolyn used to do, he allowed me to hug him for a long time. She had known I never wanted to be the first to let go.

"Do you know where my mommy's grave is?"

His question brought on a fresh wave of tears, and I pulled him closer. Helpless to release Roy on my own, I was relieved when Benjamin gently pulled him free.

Unable to speak, I pointed to Carolyn's grave.

"These flowers are for her," Roy said as he took one flower at a time from the bunch and carefully lined them up over her grave marker. I couldn't take my eyes off him. Between tears of joy, a smile slid into place. Benjamin may be the devil incarnate, but Roy was back! Prayers were answered.

When Roy finished placing the flowers, we began walking slowly back to the parking area. The knot in my throat prevented me from speaking, and I was afraid of what I might say anyway. Tension and fear crippled my gut. Why had he come home and what would happen next?

"I'm between jobs," Benjamin said as if reading my mind. "Got laid off. Thought I would come home before we settle wherever we are going to settle next." He shifted the suddenly sleepy toddler in his arms, allowing Roy to rest his head on his shoulder. Checking my watch, it was two-thirty on a muggy afternoon in June. Roy had the right idea.

Unsure about keeping my anger in check, I said nothing. We walked on, and I couldn't help remembering the day they had left.

It had seemed like a normal day, but I guess many life-shattering events happen on otherwise normal days. A six o'clock morning call from Carolyn started it all, more than two years ago. Voice filled with panic, Carolyn had said Benjamin took Roy. Mind groggy, initially I didn't get it. I thought she was telling me Benjamin had left early to take Roy to daycare. Three explanations later, I understood they had not been home when she woke and that some of their clothes were missing.

With my car in sight, anger refused to be repressed another second. "You mean I have to thank God for a downward slope in the economy? Doesn't Roy deserve to live in a stable home with people who love him? I cannot believe—"

He shushed me with a cautionary glace at Roy. "We haven't been bouncing around the country, Andrea. I love Roy very much and, yes, thanking God each day is essential if that reflects your belief system."

Benjamin was rarely if ever ruffled, always Mr. Cool, if not Mr. Smart-ass. I'd forgotten.

"Where did you go?" I asked.

"Huntsville, Alabama, then later to Florida."

"Huntsville? That's a long way from St. Louis. What did you do in Huntsville?"

"I kept books for a buddy for a few months. Somebody came through the garage where I worked and said he'd hook me up with a job in Jacksonville. I was ready for a change. A friend and I had worked out a living arrangement to help me take care of Roy, and she came with us to Jacksonville."

Working to keep my expression neutral, I responded, "She?" Another log added to my flaming rage, yet, surprisingly a twinge of jealousy flickered. I couldn't be sure if it was on Carolyn's behalf or mine, because as long as I have known Benjamin, an unlit spark existed between us.

"Yeah, you have to meet Marissa Torres. She's been a godsend."

I'd like to, right after I wring your neck. "Can you even fathom the hell you put us through? Carolyn and I notified every missing children's resource we could find. We distributed flyers in four states, and spent thousands of dollars on a private detective. Money Carolyn could have used to go back to school, to change her life."

We'd reached the parking lot. Benjamin fastened a sleeping Roy in his car seat inside a red Acura and let the windows down. We walked a few feet away. Roy didn't need to hear us, even in his sleep.

Benjamin stuck his hands in his jeans pocket. "You know how it came down, don't you? You know she was using again?"

"One act on your part created so many ripples, Benjamin."

His thick eyebrows bunched, his jaw tightened. "Carolyn created those ripples, not me. I won't take responsibility for that. I did what needed to be done."

Breathing deep, I examined Benjamin for a minute. His strong arms and sculptured physique filled out his yellow polo shirt to perfection. My emotions were all over the place. One moment I was furious, the next tearful, and in the next moment, I felt guilty for realizing I'd missed Benjamin almost as much as I'd missed Roy. I went back to being furious. It was safer and more appropriate.

"Why didn't you come home for her funeral? That would have at least been something."

"She was dead to me that night I left. Burying her was nothing more than a formality I chose to skip."

Before I knew it, my hand flew across Benjamin's face with as much force as I could muster. "Not even out of respect for what you and Carolyn once had? Don't you care that she gave birth to your child?"

The dark look in his eyes told me he had feelings under that glib exterior. "I brought Roy here today. He knows about his mother. I try to do the right thing, not the thing that looks right."

"Oh please. Save the platitudes for another day. What does Roy know about Carolyn? He's three for God's sake. All he knows is that someone who loved him vanished from his life one day."

Despite my best efforts, my tears returned. "Why didn't you call me, Benjamin? You were content to ignore her murder? Somebody shot my sister and left her to die near an alley four months ago."

He shook his head. "I don't know."

I checked on Roy before I continued to let Benjamin have it. "What don't you know? How you kidnapped Roy and left Carolyn to suffer? Or, don't you know why her life was so insignificant to you, that a phone call acknowledging her death was too much of a burden? It would have been nice to hear from you at any point, but to not call after her death? Has your heart turned to stone, Benjamin?"

Glad to vent, I stopped when a cold finger of fear brought me up short. *If I'm too angry, will he leave again?* I didn't want that, so I softened my tact. "You and me, Benjamin, we were not exactly strangers. How could you be that heartless? You know that with Carolyn gone, Roy is the only family I have."

"I thought about you a lot, Andrea. Hurting you and Carolyn was not my intention, but nothing mattered to me as much as Roy's safety. A father's job is to take care of his family. That's what I did. After Carolyn's death, well, you're right, I should have at least phoned. I'm sorry I didn't."

That was such a meager sentiment in the light of my sister's death and the agony we both had endured. "You're sorry?"

"Sorry is all I can say. You think it was easy for me to leave everything I've ever known behind and take a baby with me? I never set out to hurt you or Carolyn. I was taking care of my son. I'd hoped you'd understand."

I wiped my eyes, blew out a huge sigh and set my sunglasses in place. His logic didn't matter now. I needed to move on to what was important. "I'd like some time with Roy. Maybe I could take him to the zoo or some place this weekend? Will you be here that long?"

"Yeah, we'll be here."

"Good." Walking away from him was like walking away from a car wreck. Physically I was okay, but I shook all over. Barely aware of the light weekday traffic, I drove in a haze, unsure where I needed to be.

Automatic pilot took over. A mapmaker could not have drawn a more direct route to the police station on Union Boulevard. I'd been there several times since Carolyn's death.

There was an outstanding warrant for Benjamin. He hadn't come home for Carolyn's funeral, but I'd make sure he was accountable to the legal system. Carolyn deserved to have that much extracted in payment, to have that much of his arrogance wiped away with handcuffs.

Inside the police station, a crusty blonde with a smoker's voice asked me my name. Her mascara-laden lashes didn't preclude blinking. I worried for a second they would. "How may I help you?"

"My name is Andrea Young." I directed my voice through the hole in the bulletproof glass.

"Yes?"

"I uh…" Unsettling thoughts gave me pause. *When Benjamin's arrested, his mother will end up taking care of Roy and she might not let me see him. If I turn Benjamin in, he'll be angry and leave again.* "Could I speak to Detective Peck?"

She picked up her phone. "James, is Winston available? Andrea Young wants to see him." She listened, then continued, "Oh, okay. Sure thing, will do." She replaced the receiver and gazed at me with a bored expression.

"Detective Peck is in the field. You can leave a message, if you like."

Unfairness and confusion gnawed at me. I needed two things: Carolyn's murder resolved and Benjamin to stay so that I could have my nephew in my life again. Would having Benjamin arrested accomplish either? No.

"Is he expected back soon?" I asked.

"No, he's not. Speaking with him and arranging to meet is the way to go."

"Okay. He's—I just wondered if there had been any developments with my sister's case? I posted reward money last month, and I haven't heard anything from him."

"Peck's the one who can help you, Hon. You can leave your home and work numbers, and I'll see that he gets them."

"Yeah, thanks." How could some people not get the idea that calling someone "Hon" was condescending? I drummed my fingers on the ledge in front of her window for a second more, but then stepped aside when someone else needed her attention. School was out for the summer, so my home and cell phone number would be the only ones he needed. I left those again.

The rest of the day loomed over me like one giant itch I couldn't reach. Seeing Benjamin and Roy made me want to scratch. I called my best friend Gloria. Talking to her always helped, but she wasn't available. I left the message that Benjamin and Roy were back.

Driving home, I wrestled with my thoughts. Despite what Detective Peck had been insinuating since the beginning, Carolyn's murder didn't feel like a random drug-related shooting to me. She was not a dope dealer, which meant she had no money for someone to steal. She took the bus wherever she went, so she wasn't car jacked. One dollar and eighty-two cents zipped in her jacket pocket said her death wasn't a mugging gone bad. I had no illusions about why Carolyn was where she was the evening she died. Because she had fallen so far, shopping crack houses for her drugs was commonplace. Yet, instinct wouldn't let me believe she was another drug statistic.

At home, I headed straight for my desk in the den, pulled out my file drawer and selected the manila folder labeled "Carolyn." Inside— her funeral program, her death certificate, and the medical examiner's report.

I kept thinking that this report held the clues, and read through the narrative for the hundredth time: Fully clothed. No signs of sexual activity. No scratches or bruises inconsistent with a drug user's lifestyle. She had crack in her system and popcorn in her stomach. Popcorn had often been a cheap meal for her, so that was nothing unusual. *Where did she get popcorn that day though? Wouldn't it digest rather quickly? Do they serve snacks in crack houses?* I sneered at the thought.

Outside the window, hummingbirds that seemed to enjoy feasting on the nectar of my morning glories caught my attention. Who had feasted on Carolyn's life? Who wanted her dead? Had Benjamin gotten tired of living in exile after more than two years? Had he murdered Carolyn so he could have sole custody of Roy?

Putting the folder aside, I dropped my face into my hands and sighed. Did I really think Benjamin killed Carolyn? No, Benjamin was a man who knew his mind, but there was goodness in him. He could be arrogant and opinionated, but he wasn't a murderer. No way. Still, he had motive and means.

I kept coming back to the report. Two gunshot wounds to her head and one to her abdomen fired at point-blank range from a .38 automatic. Whoever did it wanted Carolyn dead, not incapacitated.

CHAPTER 2
Benjamin

With stealth, I grabbed a couple of washed celery sticks from the counter, but I couldn't escape the loving assault of my mother who felt the need to hug me every time she saw me.

"I'm glad you're back!" She pulled me close, giving my clothes their third dose of her signature Chanel today. "Ben, I hate to say it, but if it took Carolyn's death to bring you home, may she rest in peace."

"Millie, if you hate to say it, you probably shouldn't." Sage advice came from my stepfather, the laconic, easygoing Mr. Elrod. He sat a few feet away from us in what used to be the living room, watching Sunday football. "Sounds like you mean you're glad Carolyn is dead, and I know you didn't mean that."

"Oh, for land's sakes, Rudy. Of course I didn't mean it that way. Benjamin and Roy are back where they belong. Let me enjoy every second of it."

I had missed her. My mom was a big woman—wide, tall, and always particular about her hair, makeup, and clothes. She was right. Carolyn's death had made it easier for me to come back because there were no custody battles to wage. But, I still had a battle; how to find out if there was any chance of getting with Andrea. That could only happen if, and when, her anger resolved, so I'd do my best to help her through it.

Not that I had any choice. There was something about the woman that held my heart captive. Two years away from her had been two years too long. I thought of her every single day, sometimes two and three times a day. The only good thing about our separation was that it crystallized my love for her. This was the same love I'd been helpless to act on as long as Carolyn was in the picture.

"It's good to be home, Mom."

It was good to be home, even though I hardly recognized the house I had grown up in. While I was away, Mr. Elrod and my mother had remodeled the entire first floor.

The living room, my mom informed me, was now part of a great room and they liked to refer to it as the sitting area. The room flowed from the entrance hall, past the sitting area into a kitchen sparkling with stainless steel appliances and one of those popular cooktop islands.

The house was old, but well-preserved, just like the part of St. Louis it was located in. There was a good-sized park within walking distance, as well as a library, a grocery store, and a few restaurants that still did steady business. Those amenities kept the neighborhood vibrant for young and old families who hadn't abandoned the city for the suburbs.

Roy, Marissa, the young woman who had been helping me with Roy, and I had an open invitation to stay here for as long as we liked. I don't know who needed the security of home more, me or Roy, but I wasn't in a hurry to go anywhere. Marissa would be going back to Florida in August to attend junior college, so staying at home to have help with Roy was the perfect solution. In addition, my bank balance could stand some fattening up. Having minimal rent to pay would do the trick.

Marissa came in from the pool with Roy. The pool was what Mr. Elrod got in exchange for the state of the art kitchen my mother wanted. Mom ran a gas station deli, and my stepfather drove around to gas stations, trouble-shooting pumps that weren't working right. They were both hard working and had saved well.

Roy's green beach towel swallowed him whole. Marissa's oversized T-shirt covered her discreetly. She wore her dark, heavy hair pinned up, but now it broke loose into tendrils that fell against her long neck. Marissa wasn't tall, but she had a lean, dancer-type body. Her skin, a café au lait color, reminded me of Carolyn's.

"Mrs. Elrod," Marissa said, "I'll be right down to help you." Every Sunday, my extended family gathered here for dinner, and there was a lot of cooking to do.

"Okay, honey. Take your time. The potatoes are boiled for the potato salad, Sharon went to the store to get the scallions, and I think those plantains are ripe enough for you to fry up your specialty."

"Thank you. Come on Roy, let's find you some dry clothes," Marissa said as she and Roy went upstairs.

Marissa Torres and I had met when I needed a babysitter who could work from three to nine. She'd answered the ad I had placed on a grocery store bulletin board in Huntsville. I'd seen her loading groceries, a job I had done in high school myself. She was polite and friendly, so I was happy to hire her. It was cool that she could teach Roy and me Spanish, with Roy being her main student.

Marissa showed up for the first two days, and then disappeared. Intending to give her a piece of my mind for leaving us in a lurch, I went looking for her. I had driven her home those first two nights, so I knew where she lived.

It took me a few minutes to convince her to come to her door and talk to me. Marissa was at loose ends. Her aunt had died in a car accident.

At fifteen, I'm sure she was scared to death of the idea of living with me, but she took a chance. The other choices included living with friends or going to a social agency for support. All were risky options for an undocumented minor.

Sharon, my sister, came back from the store. She allowed her fingers to dribble across my bald scalp on her way to the kitchen. She checked on the roast in the oven, then joined me in the sitting area as Mr. Elrod left to whisper something to my mom that made her smile and swat at him.

Sharon's kit with the extra supplies for Roy—everything from Band-Aids to sample antibiotics a doctor friend had given her, had come in handy many times. That was the first thing I told her as soon as I got back, after I complimented her on how good she looked.

Tall and slim like me, she no longer slouched. There were other changes. Her blotchy skin had vanished, her ill-fitting clothes were gone, and her bangs were no more. Now she sported one of the latest short styles. It's as if she had come into her own. Two more years of med school, and then she'd do her residency. I was proud of her.

"No new beau, huh?" I wondered if there was a new man in her life who was partly responsible for the new Sharon Dunn.

"Nope, Cecil is still in the picture. I see him when I get a break in studying and he's not out of town at some comic book convention."

"Oh yeah, Cecil Chambers." That had been going on before I left. I remembered him. He was one of those political, intellectual types. His family owned a bookstore, but comic books threw me for a loop. "Comic book convention?"

"He's got over three thousand comic books. Cataloged and numbered, nearly hermetically sealed to protect them from aging. It's a huge thing with him."

"I didn't know that. What kind does he like?"

As if to say she was helpless to figure it out, she opened her hands. "Superheroes; anybody willing and able to save the universe at a moment's notice. He loves that stuff. Claims it's the artwork that turns him on, but I know better. He's into the whole hero thing."

"Well, we men, you know, we need our outlets," I said, stretching my legs onto an ottoman with the right amount of bravado while keeping a straight face.

"Yeah, I guess. He keeps asking me to marry him, and I keep saying, maybe, after I finish school, but who knows?" Sharon put her legs up next to mine.

"Are you just not interested in marrying him, or not interested in being married period?"

"Hmm, I don't know yet. I could see spending a mundane existence with him. He'd be good to me. So, what does that mean?"

"You tell me."

"Well, I guess it means it's the institution of marriage that I don't find appealing at the moment."

We glanced at the commercial that droned on in the background. "Can I ask you something, Sharon?"

"Sure, what?"

"If memory serves me correctly, there was a boy you dated for a month your first year in college, and then Cecil. That's two guys, and you are almost twenty-six years old. What's up with that?"

"Don't discount school, Ben. It's not like I've been lying on the beach all these years."

"So …"

"So what? Do the statistics reported in *Cosmopolitan* have you worried?" She laughed. "Who said monogamy was a bad thing? Maybe it's something you want to consider one day?"

"You might have a point," I conceded, and this sent my thoughts back to Andrea. I rubbed my face, surprised it didn't still hold her handprint. It had taken everything I had not to grab her and pull her into my arms, letting my lips calm her.

"And anyway, I've finally got Cecil trained. I don't want to start over."

"Now, now," I said, laughing and wagging my finger at her.

A tired, but dry Roy climbed into his aunt's lap, resting against her as if she were a human cushion. I could tell the water and sun had taken their toll on him, as he watched the end of a half-time show.

"How about kids?" I asked Sharon. "You see yourself being someone's mother?"

"That's a hard one for me."

"Because of what happened?" The abuse is what had happened. Sharon had endured a nightmare when she was slightly older than Roy was now.

"I'd be overprotective." She wrapped her arms tighter around Roy.

"How so?"

Sharon shook her head then kissed the top of Roy's. "I'll take care of kids in other ways. Let's leave it at that."

"Okay, as long as you're happy."

"Speaking of happy, I found a shrink I like."

Sharon had been visiting psychiatrists on her own volition since she was in ninth grade, trying to pull it together. She was different now, compared to two years ago, no question about that. Maybe this new doctor was the answer she needed all these years.

Dinner had gone well. My brother, Tim, and his wife and two kids had eventually made it. Seeing them and being surrounded by family reminded me of the cost I paid by leaving.

I had kitchen detail, because the rule was if you don't help on one end, you helped on the other. We had ice cream sundaes for dessert. Thinking about how my next job should be in a dairy because I love ice cream so much, I rinsed off bowls for the dishwasher.

Someone handed me a bowl. "Well, it's about time I had some—" I didn't get to say help because the bowl slipped and broke. I know it broke because I heard it, but I couldn't take my eyes off this woman who hadn't seen the sun in years. Her paleness was bad enough, but I couldn't figure out why someone dumped strawberry syrup all over her.

"Ben, that's your Mama's Sunday bowl! You better stop killing things."

My eyes flew open. Rolling over, I almost fell out of bed. I blinked and blinked again while my heart pounded double-time in my ears. Was this Huntsville? No, Jacksonville. No, no, I was home, this was St. Louis. Sitting up, I threw off the covers to cool my sweat. *Damn.* Dreams about Carolyn were the last thing I needed.

CHAPTER 3
Andrea

I had "The Question Dream" once or twice before. It took place in Carolyn and Benjamin's apartment, when the police were questioning her the morning she called to report Roy missing. Bereft, Carolyn sat on the couch, answering endless questions, and I held her hand. In my heart, the world had come to an end, because this loss would be too big for her to survive, and I had my doubts how well I would handle it. I was used to living with Benjamin; close, but never mine, but how could either Carolyn or I stand losing Roy?

Two cops ran through their litany of questions:

"How old is your son? When was the last time you saw him? When was the last time you saw your boyfriend? Where does he work? Did you two have a fight? We'll need pictures. Is this recent?" And on and on.

As I had done in real life, I got up to make coffee, but this time my mother was in the kitchen. That didn't surprise me, even though she'd been dead for five years when this all happened.

"It's a shame it had to come to this," she said. "But there is never a good ending with drugs. If I told Carolyn that once, I told her a thousand times."

My mother, thin as a twig after the cancer treatments, had already made coffee. I opened the cupboard door. Hidden behind the cups was a bag of marijuana. That was real. I had found some in the kitchen that same morning while the police were still interviewing Carolyn. In my dream, I ignored it. In real time, after the police left, I flipped.

"But Roy's gone, Mama. I feel bad." While I poured my coffee, I looked out the kitchen window and saw Benjamin driving away with Roy. Divided loyalty squeezed the breath out of me; I stood transfixed.

I couldn't scream to Carolyn or to the police, and I couldn't say anything to Benjamin. Was he right to take Roy? Was my sister an unfit mother? A former crack addict using any kind of drug was asking for trouble. But, she was Roy's mother. She loved him, and I loved them both.

Carolyn wasn't here to fight for her right to be Roy's parent, so maybe the question was moot. Except, I was here, and I had to live with Benjamin's unilateral decision to strip Carolyn of her rights.

When I let my rational mind take over, I knew it wasn't so much what he did, but the way he had done it, absconding with Roy and all of Carolyn's options in the middle of the night.

I think his leaving created the ripples she drowned in. He thinks she would have drowned regardless.

On Monday, it was cloudy and in the low 80s. Perfect zoo weather and bearable for the first day of July in St. Louis. I hadn't been able to see Roy on the weekend after all. Mondays were less crowded at the zoo anyway. My young charge and I were having a blast, but it was time to take a lunch break. Roy reminded me he didn't eat meat, and his father had reminded me to avoid caffeine and food coloring.

"So what have you been doing all week?" I asked after we found a vacant table.

"Visiting with my daddy's mommy and 'em."

"It's a big family."

"Very big."

"Shall I cut your pizza for you, Roy?"

"No, I can bite it."

"Okay, here's your napkin."

"Thank you. There are bees."

I looked over at the trashcan he stared at, then turned to face Roy. "Yeah, they're everywhere." I glanced again to a place beyond the trashcan where I'd caught a fleeting image of someone looking in our direction. He or she was gone now. "Bees won't hurt us. Here's your straw."

"Thank you, Aunt Andi."

"You're welcome, Roy." He was so beautiful. "How is Marissa? I hear you speak fluent Spanish. Let me hear."

"She's fine. Marissa is my friend and babysitter," he said in Spanish, and then translated into English for me.

"Is she staying with you now?"

"Yep. Sí."

I licked a bit of cheese off my lip and watched Roy eat. So, Marissa the nanny was still in the picture. What else did she do for Benjamin besides take care of Roy? It was too cliché to be true, and I immediately chided myself. That wasn't Benjamin's character—it wasn't the Benjamin I'd known through the years, but, of course, he could have changed.

"Roy?"

"Yes, Aunt Andi?"

"Elephants or tigers next?"

"Tigers!"

Roy and I had enjoyed the zoo immensely. It reminded me of all the time I'd missed being part of his life, and it whetted my appetite for more days with him. In that vein, I invited my reincarnated family to my place for dinner later in the week.

Benjamin's actions had probably contributed to Carolyn's downfall, but he didn't actually pull the trigger. I was convinced of that.

"This house is great; love the fireplace and the hardwood floors." Benjamin looked around with an appreciative smile.

"Thank you." I loved the oak floors and the white stucco fireplace, too. I loved everything about my two-bedroom, seventy-year-old, Spanish style house that I had purchased a couple of months ago. I found myself standing further away from Benjamin than I needed to; holding Roy's hand more than he wanted me to, hoping my pounding heartbeat was my secret. Making believe this was a regular family meal, disregarding that Carolyn never got to see this house, or that the man who had cut her heart out was here now with her son, was difficult. When Benjamin's and my eyes locked, a tremor coursed through me. I knew that if I followed my heart, the real difficulty was just beginning.

Investigating the house further, Benjamin said, "Spanish architecture is cool with the arched windows and doorways. This covered patio is a nice touch, too. Can we eat out here tonight?"

"I like eating outside," Roy said.

"Sure we can. I hadn't planned on it, but that's a good idea." I had to scramble to come up with something vegetarian to serve. Good old black-eyed peas and rice didn't let me down. I'm not the best cook in the world to start with. I planned to check the Internet for vegetarian recipes next time. If I wanted to invite them over and expected them to come, I'd have to cook what they ate. But they weren't vegetarians before they left—before Benjamin had taken them away. I sighed at another adjustment I was forced to make on Benjamin's account.

By 7:30, Roy no longer enthusiastically orchestrated the conversations between the additions to his stash of action figures I had bought him. He was falling asleep on the blue area rug in my den, leaving me alone to guide the five-inch heroes in their mission to stamp out evil.

After making sure Roy was comfortable on the daybed, we left the guestroom door ajar. Benjamin looked at me as if I were supposed to say something. There were some things on my mind, but I hadn't wanted to bring up topics that Roy didn't need to hear discussed. "You want another beer?"

He washed the few dishes there were, while Anita Baker's jazzy voice filled in the quiet spaces. I enjoyed Benjamin's company. My anger at him had distracted me from these feelings. Now that the anger was dissipating, I was in trouble.

I hadn't had a date in seven months, and no serious relationship since Eugene and I had broken up.

Eugene Sherwood was a history teacher at the high school where I taught English. When Benjamin took Roy, my world turned upside down, and I didn't have time for Eugene or anyone else.

I looked up from wiping off place mats to see Benjamin watching me. I smiled.

"Be right back. I got something for you," he said. Moments later, Benjamin produced a nicely wrapped, flat package.

I thanked him. I thought about giving him a kiss to show my gratitude, but I wasn't sure what the implications might be. I unwrapped a beautifully framed five by seven picture of Roy and me.

"Oh, this is great!" Suddenly confused, I frowned. "But, this is Roy and me at the zoo. Who took this?"

"I did."

"I don't get it."

"I was there. I needed to make sure the zoo was where you two were really going."

"What? I thought I saw someone watching us. You know, I wasn't the one who snatched him in the middle of the night when he was a baby. I can be trusted to take my own nephew to the zoo!"

He flashed open palms. "Still, I had to be sure."

I brushed past him into the living room.

"Andrea, I have strong protective instincts," he said, following me. "I'm like that with people I love."

"Yeah, well tell me something I don't know." I rearranged my mantel display a few times, looking for the best home for my new picture. I put it next to the one of Carolyn holding Roy while they both slept in a rocking chair. Sensing Benjamin right behind me, I whispered, "You should go. You don't know me at all if you think I would hurt Roy."

"Speaking of that, I was at the police station a few days ago."

I turned to face him. "Really?"

"Andrea, you should know I had called a lawyer and arranged to turn myself in. Thank God Roy was with Sharon when the police came for me."

"Oh," I gasped, my hand flying to my throat. "I didn't think about that."

"You should have thought about that before you called the police."

"I didn't tell the police. I was going to, but changed my mind."

"Well, someone called before my lawyer had a chance to set things up."

Gloria, I thought. Gloria must have turned Benjamin in. She was furious with him, and although she'd done what I'd decided against doing, I felt a need to defend her.

"Why would you expect Carolyn and everyone who loved her to be the only ones forced to deal with consequences?" Frustrated and angry, I pushed back my hair. "I don't want Roy to suffer any more than he has already because of this, so I didn't call the police, Benjamin."

"Whatever." He threw his hands up to say he didn't want to argue the point. "And Roy hasn't suffered."

"Yes, he has. You robbed him of years of love he was entitled to receive from his mother and me; love that can't be replaced."

He didn't respond verbally, but his distressed look spoke for him.

"Seeing his father hauled off in a police car would have been traumatizing. I'm glad Roy didn't see that," I said. What happened at the police station?"

"They arrested me on the outstanding warrant—for not showing up at Roy's custody hearing—and they wanted to know my whereabouts on the night Carolyn died. What did you think would happen if you had called?"

"I'm not sure. I was afraid that you would get mad and take Roy away again. I don't want Roy separated from the only parent he knows—I wouldn't do that to him—but I would like to see him grow up, too."

The couch beckoned me. Sighing, I sat and Benjamin sat next to me. "Where were you the night she died?"

"At work, apparently. It was a telemarketing job. The police called the guy I worked for in Florida, and he vouched that I was at work that day and the day following. That's as far as they took it. I guess they're satisfied."

"What happened with the warrant?"

"I have a court date in two weeks. My lawyer said the court's main concern will be why I didn't seek custody through the legal system."

"Could it have been handled differently, more fairly for Carolyn? That's been my whole issue, Benjamin." I watched him closely, wanting to peer into his heart for the answer I had always wanted.

He looked at his hands, folded in front of him, his elbows resting on his knees. "Carolyn was a drug addict, doing what drug addicts do. You know her history, as well as I do. She got hooked in college, which she didn't mention, by the way, when we first met. A year later, she started using crack. I called it off as soon as that reality hit home, but then she told me she was pregnant."

"Yeah, she didn't want to check into a rehab program. I remember her saying there was nothing special about being locked up with hard-ass warden types that would help her kick her habit any faster. She begged you to let her move in because my efficiency apartment was too small. She promised to go cold turkey, and she did."

There was a moment, after they had broken up and before Carolyn told me she was pregnant, that I'd wondered about the possibilities for Benjamin and me, despite people's eagerness to cast aspersions. Yet, I was drawn to him, no matter how much I fought it, but would have never placed myself between him and my sister. And, of course, the baby took precedence. I told myself it was easy to give up what I'd never had, but still there'd been some difficult moments, especially when I ended up practically living with the two of them that week of hell.

"The three of us got through it," Benjamin said.

We quieted a minute, lost in our remembrances. That had been three days of hell on earth, with Carolyn in constant motion, examining every speck of white she could find, in case it was a grain of something she could get high on. Determination and humor had seen us through it.

"Carolyn and I, we knew we were together because of Roy, but we were making it work. Then, when Roy was seven or eight months old, she started with the weed again and had the nerve to tell me she could handle it."

"Around that time you found the gym bag with the pipe and vial?"

"Yes. What was I supposed to do then? Believe it or not, I like stability. I'm not built for that up and down roller coaster ride Carolyn thought she could take me on. And, even if I were, my father was a heroin addict, Andrea. I've seen what happens. Drugs take over your life. You don't care about anything, not even your own children. Carolyn was out of chances as far as I was concerned. Sister loyalty has you looking at it differently, but I wasn't going to allow her to raise Roy another minute."

Benjamin absentmindedly lined up the magazines on my coffee table. "I had to leave, and I had to leave then. I couldn't wait for the court system to see things my way. I may have to explain my family history, fill the court in on what happened with Sharon and my father, but I think any decision made will be in my favor."

"I think the court will agree with you. Benjamin, how did Carolyn's gym bag get in the Dumpster?"

He looked up at me. "What? Oh, I threw it away. It's illegal to have a pipe like that in your possession, not to mention just plain stupid because of what crack can do to you. Why?"

"The police found it in the trash. Carolyn swore on Roy's life that she wasn't using crack again and that she didn't know where that stuff had come from. It was always strange to me that she would deny it."

"What else would she do, Andrea? It was in her gym bag. How else would it get there? Drug addicts are liars by default."

Tugging on his earlobe, he said, "I want stability. That's the main reason I came back." He rubbed his palms along his jeans as he stood. "So listen, Roy's learning how to roller-skate. Maybe he could practice here tomorrow if you feel like hanging out with him again."

I stood, a smile curling at my lips. I didn't relish going to his mother's home, but I would to pick up Roy.

"I can drop him off after breakfast," he volunteered, "and he can spend the day, if that's all right?"

"Perfect," I said, thankful he was making it easy for me.

"No problem. Thanks for a lovely dinner and a good conversation. We got a lot off our chests, but we never had a problem communicating, did we?" Benjamin took my hand and held it to his lips for a long moment. His eyes found mine, and we held our gaze until I had to turn away. When I wanted to pull my hand free, he wouldn't let go immediately. Braving a look at him again, I saw the yearning I'd seen years before in his eyes. Quickly, I lowered my lashes. I didn't want him to see the yearning in mine.

CHAPTER 4
Andrea

The air was heavy with humidity even this early in the morning, but that couldn't dampen my spirits. I looked forward to seeing Roy today and, if I were honest with myself, to seeing Benjamin. By seven, I had cleaned the house from top to bottom and had even watered the outside plants. I lingered a moment over the yellow daisies in planters on either side of my front door. I would always plant those wherever I lived in memory of Carolyn. For a quick second, I guiltily relived the flush of warmth Benjamin's kiss on the hand had set into motion.

By eight, the roughness of my facecloth gliding over my breasts in the shower reminded me of when I had watched Benjamin help Carolyn nurse. She'd been home a couple of days after giving birth to Roy and her milk, as opposed to the early milk—the colostrum, hadn't come in yet.

I knocked on their front door, but when they didn't answer, I tried the door and it was unlocked. I called out once and they didn't answer, so I made my way to the extra bedroom, which was now their nursery. I happened to see Benjamin kneeling before Carolyn. I wanted to turn away to give them their privacy, but I was mesmerized. He alternately suckled on the rock-hard fullness of both breasts, no doubt to give her some relief.

I pushed that memory away, but it kept coming back. At the time, I had wanted to feel his lips touching me like they touched her. Standing under the pinging water, I realized I could probably arrange that now. *How unwise would that be? After all these years and all this heartache, did I seriously think there was something good could happen between us? And what about church and my decision to remain celibate?*

Before, giving into carnal desires was just the logical conclusion to dating. That's not what I wanted anymore. *What would Benjamin think about this?*

Stepping out of the shower and drying myself off, I pondered more.

What would people think? Gloria would never speak to me again. Ignoring the comments from people at church would be a challenge, and his mother. Good Lord, She'd be fit to be tied. She never liked Carolyn, and I was not one of her favorite people. And what about my guilt? Had I rationalized it all away by now, or would it vex me my whole life, like a thorn on a beautiful rose?

Benjamin dropped off Roy. We both remarked how it was almost like old times; the summer after Roy's birth, I had baby-sat him. I asked Roy if he remembered that far back, as I accepted the car seat from Benjamin in case we went somewhere. He smiled and said no.

He was such a little person now. I loved how his brain worked. I asked him if he wanted to go swimming after roller-skating. He said we could, or we could pick something else to do since he had a swimming pool at his grandmother's house. Well, he didn't say it exactly like that, but he made his point.

Roy and I roller-skated for a couple of hours, and then we went shopping for a Big Wheels bike. I rode behind him on my own bike, chasing him around the block. By noon, we'd had enough sun, and after lunch, we watched *The Little Mermaid* until nap time overtook us.

The doorbell ringing woke me. It was four already and Benjamin had come for his son.

"Hi." I pushed the screen door open for him to come inside.

"Guess what?" he said.

"What?"

"I got a job today."

"Great, Benjamin! That was fast." And encouraging. That meant he and Roy would stay in St. Louis a while, hopefully forever.

"Where?"

"Street Maintenance. Uncle Fred hooked me up. You know Uncle Fred?"

"No, I don't think I do. You have a big family. I never knew them well enough to keep everyone apart."

"He's at the house a lot. My mom's brother."

"Oh, okay."

I gestured for him to have a seat in the living room. His cheeks puffed as he blew out a silent whistle. "You know, I had a plan for my life. I was taking classes part-time at the University of Missouri and working as a checker at Schnuck's Grocery store before Carolyn told me she was pregnant."

"I remember." I sat in the armchair to the left of the couch.

"My plan was to get a business degree and redevelop at least one block of Martin Luther King Boulevard personally. It's four years later, and I still don't have my degree, but I'm learning how to pave streets."

"You know how the expression goes. Life is what happens while you're making other plans." Carolyn never expected him to steal her son from her, or die on some crappy street.

"Yeah, you're right." He picked up an embroidered throw pillow and set it in his lap. "Not that I'm giving up on any of my goals, I'd never do that, but life is more challenging than it was before."

I nodded. "Things did get complicated along the way. It will work out, though. I feel sure about that."

"I like your optimism, Andrea."

"Life would get pretty dismal without it. You have to think God has purpose, or I do anyway. Let me wake up Roy. He's been sleeping since two."

"I'll get him," Benjamin volunteered. "He's in the den again?"

"No, in my bedroom this time."

I'd been in Carolyn's and his bedroom before, but this was a first time for him in mine. What if he didn't like what he saw? Why did I care? I crossed my arms and waited in the doorway. He looked around at the dark rose walls and the black and gold rug underneath my bed.

"I like this room. I remember that Tiffany lamp." He pointed at the lamp. "I got that for Carolyn's Christmas present one year." His gaze floated unhurriedly, then darted back to things that caught his eye.

Carolyn's art, the Tiffany lamp, and a glider Carolyn had inherited from my mother were the items of hers I'd kept. My mother's hatboxes filled with vintage hats she'd inherited from her mother were in my closet. That's all I'd kept of my mother's, except her urn. She'd wanted to be cremated to save Carolyn and me burial costs.

"Your bed is unique."

The bronze wrought iron head and footboard had just enough curls and curves to feel romantic, but not enough to get dizzy looking at them. Suddenly, Benjamin was sitting on the bed, smoothing a hand over his naked, rock-hard, pecs, but then I blinked and reality returned. The ensuing blush raced up my cheeks. I covered them with my hands, and cleared my throat. "Thanks. It's not that unique, just JC Penney."

Benjamin tilted his head toward Carolyn's sketches. "What are those? Is that Carolyn's work?"

I took both sketches from the shelf and held them. One was a living room drawn in charcoal and bold colors, and the other one depicted a sun porch overlooking a body of water, with a breeze fluttering through sheers at the windows.

"Yeah. We worked on these together. These were ideas for Eugene's house. You remember Eugene?"

"Yeah, I do. Does he still come around?"

"No. Well, he and his mother came to Carolyn's funeral, and Mrs. Sherwood stayed a long time after most people had paid their last respects and left that day. She's a nice lady." I replaced the drawings, feeling the ache of Carolyn's loss all over again and with it, the guilt of thinking about Benjamin naked from the waist up. As far as I knew, Carolyn never suspected once that Benjamin and I had—*had what? Wanted to be more than potential in-laws?*

Maybe I was making too big a deal of it. Carolyn had never said she loved Benjamin and the subject of marriage had never come up. If it had, she never mentioned it to me. Roy was who she had loved, yet, she and

Benjamin had been living together when he took Roy, trying to make to it work for Roy's sake. Oh, the more I thought, the more confused I got.

He carried Roy into the bathroom. "Time to wake up. Let's wash your face, buddy." When they came out he said, "So, Andrea, you feel like celebrating with us?"

Not really in the mood, I found something interesting to stare at on the floor. "No, you guys go on."

"Oh, come on. You have to eat. We'd love the company."

"Come on, Aunt Andi," Roy said in his best pleading voice.

Roy was another reminder of Carolyn, but a wonderful one. I didn't want them to see me cry, so I sniffed and turned away. "Okay, give me a second."

We ate at a Mexican restaurant. I half-listened while Roy and Benjamin shared how their days had gone. Watching them interact, seeing Roy rub the side of his nose while his father told him something, noting how Benjamin effortlessly anticipated his son's needs, caught my attention more than the conversation. I grinned. Being in their presence delighted me. *What if Roy had stayed here and Carolyn really had started using again,* I wondered. *If Benjamin had left them to fend on their own, would Roy still have his ready smile? Would he be this curious, outgoing, and well-mannered, or would he have learned shut up and not speak unless spoken to and be a behavior problem just to gain any kind of attention?*

As we left the restaurant, we noticed a Ferris wheel in the distance. Carnivals popped up out of nowhere these days, but this one was probably a hold over from the Fourth of July.

The Ferris wheel was Carolyn's second favorite ride, after the roller coaster. A roller coaster was the perfect symbol for her life. Benjamin had been right about that. Her life had been riddled with so many ups and downs.

"You want to go see if they have any rides that Roy might enjoy?" Benjamin suggested.

"Yeah, that would be fun."

"Yeah, that would be fun, Dad," Roy chimed in.

We found the kiddie section. It contained a train, some boats in water, and an airplane. Each traveled in its own small orbit.

We got in line for the airplane ride. "Is this how you and Roy spent most of your evenings when you were away?"

"Not every night, but we had our fun."

"Roy had already begun to talk a little before you left, but when did he start to walk?"

"He was a year old, shortly after his birthday. Man, oh man. I could write a book about child-proofing the home. Roy was into everything."

"I'll bet he was." I sighed. Carolyn didn't get to see any of that.

"He still is. You have to keep an eye on him and make sure he can't get into anything dangerous."

"I know. I'm careful."

"Good."

Before long, I said good night with a hug from Roy and a wave from Benjamin. He called me, just as I had settled into bed with a J. California Cooper novel. "I'm sorry if I'm out of line, but I'm thinking about you all the time."

He and I laughed at his poetic hello. A school-girl giggle almost escaped my lips, before I pressed my hand to them and came to my senses. Here he was, putting his cards on the table, and I had to admire that, even though it frightened and thrilled me at the same time. The seed of anxiety that had been planted years ago in case this moment ever came to fruition now blossomed, big time. I walked with the phone, rubbing my stomach, trying to soothe the fluttering. Following suit I said, "How can you be out of line by thinking about me all the time?"

"Because thoughts create action, and I want to hold you in a way that will make us both forget that I was almost your brother-in-law."

He paused, but when I didn't say anything, because I couldn't, he kept on going.

"I know how much you loved Carolyn. I know you don't want to do anything to disrespect her memory."

I remained speechless.

"I don't know what to do about my thoughts. What do you suggest I do, Andrea?"

Shaking my head, I fingered the twirls of the phone cord. *What should he do?* He'd often asked me that when he was trying to navigate his tumultuous relationship with Carolyn. Now he wanted my help to navigate a relationship with me. The thought excited and repulsed me at the same time. He had been Carolyn's boyfriend for a long time. Was this the right time to move forward in our relationship? A forlorn sound that might pass as laughter bubbled from my mouth. "I don't know what you should do, Benjamin. This is awkward. You've only been back a couple of weeks, and you know what people are going to think."

"I'm sorry. I don't know why I'm trying to rush things. I take that back. I do know why. There's been too much wasted time already."

I couldn't argue with the profundity of that statement. Life is short. My mother and Carolyn's death at their young ages had taught me that. I couldn't help the way I felt about him, but were these feelings strong enough to justify trying to take this to the next level? "Tomorrow is your first day at work. You need to get your rest tonight."

He chuckled, probably at my need to get him off the phone. "Tell you what, I'll focus on getting off to a good start at work and plan on seeing you next Thursday. Would that be okay?"

"Next Thursday? Oh, okay. I'll look forward to it."

"Okay, Good night, Andrea.

"Good night, Benjamin."

"Oh, Andrea, wait a sec. You have my mom's number, right?"

"Yes, I have it." I had called Mrs. Elrod once a week to see if she had any news to share about where or how Roy and Benjamin were. Sometimes she'd answer me politely. Other times, she told her husband to tell me she hadn't heard anything. Most of the time, I think she let her caller ID do the screening. So yeah, I definitely had her number.

I also had a week's reprieve. The attraction I always felt for Benjamin was still there. He had made it clear he felt the same about me, but I had a week to think about it, a week to decide what, if anything, to do.

Despite Carolyn's suffering, in my heart I knew I wanted to be close to him; I wanted his arms around me. When he took Roy, he was being the best father he knew how to be, and I had to give him credit for that. Since meeting Benjamin, I had to work at remembering he wasn't mine, but now he could be.

CHAPTER 5
Andrea

That feeling was back. That feeling I had in the cemetery the day Benjamin and Roy showed up. Someone was watching me. Careful to have my keys in hand, I hurried to my car, scanning Dillard's parking lot left and right.

"Hey girl, thought that was you. What's up? What's this I'm hearing about you and Benjamin Dunn?"

"Ouch!" I banged my head on the open trunk when I jumped. I was on edge, and Gloria had scared me.

As I finished loading my purchases, I braced myself for what I was in for. We hadn't even exchanged hugs yet, and she was already knee-deep in my business. Gloria had an opinion about everything, and she had loved Carolyn. That's why she had taken it upon herself to let Michael, her brother who was a police officer, know that Benjamin was back. I couldn't be mad at her about that, it's just with my feelings developing more and more everyday for Benjamin, I didn't want to hear Gloria's rundown of why I was out of my mind for even considering it.

"Look at you, you're looking good," I told her. It was the truth, and a viable stall tactic. Her red-orange hair was styled in a short, relaxed cut that worked on her. Gloria wore at least three earrings in each ear, and these days, a ring on just about every one of her weekly manicured fingers. This week she was sporting a color that had to be Rambunctious Red. Plus, no matter how much pizza she ate, and she could put it away with the best of them, she remained a size eight. Fourteens had always fit me comfortably, but I'd be twice her size in a minute. I blamed the added weight on the stress of the past two-and-a-half years. Right now, the zipper on my jeans resisted all kinds of pressure to just give up the fight and come undone.

She popped her gum as we embraced. "You know I got to know about you and Benjamin," she explained, smelling like Juicy Fruit. "Mama even asked me what I knew, and I had to tell her nothing because my sister friend, Andi, has been too preoccupied to pick up a phone. Start talking."

I closed the trunk. "Well, he's been back in town almost three weeks now. He brought Roy home, and they are living with his mother."

"I know that much. After all this time, he just waltzes back as if nothing happened? Like everybody and his uncle wasn't out looking for his sorry ass? How's the baby. How's Roy?"

"Oh Gloria, Roy's fantastic." I couldn't stop my voice from oozing praise. "Benjamin has done a terrific job with him. You have to see him."

"Personally, I hope he's the spitting image of Carolyn. That would serve his ass right. I hear there's some Chiquita chick in the picture? A little tit-for-tat is what I've been hearing."

"There is a friend that has been helping. Her name is Marissa Torres."

Gloria adjusted her designer purse strap on her shoulder and folded her arms across her chest. "They're playing house, or what?"

"Or what," I said." You want to get a cup of—"

"That's what he told you?"

"Yep."

"And you believe him?"

I shrugged. "Yeah, I do."

"So, suddenly you're feelin' him? I don't get it."

"Gloria, are you still working for the phone company?"

"Yeah, why?"

"Because I feel like I'm being interviewed for an article in the *Post,* that's why."

Face creased, her arms fell. "Oh, it's like that." She closed the space between us. "I'd rather hear about this now and not when you come crying to me when this asshole pulls some more crap. Just trying to be a friend, but hey, forget it." Gloria threw up her hands as if willing to let go of the matter. "I got plenty of shopping to do."

She walked off and left me there, twisting my mouth, debating if I wanted to apologize to her or not. Gloria definitely had a flair for the dramatic, but I knew she wouldn't stay mad at me long, because we were close. I had cried myself to sleep many a night on her couch after Carolyn's death.

As I put on my sunglasses, I noticed a black SUV pulling out at the end of my row, and a dark blue Lincoln Towncar with tinted windows slowly pull up beside Gloria. I could hear the greeting sounds long-lost friends made. Now it was my turn to be nosy. I stretched my neck as far as it would go in their direction.

"Andi!" Gloria called to me. "Girl, come and see who this is. You're not going to believe it."

Good, because I couldn't imagine who it was. As I approached, the window on the passenger side silently lowered. Barry Jordan sat behind the wheel. I hadn't seen BJ since Carolyn's funeral. The sight of him, mixed with the smell of all that luxurious leather made me grin.

"BJ!"

"Andi, good Lord! You look rejuvenated. Get in here, girl. Come on Gloria and tell me where you're getting this awesome jewelry." I clicked my remote to lock my Cougar and got in his front seat. Gloria sat behind him.

His voice nearly clapped with glee as he raised the windows. "I'm just so happy to see you both!"

I took off my sunglasses to get a good look at him. BJ was still as fine as the day is long: tall, thin, clean-shaven with tan-colored skin. His hair was cut as low as it could be cut, and he had dimples for days when he smiled. Just puppy-dog cute, always was.

"I go to Jeff City for a few months, come back to find out that you have moved Andi, and I can't get in touch with anybody! What's up with that?" He slapped a playful hand on my thigh. "Don't worry, I didn't take it personally. But, speaking of moving, I'm gonna show you my new place. It's much nicer than Ghetto Heights, ladies. Wait until you see."

When we were growing up, BJ lived between Gloria and me on a street called Garden Haven, or Ghetto Heights as we affectionately referred to it.

"BJ, this car is something else," Gloria said. "This backseat is just about as big as my whole kitchen."

"It's sweet, isn't it? I've eaten back there a time or two myself."

"Ewww! Why spoil it for a sister, BJ? Did I need to know that?" Gloria asked.

"Ha! My bad. I remember you used to like me to share all the details. That must have changed."

"No, it hasn't, trust me." I hoped my look told him Gloria still preferred to be fully informed. "What else have you been up to? This is a step up from that used Saturn with the dented fender."

He laughed. "Well, you are looking at a kept man. I met Mr. Works-for-the-Governor's-Office, and since then I'm on voluntary lockdown—for the price of this car, my condo, and a healthy monthly allowance, I should mention."

"That's what I need," said Gloria, "a sponsor. They can come get this true love crap as far as I'm concerned and stop lying to the masses."

"That's right. It's all about bargaining and trade-offs," BJ agreed.

"Um hmm. Tit-for-tat, there's a lot of that going around these days," Gloria added, for my benefit I was sure.

BJ's condo was located in the renovated heart of downtown. It was early evening, and inside the garage was brighter than it was outside, a great security feature.

The living room window featured a postcard view of the Gateway Arch on the riverfront. The 630-foot monument glistened in the sun.

"Okay, now see, this is living," Gloria said, giving herself a quick tour. "And all you have to do is see him—what, twice a week? I want your job BJ, I swear I do."

"Everybody wants my job, but everybody can't do it like I do, okay sugar? What can I say?"

"How about you just pour the wine," Gloria suggested.

BJ put three glasses and a chilled bottle of wine on a tray. We settled comfortably on his blue-green leather sectional. Even though it was the middle of August, he clicked on the gas fireplace. We wanted to be consumers of every perk available, and the air conditioner was running full blast. Content to be in each other's company, we sipped wine.

"What about you, Andi? You want my job, too?"

"No thanks, I've got a job."

"She's got a man, too, BJ. A younger one at that. Ask her about Ben Dunn."

"Wait, is he working with the street crews?" BJ sat his wine down in his excitement. "I saw this fine brother—totally chiseled—paving that street two blocks over. I said to myself, that looks like Benjamin Dunn, with his Hershey-chocolate self, bald head shining in the sun, but I thought I was delirious. Seeing all those hot, sweaty men at the same time can have that effect."

Gloria and I laughed at BJ's enthusiastic assessment.

"That's him," I said. "His uncle got him the job."

"What's up? Last time we talked, you were vowing to hand him his manhood. Are you telling me you found a better place to put it?" BJ asked.

I didn't miss BJ's humor, but I took a long swallow of wine, thinking it might help me articulate my thoughts. "I like Benjamin. I have always respected him, even when I hated him. True, he's three years younger than me, but he is a strong man, and a strong, involved father. Remember? We were glad about that because we knew Carolyn sometimes … We knew that she didn't have a lot of inner strength and sometimes she'd get …"

"Fucked up?" BJ supplied the words he thought I wanted.

"I was going to say lost."

"Yeah," Gloria said, "but everybody knew that as far as Carolyn was concerned, Roy was the reason she was put on this earth. She surprised everybody by nursing Roy well into the fall, and we all know how much Carolyn loved how she looked in those halter tops. Remember when my girl whipped out that breast at Mimi's wedding reception and Miss Prim and Proper at the next table launched into her eyebrow exercise program?"

I did recall. Carolyn had adjusted the blanket so nothing was revealed. Looking directly at the woman, she had loudly explained that she fed Roy with such style, grace and discretion that only the prudes noticed and only the backwards protested.

Reminiscing about Carolyn's devotion to Roy made us all smile for a few seconds, and then the atmosphere became serious again.

"Ben had to know it would kill Carolyn to not know where her baby was," Gloria pointed out. "And I will go to my grave believing that Carolyn was not sucking the pipe again. She was my girl; she was your sister. How is it she could be doing crack again and both of us not have a clue? Smoking a little pot—yes, but was that a reason to take her child from her the way he did?"

"I'm not defending the way Benjamin left, but if he really did find the bag with the drug stuff in it, there's no defense for Carolyn either. In that case, he was justified. That would mean she was a stone crack addict, and no child deserves that."

Gloria shook her head like she was sorry for me. "Here you are, prepared to forgive Benjamin for causing your twenty-five-year-old sister's death. Why? Because he's managed to raise her son well with the help of Chiquita, the Latin Lover?"

Rolling my eyes at her, I said, "Nothing is black and white, Gloria. If everything in life was that simple, the world would be a happier place."

"Hmph. Don't look at me like I just slapped you either, Andi. Not that the thought hasn't crossed my mind. I want you to make sure you know what you are doing if you are considering getting involved with this man."

"This is some heavy shit," BJ commented, as he reached for the small wooden box on his coffee table. "I got hold of some excellent smoke the other day." He began twisting the weed inside rice paper without missing a beat. "Was Ben shackin' up with somebody the whole time he was gone?"

"From what Ben told me, Marissa was scared and about to become homeless. She was fifteen and her aunt died. She moved in—which is different from shackin' up."

Gloria accepted the joint and inhaled deeply, held it, and then let the words flow out on her exhale in a trail of smoke, "And, of course, he's never touched her."

"Well, nowadays, you just can't get with anything off the street like you could in the old days, no matter how many Trojans you plan on using," BJ said with unmistakable longing in his voice.

"Living in the same house going on three years, with a teenage Jennifer Lopez wannabe, and all he wants is a nanny? Somebody give me a break," Gloria said.

"Gloria, how do you know what she looks like? Have you seen her?" BJ asked.

"I've seen her. She's is a J Lo wanna-be, maybe even cuter," I admitted.

"Girl, he probably found a real woman to handle his needs, that's all," BJ said. "Although, waking up to J Lo every morning might even make me want to broaden my horizons." BJ shifted in his seat and crossed his legs. "But, back to Mr. Dunn. He looks like he can handle his business; can he?"

I feigned a shocked look. "BJ!"

"Oh, now you're going to pretend to be all shy. She's going to be all shy now, Gloria. We used to talk about Allen and what was his name with the size thirteen shoe? Eugene? You weren't shy then! And, as I recall, Eugene thought you hung the moon, so I know you haven't forgotten about him."

"Oh, shush." I stopped him by showing him the hand. BJ, you're not going to make me blush, so stop trying. "I've thought about Benjamin a lot since he's been back, and I want to move forward in our relationship, but I need to think clearly. Gloria is right about that."

"It's all that time unaccounted for, that's the problem. You have no way of knowing what he has been doing," BJ said. "Ben is buff. You have to workout an hour a day minimum to stay in that good of a shape. You sure he wasn't working on some chain gang somewhere? I hear those are still going strong in places like Mississippi."

"No, I don't think so. I can tell by watching him with Roy that they have been together. Are you trying to live out some of your prison fantasies at my expense?" I teased. "Besides, he has an alibi."

"That's right, but you're talking about the actual murder, and I'm talking about the murder of her spirit, her zest, her joy for life," Gloria said. "I don't believe he was justified in doing what he did and never will. But, go ahead. Throw common sense and intuition right out the window," Gloria said. "If loyalty to your sister's memory is not an issue, and I don't know why in the world it wouldn't be, then just tell me this. How will you be able to trust him? If it's in his nature to just get up and go, how do you know he won't do it again? I mean, what if you decide to become a Mormon or something and he decides that Roy cannot be exposed to that. Is he gonna up and leave? You get involved with Ben, and he might just put you down like a bad novel and keep on steppin' whenever the whim hits him. He's already proved he can be a cold-hearted bastard."

"You're right, Gloria. I don't want to invest all my emotion in Benjamin only for him to decide one day that he can live with or without me. I refuse to do that. Not that a drug addiction and a choice of religion can be compared, but I'd rather stay celibate than get into an ill-conceived relationship with him."

"Ohhh, that's right!" Gloria smacked the coffee table with her hand and laughed. "Why am I worried? You've decided to be celibate. When Benjamin finds out he ain't getting none, he's not going to stick around. Just you wait and see."

I passed on my chance to take a hit of the herb making the rounds. One person in the family with a penchant for getting high was more than enough. I never used it.

Gloria's comments, including that last remark about Benjamin being unlikely to live without sex, made my stomach churn.

"You're right. He might not stick around. But Gloria, let me say this. You will never understand the depth of my bond with Carolyn, because if you did, you would never suggest that I could disrespect her in anyway. Carolyn was your friend, but she was my sister. I was in the room when Roy was born. When Benjamin took him, I lived through every single day of that horror with her. I identified her body. I visit her grave every month."

I could see Gloria's tough-love persona melt; she'd finally heard me.

"I have forgiven Benjamin." That surprised me. I didn't know that was true until I had said it. "I needed to release that negativity and accept that Benjamin played a part in causing the most painful days of my life. Carolyn caused a lot of that pain herself, and I have forgiven her. I can move past that. The question is, move past to where?"

Gloria stood with a heavy sigh. "I give up. Do whatcha gotta do. I'm going to the bathroom. Is it down the hall, BJ?"

"Yeah, straight back."

Mumbling to herself, Gloria left us alone.

When the bathroom door closed, BJ spoke in a softened voice, "She's right you know. Do what you gotta do. Don't worry about what other people think. And don't be afraid either. Sounds like you're look-ing for some kind of guarantee. When does that ever happen when it comes to love?"

"Love? You think that's what I'm talking about?"

BJ arched his brows and waited for me to answer my own question.

Pushing my hair back, I shook my head. "Love is something worth fighting for. There are no guarantees, but I want an honest relationship. Benjamin and I would need to want the same things out of life; some-thing beyond a physical relationship. If we had that, it's not the same thing as love, but it would be a start."

"Okay, but listen to what your heart is telling you. People want to pretend it's all shocking you could be interested in Ben. In the Bible, didn't men marry their brother's wife if something happened and they needed to care for her? Ain't nothing new under the sun. People need to get over themselves and their judgments."

Gloria opened the door and BJ's voice returned to normal. He announced, "Dinner's on me. What sounds good? And no, we are not eating pizza, Gloria. Forget about it."

"Hey," I said, taking the wine glasses into the kitchen. "Maybe dinner can wait."

"Why?" BJ asked.

"Let's check out the folks on Vernon Avenue."

"It's where Carolyn died, BJ," Gloria explained, seeing his puzzled expression. "We've been there a couple of times trying to see what we could find out."

"Yeah, cops do what they can, but with the murder rate what it is in this city, they stay on the move," BJ said.

"Even Michael has been no help, and he's been keeping tabs for us from the beginning," Gloria added.

BJ turned off the fire in the fireplace. "So you all tried to conduct business without the third Angel? You know Charlie likes it when the trio works together. Let's roll."

CHAPTER 6
Benjamin

Roy was crying; screaming. Thinking the worst, I flew down the stairs. A broken arm—a cut that needed stitches, something involving a trip to the emergency room.

Roy stood in the kitchen, mouth wide, showing his tonsils during an extended scream. His whole chest lifted in spasms to inhale. Seeing no visible wounds, I moved to a lesser stage of alert.

"What's the matter!" my mother asked.

"What happened?" I was a close second.

My mother picked him up, wet swimming suit and all, but he couldn't get the words out. Mr. Elrod arranged Roy's towel around him.

"We will have to drain the pool," Sharon said, brow creased, hands on hips. The edges of her red shorts and her white top were wet.

Mr. Elrod acted as if he hadn't heard her. "Hey, little man, we'll get another chance tomorrow. Don't cry."

Roy reached for me, and I took him and his drips. I pressed his head to my shoulder. "Roy, it's going to be okay. What happened?

"Roy was in the pool by himself!" Sharon snapped. "That's what happened!"

"I was watching him the whole time," Mr. Elrod said. "I just left the side of the pool for a minute to get my sunglasses."

"You came back inside?" my mother asked.

"No, Millie. They were right there on the patio table."

Sharon looked at Mr. Elrod as if she were talking to a brain-damaged monkey. "A minute is all it takes. You can't turn your back on a three-year-old child in a swimming pool for God's sake! I say we drain the pool, or at least put a mesh fence around it."

"Listen to me." If Mr. Elrod's voice had hands, it would shake Sharon by the shoulders. "I know about the dangers of pools and kids, I'm not an idiot. I did not leave Roy by himself. Stop saying that."

"How do you know about the dangers of kids and pools, Rudy? How many kids have you raised? None. Nada. Zero. That's how many." Sharon made a sound of disgust. "Maybe we should just bulldoze the whole damn thing if you can't be more conscientious."

My mother tensed up. By now, Marissa had joined us. With all the yelling, I was surprised it had taken her so long.

I handed Roy off to her. "Please take him and get him dressed." By silent agreement, we waited until they were gone before continuing.

"Sharon," I tried to assure her, "Mr. Elrod knows what he's doing." Stress lines evaporated from Mr. Elrod's face.

"No, he apparently does not, Ben. What were you doing anyway? If your son is in the pool, why can't you watch him? Jesus Christ! Whose job is it to protect a child? It's the adults around him. Hello!"

"Mr. Elrod says he didn't take his eyes off of him. I believe him. The table is what? Four feet from the pool? I think you're overreacting."

"It's impossible for me to overreact! Do you know how many pool accidents happen every summer? Accidents where seconds mean the difference between life and death? It's the job of the adult to think about these things and plan accordingly." She had exaggerated the "th" in think and pointed to her temple several times, with her neck stuck out like someone wanted to chop it off. I could tell Mr. Elrod wouldn't mind obliging.

Mr. Elrod, always calm, shook his head and closed the door forcefully behind him.

Face pinched in concern, my mother walked over to Sharon and rested an arm on her shoulder. I could see her loyalty torn between her husband and her daughter. Sharon folded her arms and looked down.

"It's okay," Mom said. "You're right. Rudy isn't used to having a three-year-old around. We all have to learn to be extra careful, and we'll get a fence installed. Better safe than sorry."

"I'm sure Roy would've been okay," I said, "but thanks for looking out, Sis."

"Some things are preventable, Ben."

"I know." I nodded. "I know."

"Okay then." Sharon dropped her arms with a sigh. "I hope I didn't scare Roy too much."

"No problem," I said. "What's five years of growth? He'll make it up on the other end."

"Oh, funny. How about we go to Chuck E. Cheese? I'll try and convince Roy his aunt isn't a crazy woman, and we'll watch rats dance."

"Sounds like a plan, but let's all go. Mr. Elrod included."

CHAPTER 7
Andrea

Twenty minutes after leaving downtown, Gloria, BJ, and I stepped out of the coolness of BJ's car into the humidity of St. Louis in the summer. Walking slowly, I wondered if I was the grisliest tour guide that ever lived? I pointed to an otherwise indistinct section of the sidewalk in front of an overgrown empty lot. "That's where they outlined her body."

BJ crossed his arms and looked up and down the block. "Which one of these is Carolyn's crack house?"

"You can see the back of it from here. The second house down that alley," Gloria said. "We found that out the first time we were here."

"Do you know what evidence the police collected, Andi?" BJ asked.

"No. Detective Peck said he can't share specifics, but when I ask if he has any leads he's tracking down, he always says no."

BJ looked around in disgust. "I'll bet they picked up all kinds of crap around her body, look at all this mess. He kicked a beer can and watched it roll, and then stepped on a McDonald's cup. "Were there any fingerprints on her body or any good forensic stuff under Carolyn's nails where she scratched the perp?"

I smiled at his use of the word perp. "No prints, no potential DNA evidence under her nails." Seems he and I were up on the latest crime shows.

"And they checked and rechecked Ben's alibi I hope?" BJ asked.

"Yep," I said.

"Andi and I agree," Gloria said. "Someone took vengeance. Someone wanted Carolyn dead. If it wasn't Benjamin, who was it?"

We looked at each other; no one had answers.

"Since we don't know the answer," I said, "we go door-to-door again. Let's start on the corner and work our way back here. Let's hope the third time is the charm."

The corner was three houses away. Six, if you counted houses on both sides of the street.

"Benjamin was the only one who had anything to gain from Carolyn's death that I can see. Maybe that's why I dislike him," Gloria said.

We climbed the steps to the first house and rang the bell. Gloria said, "Looks like we're in luck. Someone's coming."

"What y'all want?" A haggard young woman wearing a blue bandana and carrying a fat baby talked to us through a screen door.

"Hi, my name is Andrea Young. My sister was murdered up the street back in late February." I pulled out a flyer from my jeans pocket. "Did you see or hear anything? There's a reward for information that leads to an arrest."

The woman barely glanced at Carolyn's picture. "Don't be wasting my time asking 'bout no crack ho. My kids can't even play outside in their own yard cuz of folks like her and crap like that; needles and makeshift pipes everywhere."

Her impersonal attack was like someone dropping my heart in cold water. "My sister didn't deserve to die like that."

"And my children don't deserve to be stuck in the house because grown-assed folk like your sister decide to leave needles and pipes every damn where. Didn't nobody make her smoke that shit. Hell, I don't know nothing no way." She closed the door in our faces.

When we'd asked other people before, we'd been met with indifference or sympathy. This woman's virulent hate left me with an icy trembling.

BJ patted my shoulder. "Nowhere to go but up."

No one came to the door at the next house, but we left a flyer.

BETWEEN TEARS

At the third house, we didn't have to knock, because an older lady sat on her porch in a green metal lawn chair. This was the house next to the lot. No one had been outside when we first arrived.

"What y'all selling?" she asked. "I got all the religion, magazines, and magic cleaners I need, thank you very much." The curiosity in her eyes belied her disinterest.

"No, ma'am." I told her what I wanted.

"Lawd have mercy. Back in Feb'rary you say?" She shooed a big fly away. It was hot. The short walk already had me sweating.

"Yes, ma'am."

"Umph. Child, I can't member that far back." She chuckled a toothless laugh and adjusted her brown pageboy wig before her expression turned serious. "Why you just now asking?"

"I know." Guilt about my lack of action flitted around me, causing more irritation than that giant horse fly. "I guess I was in shock at first, and thought the police would solve this, but they don't seem interested. It took me a few weeks to figure that out."

"And then," Gloria said, "we came up with offering the reward and having these flyers printed."

"Gloria and I have been here twice before, but we were mainly putting the flyers on everyone's door on this block and the blocks nearby. We knocked at a few houses, but most times we didn't get an answer"

"Mmm-hmm," Mrs. Freelon said with a sympathetic headshake. "Folks probably thought y'all were the Jehovah Witness people or something. I don't remember seeing this flyer, but my grandson might have and just pitched it." She held the flyer and fanned with it. "Well, I'll bet you didn't talk to Betty. Y'all need to talk to Betty Tuddle. She stay across the way there. Right next to that boarded up house. She pointed a bony finger. "She don't miss nothing that happens on the block. Talk to her."

"Okay. And ma'am?"

She looked up at BJ and smiled. "Yes, young man?"

"Do you remember the police speaking to you about that shooting? I just wondered if that could maybe jog your memory."

"No, don't think they did. They could have talked to my grandson, Dale Edward."

"Dale Edward? Is he home now?"

"No, Dale Edward's in Detroit." She put the accent on the first syllable of the city. "He gave me his cell phone number, but I can't keep up with all that. Go on over to Betty's. I don't see her car right now, but tell her Mrs. Freelon sent you. She might remember something. Sorry for your loss, baby."

CHAPTER 8
Benjamin

Last night's fiasco with the pool reminded me once again that children had to come first. Now, the trick was waiting for Andrea to come around to that understanding so we could put Carolyn's death behind us. In her heart, Andrea understood my intentions—knew taking Roy away from Carolyn's influence was what any parent would have done. The fallout was inevitable and unfortunate, but I'd make the same choice over again. I knew Andrea. In my shoes, I'm sure she would have done the same thing.

Thoughts of her went joyfully and directly to my groin, and I shifted in bed to accommodate this. Andrea's mind, her body, her soul, everything about her generated a wild, hot energy that made me want to run a marathon or something. Waiting to be together after all these years was rough, but she was worth it. The crew at work even teased me about how wide open my nose was, because they'd catch me with a goofy grin on my face for no apparent reason.

She was the reason, and I hoped the time was now. Before, I'd been careful not to let my feelings for her overshadow my responsibilities with Roy and Carolyn. Had I disregarded them, not only would I have been unable to live with myself, but Andrea wouldn't have been having it. I would have lost her respect and any chance I had with her.

I showered, got dressed in a black T-shirt and jeans, and went downstairs. I didn't know where Roy was, but Chuck E. Cheese had gone well last night. By the end of the evening, Roy seemed to have forgotten the incident, and Sharon and Mr. Elrod managed to exchange a laugh about some other topic.

I found Sharon at the kitchen table studying.

"Hey, you seen a pint-sized kid, about yea tall," I gestured, "big eyes and curly hair?"

"Yep, his grandmother and Rudy took him to the Science Center." Sharon spoke while she took notes on a yellow legal pad.

"Oh, he'll love that. They didn't tell me. Do you come home this often usually, or should Roy and I be flattered?"

"Didn't want to wake you, since you're taking a day off." She finally looked at me and smiled. "A girl has to eat and do her laundry, doesn't she? And, it's not like I can't get to school in half an hour, but you're right, I missed you and Roy. Is it okay if a make up for a little lost time?"

That remark earned her a peck on the cheek.

"Are you alright?" she asked. "Need me to doctor on you? I need all the practice I can get."

"No, I'm good; just tired. Working in that heat all day is no joke. How are you feeling?"

"I'm okay."

"Did Marissa go with them?"

"No, she has a friend who lives in Clayton. She picked her up and they went shopping. They left about an hour ago."

"Oh yeah, Tricia, her cheerleader friend she met when she came to town earlier this year. I remember her mentioning it now."

"Ben, yesterday, I just … needed to yell at someone, I guess."

"It's okay. I've had days like that myself. And, you know, better safe than sorry as far as the pool goes." I looked at her for a minute longer. Something was still bothering her. "Anything else going on?"

"Dr. Fields has been out of town the last couple of weeks. I miss having someone to check in with."

"Dr. Fields? Your psychiatrist? Oh, right. Well, check in with me."

The smirk on her face said she didn't take me seriously. "Right. I know Mama can't talk about it because of the guilt she feels, but you and Tim never say a thing about what happened to me. Why do you suppose that is?"

"Why?" I put some toast in the toaster and got a cup from the cabinet. I could say what I was thinking. That life is about moving forward and not dwelling on things you can't change, but I knew I only felt that way because I didn't like to think about what had happened to her.

It was cowardly I guess, but I didn't want to deal with our heroin-addicted father allowing his four-year-old daughter to fall into the hands of a pedophile. "I didn't feel competent to help you, Sharon. I never knew the right words to say, but I've come to understand a lot of times it's about listening, even though I can't fix it. I'm ready to listen."

She didn't say anything. I pointed to her notepad. "What's this?" Sharon had drawn a house and two stick figures, hand in hand, standing in front of it. There was one tall person and the short person was someone in pigtails.

"Sometimes we have to shine light on events so they don't remain shrouded in fear or shame."

If that didn't sound like something straight from a shrink's mouth, I didn't know what did. But, it was true. I poured my coffee and added milk. "That makes sense." I pointed to her drawing again. "Is this the place he took you?" I got a saucer for my toast and sat at the table.

"That's okay. You don't want to hear."

"No, I do. Talk to me."

She wet her upper lip with the tip of her tongue, looked down, then back up. Her eyes questioned if I were strong enough. We'd find out.

"Okay." She closed the book she'd been reading with a snap. "The first thing I remember is the doorbell. It was loud enough for me to hear it buzz.

"At the top of the door were three small windows. A deep voice would mutter, 'Dunn's here.' Dad could see whoever belonged to the voice, but I couldn't. I was too close to the door.

"Clunk, clunk. Dead bolts were unlocked. A chain slid away. A fat man in a sleeveless white T-shirt let us in while a younger guy in blue jeans lurked in the background waiting for me."

I listened, wondering if her stomach was in knots like mine, or maybe she'd had to tell this story so often, she'd detached herself emotionally. Probably the latter. If she put herself through the wringer every time she talked about this, it would be too much like reliving it.

"Dad said something like, 'Thanks, Joe, for watching her for me.' Sometimes he even gave him a dollar.

"I'd follow him down a long hall into a bedroom. The whole house had a stale smell, but in his room, the smell was one I recognize now as a sex smell left on unwashed sheets. There were roaches everywhere I looked. They left trails as they made their way through the dust on the furniture. Some disappeared from view as they went up and down on filthy ass sheets."

I shook my head. I had wanted my coffee and toast, but now they sat getting cold.

"Joe offered me peppermints. He'd encourage me to take one for now and put a couple in my pocket for later. As we unwrapped our peppermints, Joe always said, 'Guess it's story time now, Sharon.' He'd pick a magazine to show me from his porn collection. What I saw was strange yet fascinating at the same time. Until then, I had no idea what adult bodies looked like without clothes.

"I would sit on a black trunk at the end of the bed. Joe would sit in front of me and turn the pages, just like it was real story time at the library—almost, except he—he touched himself.

"'The police will lock your daddy up if you tell anybody about this magazine.' Sometimes he'd say, 'Little girls like you who look at books like this get sent away from home.' I'd close my eyes when he said that, scared, but then he'd laugh and say, 'You'd better open your eyes, girl 'fore I open them for you.'"

Seeming to need to re-orient herself in her present surroundings, she asked for a drink of water.

I got it for her, then reached over the table and took her hand. "Go on."

She took two deep breaths before continuing. "Soon, we'd play the game. He said I should kiss him the way the ladies in the magazines did. He liked using his fingers on me. When he finished, when he'd ejaculated into this rag, I could watch TV in his room until somebody called to Joe and told him it was time for me to go."

Tears etched shiny streaks down her cheeks, while I fought mine back. I brought her a drink of water.

"It took Mama a month to see how he'd hurt me."

In my head, I had constructed a scenario not too far from what I'd just heard, but hearing it from Sharon made me nauseous. Standing behind her chair, I wrapped my arms around her. "Thank God she saw it and put a stop to it. I feel no remorse about Mama sending Daddy away. Some people have no business being parents."

"Even if families are destroyed like ours was?" she asked.

"Children have to come first, without question. What you said last night about adults being responsible was right. I left town with Roy for that exact reason."

CHAPTER 9
Andrea

The next day, Gloria, BJ and I were able to go back to Vernon Street and see Mrs. Tuddle, the woman Mrs. Freelon had told us about.

"That was your sister?" Mrs. Tuddle's plump, round face frowned with concern as she laid the flyer on her coffee table the next day. "Yeah, I saw this flyer, but I had already told the police everything I knew. Girl, those drugs will get hold of you and rob you of everything you ever had, then throw you back and make it so your own family don't recognize you."

That was certainly true toward the end of Carolyn's life. I didn't like to think about that. I liked to remember Carolyn pregnant, and then giving birth and how much she loved Roy. I liked to remember her gift for interior design and how she'd taken so much delight in drawing sketches of layouts for Eugene's house when he first decided to move back to Kentucky. *God, how I wish I could have seen your ideas come to fruition, Carolyn.*

The couch in Mrs. Tuddle's living room sagged under the weight of Gloria, BJ, and me, but I didn't mind. The odd plate and cup in the living room and the array of newspapers and clutter surrounding us didn't bother us either. We were glad someone wanted to tell us something.

Betty Tuddle flipped her down-the-back blonde braids and sat down in the armchair, a tight fit. "That's a shame. Yeah, well I get off work at 4:00, and I'm home by 4:30 usually, but that night I remember I had to stop to pick up my Girl Scout cookie order. Got home 'bout 5:30. I noticed a Camry parked directly across from me when I pulled up. Somebody was sitting in it, wearing a baseball cap, I wasn't sure if it was a man or a woman."

"What color was it. What year?" I asked.

"The car? Oh, I'd say ninety-one or ninety-two Camry, before they changed the body style. Kinda small and sedan like."

"Those are popular," Gloria said. "Seems they last forever. What color was this one, Mrs. Tuddle?"

"They sure are popular. My ex-husband and I used to own a car wash. They'd come through a lot. This one was dark, either gray or blue."

"Could you tell if the person wearing the baseball cap was black or white?" BJ asked.

"The lighting can play tricks. I'm not sure."

"Okay, did you notice anything else?" Gloria asked.

"That's all I saw except whoever it was kept on eating something."

"Like what?" I asked.

"Something snacky you pop in your mouth, like peanuts or grapes."

"Could it have been popcorn?"

"Yeah, it could have been. Something like that."

"You told this to the police?" Gloria asked.

"Yeah, I sure did."

"Did you hear or see anything else?" BJ asked.

"No, well, the ambulance and police sirens. From what I understand, somebody driving by saw a body lying on the ground and called the police. I didn't hear anything before then." She looked at me with a frown. "I hope you get some satisfaction. I know how hard this must be for you."

"Thank you very much," I said. The four of us stood in unison.

"Good luck," Mrs. Tuddle said.

Barely down her porch steps, I couldn't wait any longer. "Guys! The medical examiner's report said Carolyn had undigested popcorn in her stomach. Mrs. Tuddle saw her killer! Who has a car like that?"

"Not Ben, he has a red Acura," Gloria said.

BJ added, "He's the only one with a clear motive. What about the rest of his clan? His mother? What does she drive?"

"She has some kind of luxury Buick," I said. "Mr. Elrod drives a Jeep. Sharon, I don't know. Tim, I don't know."

Walking between us, Gloria grabbed our arms and froze. "Oh I know!"

"What?" BJ and I said.

"This Marissa chick. Maybe she's in love with Ben? Maybe she killed Carolyn?"

"Marissa? Well, but he and Carolyn weren't married. You think she'd kill Carolyn so he wouldn't have any custody worries and he could focus on her?" I shrugged. "Stranger things have happened. I can find out what she drives."

BJ started his car. He had to, or we'd suffocate in the heat. "Let's not reach too far with the facts. What do we know?" Facing each other, we continued to brainstorm.

From the backseat, I said, "We know our killer drives a ninety-two or ninety-one Camry, dark in color, assuming the car wasn't borrowed."

"And we know the killer snacked on popcorn, or at least it's a small leap to make that assumption," I said, "because the time frame matches the medical report."

"We know the killer knew her whereabouts. Knew where to wait for Carolyn to show up," BJ said.

"Or followed her maybe?" I said.

They nodded.

I settled back and fastened my seat belt. "Well, it's more than we had when we started out."

"Gloria, can Michael get us a list of all registered Camry owners sorted by year and color?" BJ asked.

"Well, I'm sure he could, but what would we do with a list that size? I think we have to figure out who wanted her dead first, and then look for the car connection," Gloria said.

A tap at Gloria's window startled us. Two guys tried to peer in past the tinted glass. The sides of their curved hands on the window would leave prints. One wore a do-rag on his head, and the other wore a large diamond cross hanging from his left earlobe, almost touching his shoulder. Collective thoughts inside the car made words unnecessary. Were they here to help or harass? And because we were where we were, this thought could not be stopped—what would we do if one of them pulled a gun and told us to get out or worse, got in with us?

Do-Rag tapped again and smiled like we were scouts for a toothpaste commercial.

I expected BJ to take off, but he didn't. Gloria, probably thinking it was wiser not to disrespect them by ignoring them, lowered her window two inches.

Both took several seconds to appraise us sitting in the car. "Wazup. Y'all looking?" Do-Rag asked.

"No, my friend was shot on this street last winter, and we're trying to get some answers. That's all."

"All right" sounded like "aiight" when Diamond Cross spoke.

"Peace," Do-Rag said.

"Peace out," Gloria said. After they backed away from the door, she raised the window. Another murder didn't faze them. Gloria might as well have told them she lost a hubcap.

"Let's go." Gloria's voice remained calm, but knowing her well enough to hear between the lines, I heard 'let's get the hell out of here.'

My nervousness evaporated in direct proportion to the number of blocks we put between them and us. They had wanted to know if we "were looking" to buy crack.

"Neighborhood regulars for sure," Gloria said, "and they might have seen something the night Carolyn died, but, it was something about that brother's eyes. They were dead behind that smile. Some folks you don't mess with."

CHAPTER 10
Andrea

Bright lights, Loud retro music. I wasn't accelerating my heartbeat on the dance floor, I worked out on the treadmill at the gym instead. Not my favorite place in the world to be, but a necessary one, according to my scale and my profile in every evil mirror and reflective surface I passed. Those people who could read and walk on these machines amazed me. If I had the energy to read, the rivulets of sweat blinding me would make it impossible.

But the treadmill wasn't all bad. It had a rhythm all its own that allowed my thoughts to flourish under the spell of its repetitive sound.

The church had been my only comfort when Benjamin had whisked Roy away and Carolyn sank into her drug-induced oblivion. Now that Benjamin and Roy were back, that wouldn't change. My level of commitment continues to grow, and I hoped it would include them.

Being a sensual person, I had previously derived great pleasure from the giving and receiving aspect of sex, but celibacy had become part of my way of life now. All the same, I had to admit, giving it up was almost equivalent to giving up water and food.

My Sunday-school teacher, Brother Ward, told me many people struggled with the same thing. He suggested I take my mind off the physical by singing every church song I know. It's gotten to the point where I even make up my own songs now. Brother Ward said to avoid temptation, of course, and to stay in a prayerful state of mind by reciting scripture.

I followed his advice, but it wasn't enough. I found treating myself to a therapeutic massage and shopping for my elders once a week gave me the hands-on feedback I needed to stay on that narrow path.

When I factored those two activities in with church on Sundays, Bible class on Wednesday and the Christian Singles Group that met once a month, I had something to look forward to almost every day of the week. Keeping busy had helped me cope with Carolyn's death and had given me something to do other than worry about Roy.

Now Benjamin was back. I respected him; there was a definite physical attraction, and of course, there was Roy. I wanted to explore a relationship with Benjamin and stay true to my newfound commitment to chastity.

I came back from my reverie to see Sharon Dunn looking at me, charm exuding from her radiant smile. Spandexed to the max, there wasn't an ounce of fat anywhere on her body.

"Hi Andrea."

"Hi Sharon," I said, using my towel to wipe my brow and neck. "How've you been?" I hadn't seen Sharon for several months. Neither she nor any member of her family had come to Carolyn's funeral, but they had sent a bouquet of white lilies.

She climbed on the treadmill next to mine. "I'm fine, thanks. I rarely see you here."

"I know. I'm going to get back on the stick." I patted my rounded belly to indicate why.

"I'm here no fewer than three times a week. It really helps me keep the stress in check."

"Are you still in school?" I asked.

"Oh yes, but I make the time." Then she said, "I'm so glad they're finally home. I've missed them like crazy."

"Me, too." I guessed there wasn't really anything more to say. My ten minutes on the machine ticked away into the cool-down mode. When it stopped, I got off. "Bye Sharon."

"Bye."

Benjamin didn't work on Thursdays, so we agreed to meet for lunch. This was an important day, or at least my fluttering heart and stomach said it was. We were at the crossroads now that I'd had some time to process my feelings for him and the next steps I wanted to take.

A picnic in the park was on our agenda, and maybe we could rent a paddleboat and enjoy the day. Benjamin told me he would bring the food and everything else, and all I had to do was be ready at one. He picked me up on time.

Forest Park, the largest park in the city, stirred great memories. My mom, Carolyn, and I had spent a lot of time here ice skating and going to the zoo. Grass and trees bowed in the breeze that came in strong spurts, a breeze strong enough to hold the humidity at bay.

I thought of Eugene for a second as we passed the Art Museum, which was also in the park. He and I used to visit it often. Thinking of him reminded me that school would start at the end of the month, and school meant work. I liked my job, because after six years teaching tenth grade English, I finally had some strategies that worked. But, I liked my vacation time, too. I took in the trees, watched the breeze herding the clouds along, and forced myself to stop my mind's nervous prattle and savor the moment.

"This is a lovely day, isn't it?" I turned away from my window to look at Benjamin.

"This is a great day. I've been looking forward to us being together all week. And look, there's no Roy today."

"I noticed." I did an exaggerated frown, but quickly smiled. I had managed to see Roy a couple of times in the past two weeks, but had avoided being alone with Benjamin until now. Being the persistent sort though, he called me and we'd talked almost every night. "How is he?"

"He's great. That boy is going to be President someday. Smart as he can be and the social skills this kid has got, puts me to shame."

I smiled. "Yeah, both those qualities come from the Young gene pool. Did you know that?"

Smiling back, he winked. "Yeah, I did know that."

I thought of another question. "Is that Sharon?" I asked.

"Where?"

"Thought I saw her drive by in a blue Mercedes."

"Blue Mercedes? How could she afford something like that? She's got a white Eclipse."

"Oh, okay." *Duly noted.*

We drove until we found a lone picnic table cocooned in a shady section. Benjamin impressed me by remembering a blue vinyl tablecloth and a blanket. I watched him take sandwiches, grapes and a liter of Sprite from a wicker basket. He also brought plastic champagne glasses, which I thought was a sweet, romantic touch.

"What kind of sandwiches did you get us?"

"You mean, what kind did I make us? I started with garlic hummus spread on sunflower seed bread. On top of the hummus are some caramelized onions, roasted red peppers, and cucumbers."

"That sounds really good, Benjamin."

"There's lettuce, tomato, and a touch of feta cheese, too."

I took a bite. The bread was like nothing I'd ever had before. The mixture of vegetable flavors sang a happy song in my mouth. "Mmm. Tasty. Thank you."

"You're welcome." Benjamin took two quick bites. "Andrea, looks like we are getting along pretty well."

"How can you tell? You mean because I'm learning to enjoy vegetarian dishes?"

"Sort of; only true friends can share onions, and garlic and risk bits of sunflower seeds getting stuck between their teeth."

I laughed. "You're right. Guess that means we are getting more comfortable with each other. Or maybe we just like to eat."

"Well, I always say it's fun getting your basic needs met with somebody you like." His eyes twinkled mischief. "Is this the right time to ask you if you are seeing anyone, or should I say seeing anyone else?"

Chewing, I shook my head no.

"No? It's not the right time?"

"No," I said after I took a drink. "I'm not seeing anyone."

"Any particular reason why not?"

"Yeah, there are a few of them. For one thing, I know what I want, and I wasn't finding it sifting through the typical club clientele."

"What do you want?"

The imagined spotlight made my cheeks flush. "I want to be loved and respected. I want someone kind. I want a man who is aware of his spirituality and encourages me to explore mine."

The saliva in my mouth turned to dust. After more than four years of Benjamin and me erecting a wall between us, here we were dismantling it, brick by brick. I took a second to let my tongue scan my front teeth for sunflower seeds. "If the man of my dreams has his own library card, he gets bonus points."

He laughed, but I was serious.

"He needs to have ambition, a sense of purpose for his life. Is that enough for starters?"

"Yeah, gives us a lot to talk about." He dug out his wallet and held up his library card.

I patted my chest. "Wow. Be still, my heart."

He returned his card to the slot. "What do you mean by spirituality?"

"I could find a fancier way of saying it, but not a truer one. For me that means Jesus is my role model for how I live."

His head bobbed up and down. "You're a good Christian girl."

"I hoped you could tell."

"Jesus, huh?"

"Jesus definitely."

"Yeah, I noticed. This is different. This isn't the Andrea I knew before."

"Yeah, well. What stays the same?"

"You are absolutely right about that."

"Besides, that was two-and-a-half years ago, Benjamin. I already told you, after you left, Carolyn and I needed something to anchor us. We went back to the church our mother had raised us in."

"Obviously it didn't work for Carolyn."

"It worked for just over a year, I'd say. No weed, no crack, worked every day at the bank, came to church every Sunday, but then she slowly drifted away."

"How did she drift away? How did God let her go?" He frowned as if he really wanted to understand.

"I think she tried to made a deal with God—clean up her life in return for her son—but, He's not in the business of making bargains. When Roy didn't come back ... she made another choice, and God allowed it. It's this freewill caveat of God's. That's what happened." I nervously checked to see if my earring was in place, just for something to do, and then I met Benjamin's gaze. "Would you be interested in coming to church with me sometimes?"

He unscrewed the bottle top and poured more Sprite for us. "I work on Sundays now. I'll let you know when my schedule changes."

"You want to go?"

"Well, Mama and Mr. Elrod are taking Roy with them on Sundays now when they go to church. Tim, you remember my brother, Tim? He's a deacon at his church in Ellisville. He and Maryann are encouraging me to join them there also. Maybe I should take a hint?"

"Maybe you should. How are Tim and Maryann doing?"

"They're fine. Number three is due in January. I hear rumors this one will be their second daughter."

"That's great. Did you grow up in the church?"

"Yeah, didn't we all? I fell away when I was fourteen or so; wasn't feeling it."

"How about when you were away?"

"When I was away, I mainly watched Marissa go to Mass every Sunday. Let's relax on the blanket a while?"

"Okay," I said, registering the topic change.

A few feet away from the table, Benjamin flapped open a blue blanket, and I helped him straighten out the edges. We sat next to each other, our legs outstretched. He picked up my hand and entwined his fingers with mine.

"It's funny how life works," he said. "Me with Carolyn, now me hoping to be with you. Is that likely to happen anytime soon?"

Leaning on one elbow, he flicked a speck of lettuce off my shirt with his free hand. I leaned in closer as he pressed his warm lips against mine for several seconds, then his tongue parted my lips and I received him. I was happy, because I had wanted to do that for a long time. I smiled before we stopped.

"I have waited so long to kiss you, Andrea," he said, reading my mind again. "How long ago did we meet?"

"Four years ago."

"Four years, one month and seven days, but who's counting." He grabbed the back of my head and brought my lips to his again for several delicious moments. "The way I feel about you, haven't you felt it? The whole time I was with Carolyn. When I ended our relationship, I hoped you and I would find our way to each other, you know, maybe, when it was appropriate, but then Carolyn told me she was pregnant."

"I know, Benjamin. I was there. I felt what you felt, every step of the way. But there was nothing we could have done or should have done under the circumstances."

"No, of course not. But what about now?"

Sitting up and crisscrossing my legs, but not releasing his hand, I forced myself to think logically about his question, and not about how much I wanted him. "Have you decided to stay here, Benjamin, or are you just asking me how I feel about a quick romp in the hay?"

He laughed and sat up as well. We faced each other, knee to knee. "First of all, there wouldn't be anything quick about it. Second, there is something about you that makes a man want more than sex from you, Andrea. Finally, Roy and I are going to stay."

"Yes! I'm glad." I grinned like someone told me I could have free cable. "I was hoping you'd stay." I hugged him.

"I'm glad you're glad, but don't leave me hanging here." He looked me in the eye. "Do I have a chance to be with a beautiful woman? Someone with an understanding and forgiving heart? I would mention

I totally respect you, I know how much you love Roy, and I think you are sexy as hell, but I don't want you to think I'm begging."

I smiled wistfully as I drew my finger across his cheek and gazed into Benjamin's copper, sunlit eyes. "I want the chance to get to know you beyond friends, but I have to tell you something."

"Tell me."

"I want a chance for us to get to know each other without us having sex."

He missed a beat. It got carried away on a long sigh, but he was still Benjamin, cool about it. "And this is because fornication is not a good thing, correct?"

"No, it's not a good thing. When sex becomes a part of a relationship, it changes everything, for women, anyway. Well, for me, maybe I should say."

"Change. But not in a good way?"

"Change that makes emotions go haywire and clouds the thinking. Change that creates a false intimacy before a real one can be established."

He nodded and stood. "I understand. I'm so horny that I don't know what to do, but I understand." He laughed and shook his head. "Why don't we pack up and go for a boat ride?" He helped me up.

We returned the picnic paraphernalia to the car. I didn't know what to think. I wanted to tell him that kissing him and not doing anything more physical was going to be one of the hardest things I've ever done in my life. But, maybe Benjamin had decided sex was more important than getting to know me on my terms.

After he slammed the truck closed, his finger tilted my chin into position for another tantalizing kiss. "Okay," he said, "but only because you are one helluva kisser. It might tide me over."

I had the answer I wanted, for a while anyway.

CHAPTER 11
Andrea

"Andrea Young, right?"

"Right." I shook Detective Peck's hand, glad to give up my seat in the police station waiting area.

"Listen," he said, leaning in close, "I'm going to do better returning your calls. I've had a death in my own family in the past month, and … Well, there's no shortage of investigations that need my attention, but I do apologize for taking so long to set up this meeting. You came to see me—when was it—late June and it's July already."

When Detective Peck spoke, he had a habit of violating personal space. The good news was, he had the freshest breath I'd ever run across.

"Come on back," he said and held the door for me that led to his workspace. I followed him. At five-foot seven, he was three inches taller than me, but wiry thin, like a reformed anorexic.

His desk, down a short hall and to the left, was one of four near a window. Fifteen years on the force earned him the right, I supposed. He retrieved Carolyn's folder from a green file cabinet and we sat, he behind his desk and I to the side of it.

"Okay, let me bring you up-to-date. Since Carolyn's murder on February twenty-seventh, me, my partner, and two patrol officers canvassed the block and raided two known crack houses in the area." He leafed through a few pages. "Out of twenty-seven people interviewed, three of them had information we initially considered useful, but nothing panned out."

"Yes, I spoke with one of them, Mrs. Tuddle. Who are the other two?"

He gave me the look a five year old garners for walking on furniture, but I pretended not to notice as I continued, "Mrs. Tuddle told me about the person in the Camry and the popcorn."

"Ms. Young, can we get something straight? Solving your sister's murder is important to you, but this is not a game. Tracking down information, that's what the city pays me to do, and I do my job. I'd appreciate it if you would respect that and not risk jeopardizing evidence or interfering with us making a case."

If he expected contrition from me, Michael Jackson would be on the cover of *Parents* magazine before he got it. I intended my blank look to convey that.

Skimming pages, he said, "What's this about popcorn? That's not coming back to me from any of the interviews."

I explained how I had tied in the information from the medical report to what Mrs. Tuddle saw.

Grabbing a sharpened pencil from a group of nine others, he used the eraser tip to help flip through the documents again. When he ran out of pages, he looked up and said, "The popcorn killer, huh? Food never came up in the Tuddle interview. Chances are she's blind as a bat anyway, but she did mention a Camry. Don't tell me you took the reward flyers with you."

"Well, what good would they do at home on my dresser?"

"For a chance at twenty-five grand, someone will swear their mother did it and probably has. Besides, you are making the connection to popcorn, not Mrs. Tuddle. A person eating something does not necessarily equal popcorn. In any case, I haven't gone through all my callbacks today."

"You were saying something about the Camry?"

"Yeah. The trouble is, that's not enough information—1991 or 1992 dark color Camry—to find the vehicle in question. We'd need to have at least a partial license plate number, VIN number, definite color or something, Ms. Young. Dark color is not specific enough. Is it dark blue, dark green, gray, gunmetal, dark brown, bronze, gold?"

"Did they make a gold one back then?"

"Are you missing my point on purpose?"

"Okay, maybe you should go back and talk to Mrs. Tuddle again. Ask everyone what they saw again," I suggested.

He glanced at me while he wrote something down.

I leaned toward him. "Maybe you should write this down too. There's another possible witness—Dale Edward. I think his last name is Freelon? My friends and I spoke with his grandmother. He's out of town—I don't know, maybe leaving town is relevant?"

His glare told me I was pushing my luck. "People come and go all the time."

"I know. Still …"

He skimmed down a list of names again and turned to another page in his file. "Dale Edward Freelon was interviewed. In fact, his statement supports Mrs. Tuddle's. He heard a hot rod roar by, looked out of his window and saw two people walking near a dark color sedan, but he didn't know the make or model, and he didn't see or hear anything else."

"Good, maybe something will gel from all of this," I said.

He tapped his pencil on his blotter, then leaned back in his chair and rocked a few beats. "How many times have you been there asking questions?"

"Three, but not alone, always with friends."

"Friends you say. So, it's a group effort, which may not be a bad idea seeing as how you could run into some seriously rough individuals in that neighborhood. I'm talking about people who would rape, rob, and beat you to death because their electricity got turned off and they didn't have anything better to do with their afternoon."

"Not everyone has evil in mind, but we were careful." On some level, I had acknowledged the dangerous environment, but not the conscious one.

"You're careful?" He tilted his head toward a pile of ten or twelve manila folders. "You see those? Wonder how many of them thought they were being careful before someone made sure the undertaker got paid?"

"What do you expect me to do?" As I stood, I could feel the stares of others sitting around us. "It's been six months since Carolyn's murder. I don't think her death was typical street crime like you seem to."

"Sit down, Ms. Young. They pay me, but not enough for me to tolerate you yelling at me."

"I'm sorry."

He pointed to a silver framed picture on his desk. "See her?"

I looked at an attractive woman with a mass of curly black hair, like his but much longer.

"Who is she?"

"That's my sister. I get it. If something happened to her I'd be doing all I could, too, but working against the system is counterproductive. I'm the system, Ms. Young."

"Oh." Looking at his sister didn't tell me Detective Peck's ethnicity, maybe Italian, maybe Jewish, not that it mattered.

"Do we need to take a walk?" he asked.

"No. I'm okay." I sat again.

"Forgive my bluntness, but your sister was a known crack addict who frequented a nearby crack house."

"I know that, but what did the killer want? There was money zipped in her jacket pocket."

He looked through his folder again. "Says here they found $1.82."

"See? That's what I mean."

"Consider this. The killer didn't bother with the dollar and change. Maybe the murderer took the big bills or crack, then ran before witnesses gathered."

"Carolyn was leaving the crack house, and presumably leaving her money there for what she paid for. Wouldn't she have spent all the money she had?"

His look said we don't want to go there, but I knew what he was thinking. Sex exchanged for money. "But, the medical report said there were no signs of sexual activity."

Shrugging, he said, "I have no proof, but she could have fellated someone and rinsed her mouth out. One, or several. The killer knew it, and took her money the easy, no fuss way. If your popcorn killer theory is plausible, so is this."

A prickly need to defend my actions and what was left of my sister's reputation almost raised my voice again. "Nothing can be ruled out unless there's proof, which you can't seem to find, Detective."

"That's true so far, but, do me a favor. Don't go back there. Let me handle it. I don't want you hurt."

When he walked out, I followed him. On the way outside to the parking lot, he held the door for me. I searched for my car keys inside my purse.

"You know Benjamin Dunn, the boyfriend, is back in town, don't you?"

My head snapped up a little too quickly at the sound of Benjamin's name. "Yes."

"Between you and me, if it wasn't street crime, as you say, he was the one I was laying odds on. He had the motive."

My heart was off to the races. Not wanting to get Michael into trouble for sharing information, I didn't mention I already knew this. "After you talked to him, what did you think?"

"He had an alibi. Not to say he didn't pay someone to do it, but, once again we don't have the proof."

Pay someone. That hadn't occurred to me. But no, Benjamin was not that kind of man. What about Marissa Torres?"

"Checked her out, too. Came up with zip, but I haven't forgotten your sister, Ms. Young."

I opened my car door, got in and rolled down a window. Peck leaned down.

"The case is open until it's solved. I wish I could make it go faster for the sake of so many families affected by murder. I don't have that magic wand. It takes time."

"Okay."

"If there's a break to be had, we'll stay diligent and we will find it. Meanwhile, life goes on. People get stuck, become obsessed. Don't let that happen to you." He smacked the roof twice as a way of sending me on my way.

I wasn't obsessed. Carolyn was murdered in February, and here it was July. Putting up reward money and having the flyers made didn't constitute obsession. Even though we'd only canvassed the neighborhood four times, perhaps most people in similar circumstances didn't actually interview people on their own. They probably hired private detectives.

If Carolyn and I hadn't been burned doing that looking for Benjamin and Roy, maybe I would be more open to trying a private investigator again. Something needed to be done. It was common knowledge the police were less likely to do a thorough investigation when they were already convinced they had the answer. Carolyn, I'm sure they thought, was a throw away person. He and others considered her someone who made her bed, and then had to lie in it.

The more time passed, the harder it would be to find evidence. On the other hand, it was a dangerous neighborhood. It's possible Carolyn's murder was a drug-related shooting and nothing more. The thing was, I needed to be sure. Finding my Advil in my purse, I shook out two and opened my bottle of tepid water. Detective Peck seemed sincere. I'd let him do his job.

CHAPTER 12
Benjamin

I had no intention of going to church, work schedule notwithstanding. But, I was willing to work with Andrea on the service aspects she mentioned. We needed to take care of one another, especially our elderly. I also had no problem gaining information to help me understand the Bible better, so going to class with her on Wednesday nights was fine with me.

It was convenient for Andrea to come by my mother's house on her way to Bible class, and she probably knew showing up would make it harder for me to say no. We took turns driving every week. It soon became our custom to stop for ice cream after class.

Over ice cream one evening she said, "Carolyn and I went to church because we needed to feel God in our lives to cope. What did you do to help you get through living so far away from everything and everyone you loved besides Roy?"

Here we go again. People need what they need to be happy. Andrea needed religion and I needed her. I don't need a sweating preacher reading scriptures, doing a fancy dance step in a purple robe, and I didn't need one delivering a disjointed message while passing the plate for money to fund a building extension, or the choir's tour of Atlanta, or his daughter's tuition to a historically black college.

I felt the presence of God all the time, so I knew what Andrea was talking about, but I didn't need the ritual. All I had to do was see Roy smile, or hear Wynton Marsalis hit and hold a certain note, or look at the vastness of the ocean to know a higher power existed.

I thought about my answer for a couple of seconds longer while I savored my cone of black walnut ice cream. "Mainly I hung on to the idea that we wouldn't be gone forever. I wasn't sure how long, but I knew eventually we'd come home. Until then—don't laugh now—I had fantasies of being an undercover spy on hiatus to raise my child. The enemy was all around, but I had the skills and resources I needed to survive."

"You're very resourceful because the police couldn't find you. You could probably work for the CIA."

"Thanks. The reason I left, I will always stand by the principle behind it, and Roy is my heart, but being away from everybody else who loves me and is my support network was hard. I'll never take the value of family and friends for granted again, that's for sure."

Andrea nodded sympathetically, and then I realized I was preaching to the choir. I didn't have to tell her the value of loved ones.

"I often wondered if you had help from here," she asked.

I contemplated another moment while I watched her spoon up her plain vanilla from a cup. I didn't want to lie to Andrea, but I didn't want to create additional animosity between her and my family. She hadn't said anything directly, but the negative vibes were hard to ignore. She kept turning down my mother's invitation to Sunday dinner. Still, I decided to tell her the truth. "I contacted Sharon three, maybe four times just to stay in touch. We managed okay, and I didn't need money from anybody since I worked."

"Sharon? Carolyn always suspected her."

"And who did you suspect?"

"I'm not sure. I thought it was a guy conspiracy. Maybe your brother, Tim."

"Naw, Tim has been busy with his babies the past couple of years, and now a third one is on the way. Besides, there's an eight-year difference between us. He and I are just getting to be on the same playing field in life, so to speak."

"How did you work it out?" Curiosity lit up her eyes. From experience, I knew when something interested her, there'd be no letting go. I settled back in my seat, relaxing for the rest of her questions.

"Work out what? The playing field?"

"No. How did you communicate with Sharon?"

After biting into my cone, I said, "I'd have a flyer forwarded."

"What do you mean?"

"I'd get in touch with a friend in St. Louis, and then that person would mail one of Cecil's bookstore flyers to Sharon."

"Interesting."

There was a comfortable silence for a few minutes, but she had a puzzled look on her face.

"What are you thinking about?"

"Nothing. Family, I guess. I think about Carolyn's case a lot, too. Out of the blue, it'll hit me. My sister's dead. Somebody killed her. How can I be sitting in an ice cream parlor instead of searching the streets?"

I reached over and took her hand. "Try not to be so hard on yourself. Bad things happen to people we love and we are helpless to control or change that." I sympathized with Andrea's struggle to come to terms with Carolyn's death, but unlike Andrea, I concentrated my energies on moving on, not lingering in the past. It would have been nice if Carolyn had gotten her life together, but my heart was forever numb on that subject, having served its time being torn apart by Carolyn's antics.

More silence, but she finally gave a weak smile and picked up her spoon again.

"Guess what?" I said.

"What?"

"I'm looking forward to tomorrow night." I grinned at her like a kid grins on Christmas morning. She was the unsuspecting present I planned to open.

"I am, too, I think." She smiled tentatively.

When I found out Andrea paid every week for a massage, I offered my services. She hesitated at first, saying it was like walking past a hungry wolf with a hamburger and expecting him not to want to eat it. I said I respected her commitment to celibacy and swore not to do anything to compromise our decision. Having my ankles crossed was the ticket. Everybody knows when legs or fingers cross, the promise is void.

Once in the car, Andrea headed toward Delmar. From there she turned north to take me home.

"Benjamin, there was never anything between you and Marissa, right?"

"Marissa?" I frowned. Where was this coming from all of a sudden? "No, I told you. She was Roy's babysitter while we were away. She wants to earn some money for school, so she's still helping out until she leaves for school."

"I know. I know what you told me."

What is up with this look of doubt?

"Andrea, Marissa needed a place to live, she needed help arranging for her aunt's burial, and I needed help with Roy. That's all there was and all there has ever been."

"But what about social services? I never understood that part. They allowed her to live with a man she barely knew?"

Glancing at her, I saw that hungry curiosity again. Now she was onto a new topic, definitely fishing for information. What was she after? "She was undocumented at the time. When the police came to notify her about her aunt, she didn't answer the door. She was afraid of the police. People in her apartment complex were in the same boat. No one volunteered anything."

"No one knew she lived there?"

"No one who would report it to any agency."

"How did she claim her aunt's body?"

"Her body? Andrea, why do you need to know all of this? There's no way you could be jealous of a kid like that. Give me some credit, she's not even eighteen!"

"Fine." She turned on the radio. "If you don't want me know about your past life, okay."

I listened to the end of the headline news and the beginning of the stock report before I turned the radio off. If she needed to hear this stuff about Marissa to keep the peace, what was the big deal?

"Her aunt worked at a chicken processing plant. One of her supervisors agreed to go with one of the aunt's friends to identify the body and make arrangements. They took up a collection at work, I contributed what I could and we buried her aunt. That was important to Marissa."

"I'm sure it was. What about her aunt's resources? Her personal belongings? A car for example—furniture, things like that? What happened to all of that?"

"She worked in a chicken processing plant, Andrea. Anything she had was vintage Goodwill. There was no car. She took the bus."

"Oh."

"You have nothing to worry about. Just because she was a cheerleader and all of that, in my eyes she was a kid."

"She was a cheerleader?

"Yeah. Good at it too. Her high school team even came to St. Louis earlier this year for a national competition."

"What? When?"

"In late February."

"In February? You mean Marissa was here when Carolyn was shot?"

"Yeah, unfortunate coincidence. The police questioned her about that."

Her curious eyes grew to the size of lemons.

"Oh, come on. You couldn't possibly think Marissa had anything to do with Carolyn's murder."

"I certainly can think that." Andrea pulled over, obviously too upset to drive and talk at the same time.

"There's coincidence, and then there's coincidence. More far-fetched things happen all the time. Is Marissa in love with you?"

"What? In love with me? That's totally ridiculous. Marissa is a wonderful person who happened to be in town for a cheerleader competition. You see how sweet-natured and smart Roy is? Being around Marissa had a lot to do with that. Besides, the police talked to her and she hasn't been arrested. She didn't shoot Carolyn, Andrea. Trust me."

"Does Mr. Elrod have guns in the house?"

"Yeah, safe out of harm's way. What now? You think Marissa stole one of his guns? I think he'd know if one were missing, Andrea."

CHAPTER 13

Andrea

The next morning, I kept vigil, watching the clock on the mantel. I wanted to catch Peck in his office and not in the field, so he couldn't read my number on his cell phone and decide to get back to me whenever he felt like it. I paced, sat and paced again. At nine thirty-one, I dialed his number. He picked up on the first ring.

"I need to talk to you. Can I stop by today?"

"Who is this?"

My anger and startled luck had made me forget to identify myself. "This is Andrea Young, Detective Peck."

"Oh, yes. Ms. Young." I heard papers shuffle, then his muffled voice said, "Are these the ones you contacted already?" With the receiver uncovered, he spoke to me. "No, I'm juggling ten things at once. Today can't work. What's this about?"

"You didn't tell me Marissa Torres was in town the day Carolyn died. I'm assuming it was your crackerjack investigative team that spoke with her."

"Marissa Torres." He dragged out her name. "Her high school cheerleading squad came in third place. I told you her story checked out. What details I share or don't share with you are my call. You need to understand that."

"But—" I put my free hand on my hair and tugged it back to stop myself from screaming.

"I don't have time to talk now. That reward you posted is keeping this crackerjack team hopping. We still have to check an average of ten calls a week it generates, in addition to doing everything else required for four homicide investigations."

"Yesterday you told me I needed to trust the police department. How can I trust you if you won't keep me fully informed!"

"Ms. Young."

"Yes."

"Calm down. You've made an impression. Even if you hadn't, I'm committed to doing the best I can to solve your sister's case. You keep calling me, I'll keep calling you and we'll hope for the best. What do you say?"

Calm down? I paced the floor, flexing and relaxing my hand. "So Marissa has an alibi? What is it?"

I listened to his huge sigh, as if he had hoped he could get away without telling me more. "She had dinner with friends. Her roommates vouch she was back by 7:30."

"You spoke with her friends and verified the dinner?"

"No, my crackerjack team and I take turns sampling new doughnut recipes instead of verifying information. I thought you knew that?"

If I could have crawled through the phone, I would have strangled him. "Detective Peck, you know what you can do with your sarcasm?"

"I'd venture a guess, yeah. I'll be in touch." He hung up.

My mind reeled in a hundred directions at once. *Carolyn's estimated time of death was between six and eight P.M., but that was not exact. And who were these friends? Who did she know in St. Louis? Benjamin's family probably. If they had dropped her off at the hotel at 7:30, who's to say she didn't leave again and get a cab ...* No. I massaged the tension in my neck as I continued to pace. *Marissa would have had to know someone with a car like Mrs. Tuddle described. And, the gun? If Mr. Elrod didn't give it to her, maybe she stole it.*

Unable to figure it out, but unable to let it go, I walked outside and sat, transferring my energy into the back and forth movement of the glider on my patio while still holding the phone. *Did she bring it with her?* You can't bring a gun on an airplane. Jacksonville to St. Louis had to be close to a thousand miles. A long bus ride, but doable. So she could have brought it with her, in which case, we would never find it.

I almost pushed redial, but got up and got my keys instead. If I hurried, Peck would still be there.

Not making a pest of oneself was normally a good thing, but not today. The squeaky wheel got the oil and Gloria was always telling me I should be more assertive. Of course, compared to Gloria, Donald Trump, was a mild mannered pushover, so it was hard to live up to her standards.

Peck said I had made an impression—I didn't think he meant a positive one. I stopped at Starbucks for a truce offering. There was no point in having an adversarial relationship with the person I needed to depend on. Eighty-seven degrees not withstanding, caffeine and cop work went hand in hand.

Thirty-five minutes later, I pulled into the police station parking lot, scanned the vehicles and noticed several detective-type cars. Which one of those large, non-descript four-door Fords was his?

Inside, behind the bulletproof glass, a white-haired gentleman in uniform said, "Good morning."

"Good morning. Is it possible for me to get a note to Detective Peck?" I figured if I just asked to see him, he'd say no.

"Peck? He's still here, I think. What's your name?"

"I spoke with him once this morning, and he already told me he couldn't see me. But, I just need one minute of his time." I held up the coffee.

"Oh, well, let me see what I can do. The coffee's a nice gesture, but you might be some crazy who laced it with arsenic. Are you?"

My hand rested on my chest in a you-don't-mean-me gesture. "What? No!"

"Yeah, that's what they all say."

I thought he was kidding, but I couldn't be sure.

He put on his reading glasses, then looked over them at me. "What's your name? I'll tell him you're here bearing gifts."

Ten minutes passed before Detective Peck pushed through the gray door and came over to me. His crisply pressed brown suit and freshly trimmed dark hair said dapper Dan, but dark circles under his eyes said sleep deprivation.

Looking at me, he rubbed his bottom lip a couple times with his thumb. Reaching for the coffee, he remained standing.

"Regular?" he asked.

"Yeah."

He opened the lid. Steam swirled up and away—it helped that I'd gotten a venti. "Did we leave something unsaid this morning?"

I leaped from my chair, ready to make my case. What was it with arrogant men like him and Benjamin blocking my need for answers? I reached for my hair again, this time tucking my natural curls behind my ears. "I'll be real quick. If Marissa went to spend time with the Elrod family, she could have taken one of Mr. Elrod's guns. He has guns. Could you please check that out?"

Detective Peck took a couple of leisurely sips. "Ms. Young, when I spoke to the Elrods, I covered as much ground as I could. There's no way I could get access to his guns, if he has them. There is no probable cause."

"Oh," I said, sagging into a chair. That meant no connection to the crime strong enough to warrant invading Mr. Elrod's privacy. The bright glare of reality wilted my inflated assumption. Was I so desperate for answers that I would accuse a seventeen- year-old babysitter, who's only known crime was being a cheerleader in St. Louis at the time of Carolyn's murder? Looking away, I sighed. "It's just that …"

"I'm feeling you, Ms. Young. Roy's babysitter was in town the same time Roy's mother was killed. It's just not enough to go on. Thanks for the coffee."

"You're welcome, Detective Peck." Was my face red with embarrassment?

"So you think Benjamin and Marissa have more than just a working relationship? Is that what you're suggesting?" he asked.

I shook my head, admitting my error again. "No, Benjamin wouldn't do that. It's just that a woman can become obsessed with a man, you know. Feelings don't have to be reciprocated. If one person gets an idea in her head … never mind. Forget it."

"It's forgotten." He walked a few paces before turning around. "Next time, just so you know, I like it black."

CHAPTER 14
Benjamin

I surprised Andrea by showing up with our very own massage table the next evening. Obviously, based on our conversation about Marissa, this night would do her a world of good. Carolyn's murder had her overwrought and grabbing straws out of thin air, trying to figure out Carolyn's murderwhich was a waste of time. They'd never find out who did it. But hey—she needed to grieve for her sister in her own way. Besides, I'd taken Marissa to the airport this morning, so maybe her being gone would let things chill out.

Did I look like a man who would take advantage of a child? Especially one who depended on me for her livelihood? Andrea knew better—it was just the stress, and I was the man with a plan to fix that.

"Wow, this'll be much more comfortable than working on the floor," she said. "Where'd you get it?"

I looked at her white oversized sweater, over black pants and her warm, open smile. "Somebody at work knew somebody getting rid of it. I also bought some scented oils and this bottle of wine to help you relax."

"Uh-huh," she said with a bemused look. "I suppose you're planning to light a fire and play some music, too?"

"Now you're thinking. Why don't you go ahead and uh, get undressed while I set things up."

"Benjamin, we agreed to a therapeutic massage, not a seduction, right?"

"Oh, definitely. I just want it to be nice for you."

"Uh-huh, are you sure you're not trying to test my resolve?"

"Me? Don't be silly. Go on, get ready."

Andrea came back wrapped in a floral sheet, no bra. Guessing what other article of clothing might be missing made it difficult for me to blink. As I handed her a glass of wine, she smiled and said, "I wouldn't trust any other man, Benjamin, but I trust you. I'm blessed to have you in my life."

What did she have to go and say that for? I only wanted to see how many parts of her anatomy I could squeeze and stroke, hoping for a chance to give her some pleasure. At this point, a look at it would do. I wanted to refresh my memory, that's all. That idea faded in a way my hard-on refused to do.

It was too late for me to back out of giving her a massage now. *Lincoln, Washington, Jefferson …* I tried to remember all the Presidents' names while I kneaded the soft flesh of her shoulders and back. She turned her head. The straining bulge in my pants was inches from her cheek. Fortunately, she kept her eyes closed, and I could move to the other side of the table. *Ford, Eisenhower, Grant.*

I rubbed her lower body. *Madison, Roosevelt, Truman.* I knew those thighs were my road home, but there might as well have been orange cones and a traffic sign flashing "Detour at Sweet Juncture." *Taft, Johnson, Harding. Harding, oh Lord.* By the time the massage ended, I had remembered thirty of our nation's leaders and all parts of me had calmed down.

Shaking my head, I folded the table. There was no way I would put myself through agony like this every week. Andrea would have to continue to see her massage therapist unless I figured out how to keep my lust under control. There wasn't enough cold water in the whole state of Missouri.

CHAPTER 15
Benjamin

"My mom wants to know if you're coming over for dinner this Sunday? Since we've been going out a few months, she thought it was time," I asked Andrea with my arms wrapped tight around her waist and my lips grazing the back of her neck. We were at her place, cleaning up after dessert.

"Sunday? I have my Singles Group meeting." She dipped a plate in the water and gave it another swish with the sponge as she leaned back into my chest.

"Singles Group?"

"Yeah, you remember. The last couple have been canceled for one reason or another. Gloria and BJ come sometime, too. You're welcome to join us."

"Okay, maybe next time." *Next time, hell.* Gloria hated me, and BJ, well, I wasn't going out of my way to spend my time with gay-boy. Besides, I didn't need another church group. I was doing enough to develop my spiritual side by going to Bible class and helping Andrea when she did shopping for some of the folks in the retirement home.

"Next Sunday then?" I asked moving to stand beside her while I grabbed a dishtowel.

She looked at me with frustration in her coffee colored eyes. "Benjamin, I know it's been four months since you've been back, and I know she's your mother and she is Roy's grandmother, but I can't forgive her lack of compassion for Carolyn. I think it will get better in time."

"I accept you need time. But I don't get why having dinner together isn't a good way of working toward forgiveness, you know, that well-touted Christian doctrine?"

She dissolved into a kitchen chair, her leg folded under her. She rested an elbow on the table with one hand covering a brown cheek as she watched me dry the dishes. I felt guilty sweating her. She had, after all, forgiven me for taking Roy. I just didn't get why she was being this way about my mom. "I'm sorry I said forgiveness was a Christian doctrine. I know you of all people know that. It's this dinner thing. It's a stumbling block we need to find a way around, Andrea. What will it take?"

She twisted her mouth to the side in thought. "Maybe a letter."

"What?"

"I'll write your mother a letter and she can respond. It's a legitimate technique. People who have major problems like this often find writing is a good way to sort out feelings."

I don't know why I was surprised when my mom put the letter on my lap three days later while I was trying to catch the evening news. I'd open it later because I already knew what it contained. It was Andrea reaching out to my mother, trying to find a way to handle their differences. Tapping the envelope against my palm, I watched my mom and waited.

"I don't know that I like her tone, Benjamin. She wants an apology. I didn't do anything I wouldn't do again this very minute if the same situation."

She sat on the love seat next to her matching floral sofa, clearly peeved.

I clicked the TV off and sat forward. "It's not easy for anybody, Mama. I'm tired of being caught in the middle, I know that much."

"You're in the middle? I thought I was."

"I want a wife, a home, and all that good stuff for Roy and me."

"A wife? When did you decide that?" My mother looked at me like her shoes were too tight.

"I've been thinking about it I guess. I haven't asked her."

"Are you going to move into her place?"

She'd prefer to know that, than ask if I were in love. Love that makes the heart do flip-flops had never existed in her world, as far as I could tell. For my mother, love equaled loyalty and living up to one's obligations; nothing less and nothing more. Well, I'd tried that kind of love with Carolyn. This time I wanted, needed, demanded a love that thrilled and inspired. Not a love that only made me feel morally correct.

"Andrea and I haven't discussed it. Do this for me, Mom. Can you please just write her back and open a dialogue?"

"Maybe; I don't know. She can't bring herself to grace my doorstep." She drew back and raised her eyebrows in exaggerated disbelief. "What kind of Christian is she supposed to be when she can't even come inside my home to wait for you so you can go to Bible study? No, she has to sit outside in the car and wait for you. I may not have time to write a letter. I'll see."

"Okay." I knew when not to press.

"I don't think it is a good idea, if my opinion matters."

"What isn't a good idea?"

"Andrea is not ready to be Roy's mother. If she was, then she would understand what I did. I got a letter from Marissa the other day. I'll write her back. If you're going to consider marrying someone, let me suggest you take another look."

"What are you talking about, Mom?"

"I know Marissa's young, but she'll be eighteen by the end of this month. That girl has a heart of gold. You know how good she is with Roy. She cooks, she cleans, she's smart and she's pretty. More important," she pointed to the letter, "Marissa doesn't have all this extra baggage Andrea has. How do you think you're going to build a marriage on a rocky foundation like that?"

I didn't know how, I just knew that we would.

Days passed, and then before I knew it, another month went by and nothing had improved because my mother and Andrea still did not talk, or write to each other. I know it's something out of a bad made-for-TV movie, but I had to get my mom and Andrea together. I invited them both to brunch without letting the other one know.

When Andrea walked up to our table, her smile faded for a second, but she recovered well. I helped her off with her coat. She had on a short black skirt and a pink sweater. Her supple, shapely curves always got me going. She joined my mother and me as we sat around a red tablecloth and fake crystal goblets. I could tell Andrea was uncomfortable, because she kept running her hand through her hair.

My mom kept pursing her lips and clearing her throat. I was relieved when after several minutes, Mom said, "Let's talk about the letter, shall we?"

Suppressing an urge to excuse myself, I drank from a tall glass of water. I would stay and watch and hope they wouldn't need a referee.

"Okay." Andrea put down her fork with the uneaten egg still on it. "I can't erase the picture of Carolyn knocking on your door, Mrs. Elrod. She begged you to tell her where her baby was. She knocked until her knuckles were raw and her voice was gone, and you'd yell through the door you didn't know where Roy was. All the time you knew. I'd try to stop her, but when I couldn't you would call the police and have them drag Carolyn off your front porch."

"Carolyn was a drug addict," my mother began after clearing her throat for the thirty-first time in thirty minutes. "I protected my grandson and my son. I know she was your sister. I realize how she must have suffered, but yes, I chose not to lessen her suffering because I was afraid for Benjamin and Roy." She took a sip of coffee, and then returned her cup carefully to its saucer.

"All she wanted to know was where Roy was. Couldn't you see how she deteriorated before your very eyes?"

"If you mean did her appearance let me know she was a crack addict, yes it did." My mother's eyes flickered with anger now. "There was a warrant out for Ben's arrest. Would Roy end up living with a drug-addicted mother again? Would Benjamin go to prison? This is what I had to deal with." She let out a long breath. "Besides, it was for Benjamin to decide to contact Carolyn, not me."

"Intellectually, I understand that. Still, the picture stays," Andrea said. "I can't help it. I can't walk up your front steps, let alone knock on your door to come in. I don't think I will ever be able to. There are too many bad memories. It's not like you ever liked Carolyn, Mrs. Elrod."

No one could deny that. My mother had been polite on the surface, but everyone had known how she felt about Carolyn. Carolyn had said my mother would never pick someone like her for me. After all, Millicent Elrod raised kids motivated to do well in school because we bought into America's rally cry of no limits, just challenges. All of her kids graduated high school and circumvented the drug scene and prison systems, pitfalls for so many others living in the inner city. To have one of her children invite drugs into their lives after years of her good counsel, not to mention having our dad as the anti-role model, had been unsettling.

Mom shifted from side to side, stretching her neck high and back like a swan about to attack. "Do you realize Sunday dinner at my home is a tradition this family respects? Benjamin's brother and sister come with their friends and family."

Andrea took in a deep breath and let it out slowly. "I would never deprive Benjamin or Roy of a family tradition. I cannot come, but I have appreciated your invitations."

"Andrea, I can't move to a different house. I can't say I'm sorry for what I did either. What I can say, and mean with all my heart, is that I'm sorry Carolyn died not knowing where her son was. As a mother, I know how horrible that must have been. If you can't come for Sunday dinner, you can't come. That's between you and Benjamin, but know you are always welcome."

They both looked at me at the same time. Neither of them spoke. I had to select my words carefully. "Andrea, your decision not to come to dinner creates a void for me, but I didn't know until I read your letter that Carolyn knocked on the door like that. It's more than just my mom not telling you where Roy and I were. I see now." Turning to face my mom, I leaned in toward her.

"And, Mom, you're right. It's an important family tradition I won't miss again as long as I am able and Roy has to be there. How about rotating the location of dinner?"

Her eyes got as round as the saucers on the table, then her mouth formed a flabbergasted o-shape. "Certainly not! I have no desire to play gypsy, roaming all over, planning around people's schedules. Sunday dinner stays put."

My one and only idea crashed and burned. I drank some mimosa in its honor.

My mother pushed her plate back and folded her hands on the table in front of her. "Eventually, Andrea, you might be able to perceive what is best for Roy and for Benjamin. At some point, what is best for them might become your primary consideration, maybe not. Time will tell."

Andrea snatched her napkin from her lap and threw it on her plate. "Okay, now I'm a selfish bitch, only interested in what's best for me? Is that what you are saying?"

"I'm asking you if you are part of something bigger, or if it is all really about you. I'm sure I'll find out when you find out. Goodbye."

Watching my mother leave, I almost wanted to go with her rather than face Andrea, who sat with her hands over her face.

I touched her shoulder, hoping to communicate that she and I were still on the same page no matter what my mother had said.

Andrea slowly dragged her hands away from her face, shaking her head. "She's right."

"She's right?" I repeated.

Andrea looked as if she'd just missed the shot that would have won the game. "Absolutely. Is this an 'us thing' or a 'me thing?' Your mother's right. I couldn't see it until now."

My soul filled with joy. I wished I'd brought the engagement ring I'd purchased in an optimistic moment. This would have been the perfect time to give it to her; the last pillar standing in our way had just fallen.

The tip of Andrea's tongue peeked out from burgundy lips. "I'm not ready for it to be an 'us thing,' Benjamin. Right now it is about me and my need to heal."

I stared at her as if staring would make her come to her senses. "What? You don't mean that, Andrea. you're just upset. We have something solid developing between us. I know it. You know it."

"I wanted to know it. I thought I knew it. I don't know it; I'm not there yet. I think we have to stop seeing each other."

Weak, sardonic laughter let loose from someplace, and I realized it was coming from me. "What? Just like that?"

"Well ..." She removed the napkin from her plate and folded it into parts. "I think maybe we can ask your brother to bring Roy by my place three, four times a month, if that's okay."

Now I picked up my napkin and slapped my plate with it. "That often?" My head started bobbing up and down as if it were motorized. "Yeah, yeah sure thing. Not a problem." Call it male ego, but I was pissed. She'd dismissed me from her life as easily as you cancel a newspaper. Nonchalantly, I smoothed out my left eyebrow. "We'll arrange for you to see Roy around your schedule, don't worry."

She looked at me as if I was the one being contrary. "You have to admit it's complicated, Benjamin. Sometimes when things are complicated, we need to heed the warning signs."

"For God's sakes, Andrea. Life is always complicated. If you let complications stop you, you will never get anything you want out of life."

She left without saying anything else. I sat at our table thinking about going home and listening to Sarah Vaughn sing "What a Difference a Day Makes." Was it hot in here, or was it me? I wiped the sweat off my forehead. We'd come this far, got this close for me to find out I meant so little to her. How could I have been so wrong about us?

Hell, I never liked Andrea's friends anyway, and this celibate lifestyle was questionable on its best day. When the waiter walked by and asked me if everything was alright, I had to say, "Hit me with another mimosa, will you?"

I sat there drinking, appeasing my hurt and anger as much as orange juice and champagne would allow. Andrea didn't know I wanted to marry her. I had never told her I loved her. By the time I finished my drink, it was clear she should be aware of my intentions before she decided to walk out of my life forever.

I pulled out my wallet to pay the bill. When I looked up, Andrea was standing next to me with a tear-streaked face. "What did you forget?" I asked as casually as I could.

"As soon as I said we should stop seeing each other, I regretted it. As complicated as this is, I can't imagine not being with you. I love you, Benjamin. I want you to know that. I hope we can work it out, but even if we can't, I want you to know I love you."

God, just to hear her say those words moved me in unexpected ways. Women have been making a big deal about them since before dirt, but now, for the first time, I finally understood what three simple words could mean. Relief flooded my soul in a way only a love song can come close to explaining, but I wasn't ready to let her off the hook yet. "You love me. What was all of that a minute ago about 'not being there?'"

Rubbing her temple, she sat down again and took a moment, as if she needed to phrase this just right. "I have these feelings of love and hurt all mixed in my brain and in my heart. Some days, I'm the happiest woman in the world, and some days I'm so miserable and confused I don't know what to do. I've been praying, trying to get some help with this, but I'm still struggling. What am I going to do, Benjamin?"

"This is what you can do." I stood up and pulled her up to me kissing her gently. Grinning, I kissed her again in a way that could leave no doubt in her mind about how glad I was she came back. The other restaurant patrons applauded my moves.

"I've got something else to give you that'll solve most of your confusion," I whispered.

"Oh really?" she said with cautious interest and a raised brow.

"Not that. That's off-limits for a while, but you'll see."

CHAPTER 16
Benjamin

I chose a three-quarter-carat diamond with a round cut in a platinum setting. It spoke of elegance and simplicity— how I thought of Andrea.

Although the Sunday dinner problem remained unresolved, I decided to propose the week following the infamous brunch. I knew who I wanted to spend my life with.

Andrea's not joining us for Sunday dinner was impossible to ignore because it came up every week, but I understood. It represented Andrea being true to Carolyn's memory in the only way she had left. At least, that's what Sharon told me, and it made sense. After years of counseling, I figured Sharon might have a handle on some things.

Andrea had forgiven me, but she still needed to have someone to be mad at for the way Carolyn's life turned out. My mother was the recipient of that anger for now, and that's just the way it would be until something changed.

Andrea and I had two standing dates during the week; Bible study on Wednesdays and shopping on Fridays for the nursing home residents. I could have asked her to marry me on one of those evenings, but I arranged for another massage night. Nothing else would support the mood I wanted to create.

I rang the bell, and then let myself in with my key. She'd given it to me to wait on a delivery and never asked for it back. I felt my pocket for the ring box one more time before I set out to get a fire going. Andrea had beaten me to it. The fire blazed, as it should on a cold November night. I retrieved the massage table from her den.

Our paths crossed as I carried the table into the living room, and we kissed hello. Her hair, caught up in one of those claw barrettes, allowed gold hoop earrings to swing in full view.

"I'm getting dinner started," she said.

I moved the coffee table to make space. "Why don't we go out to eat after we're done?"

"The last time I had one of your massages, I felt like melted butter when it was over. Can you take melted butter out for dinner?"

"Only if I'm having lobster."

"Very good." She laughed at my snappy comeback as she returned to the kitchen. "What's in the bag?"

I yelled a little to be heard above the pots she rattled. "Some new massage oil. It's called orange sesame."

"Sounds interesting. I'll be a willing test subject." She rejoined me in the living room, maneuvering around the massage table to get to the CD player. "Do we want Chopin or Luther?"

Chopin could play the hell out of the piano, but my choice for marriage proposal music hands down was Mr. Vandross. "Luther." *Classics never die.*

"Luther it is," she said, touching my cheek. "Why don't you go first tonight, Benjamin. You look a little stressed."

"All right. Sure." I changed in her bedroom and came to the table wrapped in a towel.

Andrea stood at the head of the table, stretching my neck muscles with soft hands. With no hair in the way, she seemed to enjoy spending a few extra minutes on my bald scalp. Her inspired hands told my body to unwind.

"How was your day?" she asked.

"Cold, like it's been everyday since Halloween. Mmmm, Andrea, you are so good at this." My tension dissolved. "That job is killing me." After another few minutes, I said, "We could make a fortune taking this table and going to everybody's house I work with."

"Thanks." She laughed. "I always wanted a man who appreciated me enough to share me with others."

She worked my shoulder muscles. "Keep the pressure right there, don't stop."

"Harder?"

"No, that's it. Keep going … ahhh, yes."

What she was doing felt wonderful, but the bundle of nerves jangling in my stomach wouldn't let me relax too much. What if she said no?

I remember asking Carolyn to marry me. "You don't love me, Ben. You want to make us official for Roy." She'd been right.

Andrea's hands moved to my lower back. I thought about the other women in my past. Debbie, my high school sweetheart, had gotten married her first year in college, breaking my heart. At the University of Missouri, Angela, Cherise, and Lakeisha had given me a chance to learn outside the classroom. Carolyn next, then Anise, a woman I'd had a one-night fling with while Carolyn and I were together. Finally, there was Gina, a waitress in Jacksonville. Andrea would be the last.

I thought about my family. My mother would be less than thrilled about my engagement. Sharon and Tim would be happy as long as I was happy. Roy already loved Andrea, so there'd be no problem there.

"Okay, Benjamin, you're done." Andrea flexed my toes forward and backward and pressed her thumb into my arch one final time.

She changed clothes in the den, giving me the privacy I needed to pull myself together in the bedroom. I disposed of the ring box.

Back at the table, an angel appeared, hair loose and flowing, a pink sheet tucked under her arms.

"Did you like the oil?" she asked.

"What? Yeah." Her beauty distracted me. "I warmed it up in the microwave for you."

"Thank you."

She settled onto the table. I rubbed her neck, her shoulders, and then down her right arm. She sighed, relaxed. I moved to the other side of the table to work on her left shoulder. When I got more oil, I transferred the ring from my pocket into my hand, then I slipped it on her finger. It fit perfectly.

"What did you do?" She raised her head and peeked at her newly adorned finger.

Grinning at me, she sat up, pulling her sheet around her, but never taking her eyes off the outstretched fingers of her left hand. "Benjamin! What have you done?"

"Andrea, this ring is a token of my undying love and affection. I would like it very much if you would be my wife." *Where had that lame proposal come from? Dorkese for Dummies?*

"Oh, Benjamin." She kissed me with her lips, and her heart. I could feel it. "This ring is beautiful, but …"

Oh God. She's going to turn me down. My lungs forgot to breathe.

"Benjamin, are you sure?"

"What do you mean? I've never given anyone else a ring." I'm sure that bit of information was logical on some planet.

Trailing her fingers along the side of my face, she said, "I want us to be sure. You've only been back a few months. Do you really love me?"

"I love you, Andrea. Haven't I said it enough?" *Again with the faulty logic.*

"You haven't said it at all. I mean, it's not that I haven't felt your love, because I have, but hearing that you love me is good, too."

"I meant to say it. I've been wanting to say it for a long, long time, probably my whole life. I love you. I swear to God I love you. You are the only woman I've ever loved."

Her eyes sought mine, and I saw doubt in them. "Why? Why do you love me?"

Despite the doubt, her question was easy for me to answer. "Because you're honest, straightforward, and not afraid to be passionate about what you believe in." I picked up her left hand and brought it to my lips.

"You have a good heart, a good mind and a great sense of humor." I kissed the open palm of her right hand. "What I love most about you is how you expect life to be full of possibilities and I don't want to miss sharing any of them with you." I kissed her lips, then hugged her.

In our embrace, she whispered, "Yes, I will marry you."

I looked at her and laughed. "Oh man, you scared me. I'm lucky you want to be with me, Andrea. We're going to have a great life, I promise."

She was too excited to finish her massage. I watched her hurry off to dress for dinner. My gaze traveled toward the ceiling. *Thank you, God*, transformed from thought to words.

CHAPTER 17
Andrea

I acquired a cart from one of the corrals on the grocery store lot. Yogurt was on sale this week—three for one dollar. Gloria had asked me to pick up twelve for her mom on my way home.

Maneuvering through the fresh vegetables and fruit aisle, past the cold cuts, I found the yogurt across from the orange juice, between the organic milk and eggs. The last six were pineapple banana, and Mrs. Wellborn didn't want that flavor.

The roasted chicken aroma made my mouth water as I spotted someone to help me in 6B. He said he'd check on the yogurt for me.

I backtracked to the baking needs row and picked up flour for the holiday cookies, or in my case, anytime cookies. Rounding the corner, I almost ran into Eugene.

He put his hand on the cart to prevent it from tagging his lower thigh. "Well, hello there."

The deep resonance of his voice vibrating through the cart handle was the first thing I had noticed about Eugene Sherwood.

"Eugene, hi." I smiled. "I haven't seen you in a while. You transferred this fall." Of course, he needed me to tell him that he had switched high schools. "Where are you now?" We began to stroll along. Or, I strolled, Eugene, large and bulky, lumbered along like a tired defensive lineman, but after a day of teaching, that's been known to happen to the most energetic among us.

At six-feet-three, three hundred pounds, Eugene sounded like Barry White. His beard was gone, but his mustache remained, salted with age.

"I'm over at Metro High School now. I know the principal. He wants quality staff and asked me to make the move. Been thinking about you, tried to call you. You've changed your number?"

"Oh, I've moved."

"Where'd you move?"

"Off of West Florrisant. Did you want something?"

"Want something? Oh, you mean why was I calling? I was just thinking about you, looking at some pictures, remembering."

"Really." I cleared my throat. "Well, I hope you like it at Metro." Metro was a magnet school with an International Baccalaureate affiliation, and was probably a good place to work. We'd reached the yogurt section, but the guy hadn't returned. "I'm waiting for more yogurt," I explained.

Eugene picked up a container and examined it." "This stuff any good?"

"It's okay. I've had it before. I'm getting some for Gloria's mom. Are you shopping for dinner?"

"I'll buy, if you cook?"

"Umm, no." I made sure the tone of my voice trailed up the scale pleasantly. Did he think I wanted a dinner date?

"You've got plans?" he asked.

"No, but I'm engaged now."

"Engaged? Now that's big news. When did this happen?"

"Last month."

He swayed his head and shoulders like a rat searching for cheese. I knew he hunted my engagement ring. I showed him. Immediately, he focused an invisible magnifying glass over my finger while he rubbed the stone with his thumb.

Annoyed, I said, "Eugene, this ring is awesome and you know it."

"Sweetheart, what I know is I would have given you something three times as large."

"Oh well." I snatched my hand back. "Things work out like they do for a reason."

"Who's your new love?"

"Benjamin Dunn."

He looked at me like I'd asked him to buy green meat. "Benjamin Dunn? Your sister's Benjamin Dunn?"

"Imagine that." A fake smile masked my irritation.

"Damn. When did he get back in town?"

"This summer." *Where is this guy with the yogurt?*

Surprise, mixed with contempt, spread across Eugene's face. "You're engaged to marry your sister's man? The one who took her baby and made her do drugs again?"

A passing shopper looked me up and down with a vitriolic stare. I had come to expect this kind of response. People at work and church often gave me the same looks when I told them about Benjamin and me. What could I do about it? Tell them cupid's arrow didn't discriminate?

"Oh, pardon my lack of social grace. My mama really did raise me better. Congratulations, Andi."

"Thank you." And thank God the man had arrived with the yogurt cases on a dolly. We watched him open a box to restock the shelf.

"How is your mother?" *Time for a different topic.*

"Well, she's doing reasonably well. She's got cancer, you know. It's hard to say how long she has, but her days are numbered."

I gasped. "Oh no, Eugene, I didn't know. I'm so sorry to hear that. Please give her my best. I'll keep her in my prayers." I thought of what my mother had gone through and shuddered. *Poor Mrs. Sherwood.* She was a nice woman who had always been kind to me. I'd have to make plans to see her before it was too late.

Eugene didn't offer more details about his mother, so I respected that. I turned to the grocery clerk. "Would you mind opening a box of vanilla? That's the kind I want."

"Sure thing, ma'am."

"Did they ever catch whoever shot Carolyn?" Eugene asked.

I shook my head.

"Yeah, it'll be a miracle if they ever do. Guess I'll try a couple of these," Eugene said. "Mind if I set them in your cart?"

"I'm ready to check out," I said by way of protest.

He placed two blueberry-flavored yogurts in my cart, being his usual pushy self. "Me too." We made our way to the express lane that, of course, had a line five deep.

"You're not shopping after all?" I asked.

"No, I'll pick up some ribs or something. Say, the house is almost finished."

The house? It was actually finished? My heart beat faster wondering how he'd used Carolyn's input. I was dying to see it. "Is it the way you envisioned?"

"Like Carolyn envisioned, you mean. It's da bomb, Andi. Really, Carolyn did a hellified job. The girl had talent. She had the eye, didn't she? Why she wasted her time working at a bank, I'll never know. And your part came out nice too. Took a little longer than I thought, but there are always delays with different permits, companies going bankrupt and all kinds of problems, but it finally came together."

He had my full attention, and I couldn't stop smiling. Heart full of pride, I knew Carolyn would have had a career in decorating, if she could have kept her life together, but drugs got in the way. "Yeah, I hear construction always takes longer than you think it will. I'm glad you're pleased."

"You think you can come to the open house? Won't be for a couple of weeks, and my mother sure would get a kick out of seeing you again. And the house, you know it's really a tribute to Carolyn's talent. You have to see it.

"It would be great to see your mom, Eugene, and I'd like to see the house. I can probably work it out, but I'll let you know, okay?"

He handed me a pen and a forgotten receipt for me to write my phone number on before he loaded the cart contents on the conveyor belt. He paid for fourteen containers of yogurt and two five-pound bags of flour, ignoring my attempt to pull out my wallet.

"Work it out," he told me. "Work it out. You'll be glad you did. Seeing how all the pieces fit is going to be a real treat for you."

"Thanks. Goodbye, Eugene." Seeing Carolyn's vision come to fruition would fill a void for me, but I wasn't sure Benjamin would agree to accompany me to my ex-lover's house. Men could be so territorial at times.

Eugene hugged me and kissed my cheek. "I'll send you that invitation and expect to see you there." He exited through a different door than the one I headed for.

Alrighty, I thought. *This can work. I can see Carolyn's work and I can visit with Mrs. Sherwood. When I explain why I need to go, Benjamin will understand. And besides, I want him to come with me.*

When I got to my car, I was less annoyed than I was when I first saw Eugene tonight. He and I had started out okay as most couples do, but he demanded more of my time and attention than I'd been willing to give; and his clingy, controlling nature was becoming a problem, even before Benjamin took Roy. After that whole nightmare began, Carolyn was my priority. Eugene whined and complained that we never saw each other. Finally he's said, "Soon as you find Roy, come find me. In the meantime, I'm out."

He called the next day, asking me if I'd learned my lesson, obviously thinking I'd be a wreck because he'd dumped me, but I was actually relieved and told him it was for the best.

Tonight he hadn't even asked about Roy. Yep, things work out like they do for a reason, and getting to see Carolyn's ideas come to life may be the reason I bumped into Eugene today. His black Expedition pulled out behind me. I waved to him in my rearview mirror.

CHAPTER 18
Andrea

Benjamin fixed a sagging shelf in my kitchen. I sat at the table, giving myself a home manicure, watching him.

"Why do you have a jar of onions in here?" He was emptying the cabinet.

"Onions? I'm not sure. Probably brought them for some recipe."

He set his level on the counter. "I'm going to put two supports here, close to either side so they won't be so noticeable. That will stop the wobbling."

"Great. Thank you. I saw Eugene yesterday."

"Oh really? Where?"

"Grocery store."

"How is he?"

"He's fine, but his mother's not doing too good. He invited us to his housewarming party in Kentucky."

"Oh, yeah. I remember he has family there. When is it?"

I waited for the power drill to stop so I wouldn't have to yell. "In a couple of weeks, on a Saturday. If you ask now, can you get off?"

"No. This is the holiday season. I was the last man hired, so that means I'm going to be busy covering people's vacation time. Sorry. Send our regrets and a gift."

"Benjamin, would you mind if I went? If Gloria and I went?"

He let his measuring tape snap closed and looked at me. "He knows we're engaged?"

"Yes."

"So he invites his former girlfriend who is engaged to his house in a different state. Why?"

"He mentioned how the house turned out really nice and he thanked me and Carolyn for the work we did. I really want to see Carolyn's work. See something she did I can be proud of. See something that will bring good memories."

He nodded, and then shook his head. "I'm not comfortable with you going without me, Andrea. After the holidays you can call him and finagle an invitation, and we'll go see the house. How's that?"

"I know. It's just, I look at Roy and have to fight back the tears some days. I miss my sister. I took out some more of her sketches. She was so alive and happy when she drew them. Other than Roy, I'd never seen her so excited about anything in her whole life. She'll be reflected there in his home. I need to feel her. Does that make sense?"

He'd been looking at me, but he picked up his hammer and started to drive a nail. "Yeah, I saw them on the coffee table. Carolyn had talent."

"And there's his mother."

He stopped hammering. "Who?"

"His mother. Mrs. Sherwood called this morning and invited me. She was such a comfort to me after the funeral and coming here was hard for her. You know she's blind and doesn't get out much. Do you really mind?"

"His mother, huh?" I heard him sigh from across the room. "Well, far be it from me to whip out the ball and chain. If you need to go, you need to go. Since Gloria's going with you, I guess it's all right."

It was the second week in December. Not officially winter, yet the icy temperatures delivered a cold promise of events to come.

I'd called Gloria and asked her to meet me for lunch. I removed our food from a tray, took off my hat and coat and settled in my seat across from her. A second later, the juice dripping down my chin testified to the moist delicious goodness of the double cheeseburger I bit into. Gloria handed me a napkin.

"No, don't think of Eugene as my reject." I continued the conversation we started in the Burger King line a moment ago. "Eugene is a professional who just finished building his dream home on land his family owns in Kentucky. This could be a match."

Gloria's eyebrows knitted disbelief. "Girl, what am I going to do with some clingy-ass man? You don't have to come up with something this whack to get me to go."

"Everybody would like to be the center of somebody's world, but Eugene and I didn't click like that. I don't think he's beyond hope."

After swirling her French fry until it was loaded with catsup, Gloria munched a minute. "When you put it that way, this might not be the worst idea I ever heard. It's not like decent prospects are lined up around the block." Her eyes cut to the leering, short guy at the next table. He had bad acne and a gold tooth. "Are you sure Eugene's over you? He tried to be your shadow for a while."

"We're history. He called last week to make sure I was coming to the open house. He sounded lonely, and I thought about you two."

"I don't know, Andi. Even though he's big, he's kind of quiet. I'm more than most quiet men know what to do with."

I laughed.

"So tell me, what does Mr. Wonderful have to say about you going to see a former boyfriend?"

"Benjamin doesn't want me to go. He said I should get a gift and leave it at that, or arrange to go later, when he's free. I want to see the house now. I don't want to wait to see Carolyn's ideas, and another reason I can't wait is because Eugene's mother is ill with cancer."

"Okay. Makes sense to me. I'm in."

"Thanks Gloria."

BETWEEN TEARS

A cold and dreary weather pattern had held on for the past week. I hoped it would warm up the farther south I drove, but the temperatures registered at about forty-five degrees throughout my trip. Radio stations regaled with long stints of Christmas music, so I sang all the way there. I was in a good mood when I arrived, three hours and fifteen minutes later.

Benjamin crossed my mind, but I thought he'd be busy at work and I didn't want to confess I'd driven alone anyway. I'd just tell him all about my visit to Eugene's house when I got back. He'd understand it was too late to change plans when Gloria had to cancel at the last minute.

Summerville was a town outside of Paducah, Kentucky. Mostly rural, the townsfolk were content to leave all the big city ways to the big city. None of those fancy big box stores, mall strips or la-di-da housing developments existed here. They wanted the quiet, lazy river kind of life where cordiality and good old American values were prized. Summerville's particular brand of Southern lifestyle embraced an interracial family like the Sherwoods. Mrs. Sherwood was a white woman who had stood her ground and married Eugene's father, a black man. Or, perhaps it was Eugene's father who had stood his ground.

I hoped his mother would pull through her illness okay. She'd already had a lifetime of struggle with her interracial family, her blindness, which was the result of a boating accident when she was in her thirties, and now cancer. Even with all this, I knew bitterness and self-pity would always be strangers to her. I was grateful for a chance to see her now, in case her health took a turn for the worse.

As I drove past the one traffic light, I remembered how quaint I thought the town was the first time I'd seen it when Eugene and I dated. On our last visit, the annual quilt show was underway, and we enjoyed the works of art displayed. I had even given a passing thought to relocating here, because he'd shared from the beginning of our time together his plans to quit his job in St. Louis and move back home to take care of his mother as she aged.

As I found a space in his car-filled driveway, unblinking, white Christmas lights adorned every possible space on the three-story, A-shaped house. The thrill of what awaited me inside made me giggle.

A woman who introduced herself as Sally opened the door. The navy blue, white, gold, and green Mediterranean tiles in the foyer wowed me, as did the light fixture. *This is all Carolyn!*

"Mrs. Sherwood, it's Andi." In the green and black kitchen, Mrs. Sherwood was putting the finishing touches on a cheese and olive tray, but I could tell she didn't feel well. *Thank God I made it before it was too late.*

"I'm so glad you made it, Andi." She hugged me close and whispered, "Between you, me, and these walls, I don't know what Eugene was thinking to let you get away."

I quickly took her in. Mrs. Sherwood's shoulder length hair was as it had been—mostly white with a shock of black running through it. Her skin was soft and pale, and she wore a red silk scarf loosely tied around her neck over a cream-colored pants suit. She had on dark sunglasses, which she didn't wear unless there was company. "Thank you. I'm sorry you're not feeling well."

"Well, after a certain age if it's not one thing, it's two or three all at once. The body just starts to have its way with you. But, enough about me. Eugene told me you're engaged now, congratulations! Let's see." She removed the clear plastic gloves from her hands so her fingers could examine my engagement ring. "Oh, nice! I hope you two are very happy. Have you set a date yet?"

"Not yet. Thank you. I've known him a while. He's a wonderful man."

"I'm sure he is. May I give you a tour of the house?"

"No, that's okay. You should go lie down if you don't feel well but, I love what I've seen so far. As you drive up to the property, the steep pitch of the roof and the windows are so striking."

"Yes, a lot of people comment on that. I think the windows contribute to the atmosphere here as well. I sense a kind of energy here that's hard to put my finger on, so I don't even try to understand it. I just enjoy it." She squeezed my arm as she departed. "Thanks for coming, Andi. I wouldn't have missed being here to say hi to you for the world, but yes, I'm going to lie down now."

"Let me walk with you, I'll just get my coat."

"No, no. You just got here. Sally will walk with us. Stay, enjoy, but call me sometimes."

"I will."

She left with Tess, her faithful dog, saying goodbye to a couple of other guests on the way out.

Being here not only brought Carolyn to life, but Mrs. Sherwood's cancer called up memories of my mother as well. My hands trembled because of that one word—cancer. The idea of discomfort and struggle accompanied that word, even today.

Soon guests surrounded Eugene. I joined them in time to hear him say, "I invited Reverend Richards. It was my mother's idea to ask him to bless the house, but an emergency came up and he can't make it."

"Too bad," I said. That would have been a wonderful way to begin in a new home. When I moved in to my house, Reverend Tolley, my minister, came over for dinner and went from room to room saying a prayer. It put me at ease."

The conversation moved on to a different topic. Standing still, I realized I was inside another one of Carolyn's sketches. The fluffy sheers at the windows, the striped love seat and couch, even the massive abstract painting on the wall was as she had depicted.

"Eugene," I called to him. I wanted him to tell me the details about which store for each item, but being in the middle of a conversation, he held up his hand signaling he'd be just a minute.

While I mingled with others on a self-guided tour, tears trickled down my cheeks. Carolyn's sketches were exact reproductions in many of the rooms. She would've had a wonderful future as an interior designer, if she could have just pulled her life together. My stomach knotted with guilt. I hadn't been able to help her.

We ate and drank, and then somebody noticed it was raining outside. It was only three, but I thought I should head back. I had made my way to the room with the coats, when Eugene caught up with me.

"Andi, what do you think?"

"I think it's fantastic! Are you happy with the Mediterranean tile in your foyer? I think that's my favorite thing."

"It adds unbelievable elegance. Carolyn had such vision.

"She really did," I agreed

"I think most people are taking off. Let me see them out."

"I'm going, too," I said.

"Wait a few more minutes. You came all this way and I'd love it if we could chat."

Completely clueless, I stared at him. "About what?"

"I have a couple of Carolyn's letters I wanted to give you."

"Carolyn's letters?"

"Yeah, you didn't know we wrote back and forth for a time? She mainly answered design questions for me. This was after Roy had been taken, and you and I had broken up, but before she drifted downhill."

"Really? She never mentioned them to me. I'd like to see them." Sure it wouldn't take long, I said, "I'll wait."

CHAPTER 19
Benjamin

I was thinking about Andrea, wondering if she was enjoying her trip, when the phone rang. Sharon, who had come home for the weekend, yelled, "Ben," It's for you."

I picked up the kitchen phone. "Hello."

"Hi, I wanted to let you know I'm going to spend the night here in Summerville." It was Andrea.

"Why?"

"Freezing rain. It's not safe to drive."

"Oh okay." I slumped into a kitchen chair. "How's the house?"

"It's great! Eugene found a good architect. The ideas Carolyn had about the pocket doors and ceramic tile instead of carpeting worked out well."

"Sounds nice."

"I love it. I hope you'll see it one day."

"I'd like to see it. What does Gloria think?"

"Gloria didn't make it. Her mom woke up sick, so she decided leaving her alone was not a good idea."

"Oh?" *Going alone to see Eugene was not a good idea either.* I shook my head.

"I've made the drive plenty of times before to visit with Mrs. Sherwood. It wasn't a big deal."

Andrea had to know the drive was not my issue. I found something in the corner of my eye to pick at while I phrased my next question. "Did many people get caught by the weather?"

"Well, yes and no. The ones that live close by are going to inch their way home, and the others from St. Louis left earlier. They probably missed most of it."

"It's just you spending the night with Eugene?" It was 5:44. Shaking my head again at the answer I knew was coming, I turned away from the clock. Too angry to bring myself to ask why she hadn't left when the others did, I remained silent.

"Don't say it that way. Don't be angry. I know I should have left earlier, but—"

"But what?"

"He had letters from Carolyn. I read them, and by the time I pulled myself together it was after five. Time just got away from me."

The raw emotion in her voice told me the letters had been difficult for her. I guess being in the house had been a mixture of joy and sorrow. Though I understood why she needed to go, why she needed this closure, I couldn't ignore the fact that this was her ex. "Andrea, why can't he take you to a hotel?"

"I'll be fine. With the weather like it is, we shouldn't go anyplace we don't absolutely have to go."

"What about his mother? Why can't you stay with her?"

"The woman's dying. I'm sorry, but I'm don't feel right imposing on her."

"Let me speak to him."

"What?"

"I want to speak to Eugene." I stood as if standing could calm my increasing anxiety. Speaking with him was as close as I could get to guarding what was mine at this point.

"He's outside putting down salt."

"I'll call back then. I want to thank him for taking care of you."

When she paused, I hoped she was thinking twice, but no such luck. "I'll be fine. I love you, Benjamin. Nothing's going to happen."

Famous last words. "I'll call back in ten minutes," I said and pressed end on the phone to hang up.

"She's stuck in Kentucky at Eugene's house I gather?" Sharon asked. She'd come early to babysit for Roy tomorrow while I went to work. My mother and Mr. Elrod had taken a weekend trip.

"Yeah."

"Are you worried?"

"Nah." I shrugged. "I guess not. It's just, I know Eugene was crazy about her. He's got two degrees, this fabulous sounding home, and what do I have?"

"Yeah, but, if Andrea had wanted him, she could have had him years ago." Sharon stood behind the cook island, folding dishtowels that had been washed and needed to be put away.

"But who knows what would have happened between them if Carolyn hadn't been so needy? And now Andrea has Roy and me, and I make and spread tar for a living."

"You do a damn fine job of it, too," she said with mock seriousness.

"Can't argue that, although I'm sure my supervisor would."

"Ben, you'll be taking classes next month when the new semester starts, and you'll have your degree in May."

"It will be about time, too. I'm going to call Eugene back." It rang six times and nobody picked up.

"Try her cell phone," Sharon said.

I held the phone up so Sharon could hear what I was hearing. "Sorry I missed your call. I'll check my messages soon and get back with you. Leave your name and number."

"From years of counseling, I'm told it comes down to trust when it comes to relationships."

"Trust, huh? I guess I don't have a lot of experience putting that into play."

"Me either. I'm more of a hands-on kind of gal." She put the pile of folded dishcloths into a drawer. "I'm going to check on Roy. Why don't you pick a movie? The popcorn's ready."

"Okay," I said. But first, I'd have to check the weather channel.

CHAPTER 20
Andrea

Eugene and I stood in his central foyer removing our coats. I'd kept him company outside while he finished salting the path.

The phone rang as he picked up the glass he'd had earlier. He answered, looking down at the floor, rotating his glass making the ice tinkle, then his eyes drifted up and settled on me. "Oh yeah, you know I'll take good care of her." And then, "No problem, man." He threw back his head, emptying his glass as he handed the receiver to me.

Benjamin wanted to know why no one had answered earlier. I explained about being outside. I could hear the anxiety in his voice, but all I could say to console him was, "I love you. See you soon."

"You must have gotten with that loser when he was with Carolyn."

"Excuse me?" I'd heard him correctly, but I frowned in puzzlement. One minute we could joke about how he'd resembled a dancing bear on ice, and the next minute he could say something clearly intended to hurt me. "What are you talking about, Eugene?"

"Calls here like he has some say as to what I do in my own house. I must not be the only motherfucker drinking tonight."

"Okay," I drew out the word slowly, my heart rate rising quickly. Exit Dr. Jekyll, enter Mr. Hyde. Eugene obviously had had more to drink than I thought. Thinking back, he never could hold his liquor. "I'll just say goodnight." I walked toward the bedroom I would use.

He held up his hands to encourage me to stay, blocking my way. "Sorry, sorry. That's your man now, don't mind me. My hurt feelings are talking. I was willing to offer you me, this house, and this land. None of that appealed to you."

The high I had from standing in Carolyn's dream come true quickly turned to uneasiness. He was too close and too drunk. I wondered if the panic showed in my eyes. "Well, it wasn't the right time for us."

"My timing was off? Maybe I should try again? I could remind you of how good we were together."

Something had changed in Eugene. There was a craziness in his eyes I'd never noticed before. An icky, spider-crawling sensation walked over me along with sudden clarity. He had been the person at the cemetery watching me. He was the one in the mall parking lot, and maybe he was the one at the zoo. He'd been following me God knows for how long. The meeting in the grocery store was all a set-up, and I walked right into his trap. *Think Andrea—think. How are you going to get out of this?*

He grabbed my shoulders. I pushed, but this six-foot cinder block didn't budge. Whiskey-coated lips descended. I got my hand up between us. When I turned my face away, my ring scratched me. "Ouch!" I yelped.

Eugene jumped back as if I'd scared him instead of the other way around. He handed me a cocktail napkin to catch the dripping blood. "What happened?"

"My ring." Pretending to want to see the wound, I rushed into the powder room to get away from him, but he followed too closely. A red scar angled from my nose to outside my left eye. It looked as angry as I felt, but there'd be no permanent damage.

Eugene removed some peroxide and a cotton ball from the medicine cabinet. "Here, use this. I'm really sorry." As I took care of my injury, he watched.

Now what? Was that the end of his assault? Did he mean it when he said he was sorry? My body shook.

After a few stinging dabs at the affected area I said, "Excuse me." I carefully sidestepped him to get back into the living room. I eyed the front door, but didn't think I could outrun him. I grabbed my purse from the sofa, then hurried to the bedroom where I closed the door and locked it, collapsing with my back against it. Berating myself for being in this mess in the first place, I took out my cell phone. Holding it comforted me. Benjamin would come and get me, but should I call him? Did I want him to drive through an ice storm to rescue me? Did I want to admit how stupid I'd been for coming and agreeing to spend the night?

Unsure what to do, I sighed and looked at the ice-encased shrubbery outside my window. Eugene's mother lived fifty feet away, but she was sick. I shifted my gaze in time to see the doorknob jiggle. I took in a sharp breath. A low rapping came next.

Round two. I breathed deeply but couldn't stop the sensation of the walls closing in around me. "I've got my phone, Eugene! Go away or I'll call the police!"

"Now why would you want to do that? I said I was sorry. I just need to know that you're not going to stay mad at me."

"I'm not mad. Good night."

"Good night? It's barely six."

"Well, I'm tired from the drive."

"I don't believe you. Open the door. Please. I have a key, you know. I don't want a scene. I just want to make peace."

The key comment cinched it for me. I wasn't being paranoid, and if I was, so what—better safe than sorry. I didn't know what to do. I called 911 and actually got a busy signal. *Ugh!* Maybe people calling about the ice storm tied up the line.

I snatched open the door and swished past him before he could locate a key. "I'm thirsty." If he was going to get a key, the space in the living room provided better maneuverability.

I hoped my racing heart would not belie my acting calm and in control, instead of the trapped lab rat I felt like. I wondered how many obstacles I'd have to overcome to get out of this unscathed.

Taking a glass with trembling fingers, I filled it from the tap. "You want some help with these dishes, Eugene? I thought you were cleaning up?" When he moved closer to me, I stiffened, and then flinched when he took my hand. If he noticed my fear, he didn't care. I held onto my glass in case I needed a weapon.

"I gotta tell you. I had planned to ask you to marry me. Seeing this other man's ring upset me. I just want you to be happy."

Thinking he was Dr. Jekyll again, I wriggled my hand free. "Thank you. Benjamin, and I are going to be fine. What do you say we get this stuff cleaned up?"

He looked at the used party fare with a tired expression. "Yeah, might as well."

It took an hour to get the kitchen squared away before we said goodnight again. I felt sure the situation earlier had been diffused, but the faster I could get away from this man, the better. I couldn't trust him. I watched him go into his room and close the door, and then I got my belongings.

If I was lucky, I'd remember Mrs. Sherwood's number so she'd be expecting me. If I couldn't get through, it didn't matter. Once I crossed the salted path and was standing on her front porch, I knew I'd have a safe place to spend the night.

Not wanting to upset Mrs. Sherwood, I hoped the adrenalin surging through my body didn't give me away. I warily flitted from window to window under the guise of commenting about the ice, while I really checked to make sure I didn't see Eugene barreling over here after me. He'd apparently calmed down, and I didn't think he'd upset his mother by making a scene, but my blood pressure had to be off the charts with worry.

I would never see Eugene Sherwood again in this lifetime and pray that our conflict ended here.

When Mrs. Sherwood and I had retired to our separate bedrooms, I wept. I pushed an armchair against the door for added protection, then crumpled into it, attempting to stifle my sobs as salty tears stung the scar from my ring. I'd been lucky. No, not lucky, blessed. More tears descended when I thought again of what had almost happened and of Eugene's treachery.

After several minutes, I stopped crying, took off my sweater and pants and climbed between the sheets, bringing my purse with me. When I was sure my voice wouldn't betray me, I called Benjamin and told him that I had reconsidered and taken his advice and would spend the night at Mrs. Sherwood's house.

I couldn't tell him the truth. He'd come for me and there would be an ugly confrontation, assuming he made it here alive through the ice storm. No, I'd leave as soon as I could and never see Eugene again.

The next morning, I had to wait for the temperature to rise above freezing before I could leave. I met Mrs. Sherwood in the kitchen, which looked like a 1950's decorating book. We sat at a gray Formica table with matching red vinyl chairs. These were antique items in today's market. She covered her mouth with her hand and yarned noisily.

"Are you still tired?" I asked.

"Yes, I am. Chemotherapy exhausts me and those trucks coming in and out—all that sawing and hammering has made it hard for me to catch up on my rest, but I'll be all right."

Tess sat by her master's side, tongue hanging. She stared at me with a "how may I help you." Her mostly black coat shined.

"Help yourself to some coffee."

I helped myself and refilled her cup.

"Andi, I'm happy Eugene's back home with us."

Murky gray eyes that couldn't focus turned in my general direction. "I love the house. The sun porch on the back overlooking the river, I'm sure that's a lovely view, and the kitchen is well laid out. He'll get much enjoyment out of that house. I thank you for your input into its design."

"You're welcome. Carolyn and I enjoyed doing it."

"Oh yes, your poor sister."

I looked down at my coffee, then outside at the mist still lingering. It was only 8:30. I couldn't have run out of conversation already?

Eugene's behavior was on my mind, but I couldn't talk to his mother about that. "What good books have you listened to recently?"

"There have been several, but I forget the names. I like women's stories of love and family. Sandy is good about bringing me books on tape from the library."

Sandy was her friend who lived a half-mile down the road, her closest neighbor. "I like stories about love and family, too," I agreed. "You know they're good when they can make you laugh or cry."

"Now, that's the truth."

About 10:30, flat chunks of melting ice slid down my windshield. It was time for me to go.

"Mrs. Sherwood, thanks for letting me spend the night. Is there anything you want me to do before I go?"

"Oh, is it safe to travel now?"

"Yes, ma'am."

"I turned the heat down to save on my bill. Hope you found the blanket last night. Would you mind checking in my extra bedroom for my cardigan? I can't find the one I want, maybe Sandy put it there."

"Sure."

Large, scary aquamarine and gold flowers that don't grow in nature grew on the wallpaper in the second bedroom that had been my refuge. I wondered if Mrs. Sherwood had selected it before or after the boating accident that left her blind thirty years ago. I flicked the light and went to the closet of the neatly kept room.

A wooden pole spanned the width of the closet. I began struggling to make space enough to get a look at anything I thought was a cardigan. The clothes were tightly packed. I found one and slid it off its hanger. A mouse scurried over my foot.

"Aghh!" I jumped up and back six inches.

"What's the matter, Andi? Can't you find it?" Mrs. Sherwood yelled to me.

"No, I found it." Back in the kitchen, I handed it to her. Tess stood, tail wagging. I imagined she would give her eyeteeth for a chance to play hunter. "A mouse ran out of the closet and scared me."

"Oh yes. They come inside for the warmth. I'll get Eugene to move his boxes of camera equipment over to his place, and put down traps."

When Mrs. Sherwood kissed me goodbye, her fingertips imparted information her sightless eyes could not. I recoiled slightly because of the tenderness.

"What happened?"

"My ring scratched me when I took off my sweater last night." I prayed that explanation would work for Benjamin, too.

As I pulled onto Interstate 24 a few minutes later it came to me. What camera equipment? Eugene must have a new hobby.

CHAPTER 21
Andrea

Back in town by two, I stopped at Hamilton's Jewelry store, needing to unload some of my anger and guilt about how my eye could have been scratched out. Some unsuspecting, but polite employee endured my wrath.

Three o'clock came. A steaming soak in the bathtub, and the gospel music coming from KATZ radio station took away the residual tension, most of it anyway.

By four, the aroma of vegetable lasagna permeated the house, and by five, Benjamin and Roy were knocking at my door.

"Hello pretty…lady. What happened?" Benjamin asked, unable to conceal his shock.

I swooped up Roy into my arms for a hug. He kissed my cheek. "Hi, Aunt Andi. Do you need a Band Aid?"

"My ring scratched me. I'll be okay without one, Roy." I set him down, helped him remove his coat, and ushered them into the kitchen.

"Your ring? Let me see it?" Benjamin said.

"Let me see," Roy copied his dad.

I extended my hand for them to examine. "I stopped and had someone at the store file the prongs down before I came home today."

"Who did you talk to there?"

"I fussed at someone named Christopher."

"You should have. Let me look at you." He touched my chin, gently positioning it to acquire the best view. "Did you put some Neosporin or something on that?"

"No, just peroxide, but Neosporin is a good idea."

"You might need to get an updated tetanus shot, too, Andrea. That's a nasty scratch."

"I thought about that. I had one about five years ago, so I think I'm okay. I'll call my doctor tomorrow."

"Yeah, check it out to be sure. And they were able to sand it down the same day? I thought it took longer?"

"Really? Hmm. Well, I asked and they took care of it."

"Good then." He rubbed his hands together and looked around. "Something smells good. I'm starving."

"You two go wash your hands, dinner is about to be served."

After we said grace and the vegetable lasagna was making the rounds, I said, "What's Sharon up to these days?" I wanted to know Benjamin's family better. Not going to their family Sunday dinners kept me out of the loop, so, the least I could do was ask about them.

"Aunt Andi, did you know that Aunt Sharon is going to be a doctor? She could fix your boo-boo."

"Yes, I did know that, Roy, and I'm sure she could fix my boo-boo."

"Same old, same old," Benjamin answered as he filled Roy's plate. "School, Cecil, school. That's pretty much her life."

I nodded. "Do they live together?"

"No, she's in that off-campus housing near the school on East Gate. When she's there, that is. She's home at least three times a week."

"Maybe we should get together. Go bowling or something," I suggested.

"Yeah, we'll have to do that. So, you had a good time seeing the house? Glad you went? I'll bet his mother was glad for the overnight company."

"Roy honey, be careful with your drink," I said. "Yes, the house was wonderful, and I'm very thankful for the time I got to spend with Mrs. Sherwood." I gave a half-hearted smile, ashamed of my carefully crafted answer. After dinner, I put out the Lincoln Logs and the Matchbox cars Roy never seemed to tire of. Benjamin and I played with him in the den for about twenty minutes before we made our way to the living room for some alone time.

We snuggled in front of the fire with his arm over my shoulder. Not only did I feel safe, I felt loved. I never wanted to leave his side again. Some of it had to be backlash from my Eugene ordeal, but that experience yesterday helped me prioritize.

"Benjamin, can we talk about our wedding?"

"Sure we can."

"I don't want a big wedding, but I do want a beautiful wedding gown, something right out of the pages of *Bride Magazine*." I got teary-eyed just thinking about it. "I'm too practical to spend a fortune on it, but I want to feel special wearing it. I'd like to get married at my church, but I don't have a particular place for the wedding reception in mind."

Benjamin never got that glazed look in his eyes that men do while they wait for you to say something they can relate to. Another reason I loved him. "Whatever you want, Andrea, is fine with me. When?"

"Anytime now." I grinned.

He pulled away from our side embrace to look at me fully. "Anytime? You mean as soon as we can arrange it?"

Glad excitement stirred in his voice, I nodded. "Does that work for you?"

"Yes it does. It works for me." His eyes danced a joyous mambo. "Then what we need to do is contact the church about a date. But, I guess the date depends on how long it'll take you to find the dress you want, right?"

"Well yeah, finding it, getting it fitted. I'd say I need two months minimum."

"Maybe Valentine's Day?"

"Hmm." I looked away, feeling my enthusiasm slip a notch. "Well, maybe not then. I know it's your birthday month, but Carolyn died that month, too."

"I'm sorry. I should have thought about that."

Wanting the mood to stay upbeat, I quickly added, "But March is a good month. That's my birthday month."

"Then let's do it on your birthday."

"I'll get a calendar." Looking back as I walked into the kitchen, I smiled at Benjamin sitting on the edge of the couch in anticipation. "The calendar must be in my bedroom. Let me check."

The phone rang. I couldn't seem to put my hands on the calendar, but I knew it was here somewhere. "Benjamin, can you get that for me?" The phone stopped ringing, and I continued to search.

Fury had overtaken his expression when I walked back into the living room. Whatever it was, whoever had called— it was bad. I hurried to the kitchen extension and heard Eugene's voice.

"Like I said, man, I don't know what came over me. Congratulations, by the way. You are one lucky man. I just called to tell you both how sorry I was and to make sure Andrea was all right."

"I'm all right, Eugene," I cut in. "I got home fine and the scratch will heal eventually, but you already apologized."

"Okay, I wanted to be sure," Eugene said. "Good night then."

"Good night," I said.

Benjamin slammed the phone down when it was just me on the line. Frozen in place with dread, but knowing Benjamin had walked up behind me, I replaced my receiver slowly and turned around.

"Let me make sure I have this straight." Benjamin stared at me with fiery eyes so hot the devil might envy them. "Eugene tried to kiss you. You put your hand up to stop him and that's how the ring scratched your face?"

I squinted as if the glare of this truth hurt. "Yes."

"Andrea! Why didn't you tell me? Why did I have to hear that from him?"

"I don't know. Eugene apologized. I wanted to minimize things rather than have it be a big deal."

"What? What kind of sense does that make? It is a big deal. He could have hurt you." He walked back toward the living room mumbling, "I knew he was going to try something like that."

I followed him. He stopped walking abruptly and turned back to me. "But, then again, you had no business being at the man's house to start with." The way he shoved his hands in his pockets, I could tell they needed to be there or he'd be tempted to place a scolding finger in my face. "You put yourself in a hell of a situation."

"Don't you think I know I messed up? The reason I didn't tell you is because I didn't want to hear you say I told you so. It's over. I'm okay. Can we please drop this?"

He didn't respond right away. "Okay, it's over. But you know what? There's no reason for you to ever see this guy again. Do you agree?"

"Yes." I nodded.

"I'm not trying to tell you who you can and cannot see, but it's clear the man still wants you."

"Yeah, I got that, too. I won't see him again."

He nodded, breathing hard. "Come here."

I went into his arms, his pulse raced. After a few seconds, its beat slowed to near normal. "The thought of him hurting you, Andrea, is more than I can take. I can't think about it anymore."

We returned to the couch and sat quietly, until Roy joined us in the living room.

"Daddy, are you finished yelling now?" Roy's big eyes filled with trepidation.

"Was I yelling? I'm sorry. Come sit with us, Roy."

I raised my eyebrows to ask if I needed the calendar at this point. Benjamin gave me the go-ahead. Opening to March on the calendar, I said, "My birthday is on a Monday next year. We could do an evening ceremony, say around six, and then have a dinner reception at seven. How's that sound?"

"It sounds like something I will enjoy every second of."

"Maybe we'll wait until school is out and go away for a few days. Maybe even to Disney World," I said, but I mouthed Disney World so Roy wouldn't get too exuberant, too early.

"We'll see. Let's make our wedding happen first."

His eyes shone with their normal brown clarity and devotion again. I rested my hand on his arm.

He brought my hand to his face and kissed my palm." I love you, Andrea."

"What about me?" Roy asked.

"We love you, Roy," Benjamin and I said in unison.

Roy giggled.

CHAPTER 22
Andrea

"I'm back at Mrs. Elrod's house, Gloria." I turned the ignition off. Gloria sat in the passenger seat next to me, her somber demeanor reflecting mine.

"Last December, I sat here for five minutes crying, watching Carolyn throw up on Mrs. Elrod's lawn," I pointed to the exact spot, "and here I am again. Carolyn had dropped to her knees at first, and then, as the vomit kept forcing its way out, she fell to her hands and knees, slowly lowering her hips to the ground. She sat there, Gloria, not even bothering to wipe the dribble off her chin. She talked to herself, too. Cursing. Something about how the bastards kept her son away from her while they had the nerve to have reindeer on their lawn."

Gloria shook her head, patted my arm and sighed. The reindeer were back this year.

"Yep, that's how Sharon shook her head that day. She was already helping Carolyn stand when I finally wiped my tears and got out of the car."

"Two months later Carolyn was dead," Gloria lamented. "Tell me, what are we doing here again? Between you, BJ, Benjamin and me, we could put together a fabulous wedding. I'm talking about something romantic and memorable, Andi. We don't need her help."

"I know we could, but I don't want to go into another year with this rift between Benjamin's mother and me. She threw down the gauntlet at our brunch. She hadn't called to congratulate me on our engagement so I finally called her."

"What did she say?"

"We exchanged pleasantries and then she said, 'My son showed me the ring he bought for you. I like his taste.' Then I asked if she liked his taste in rings or his taste in brides."

"Ha!" Gloria said, "What did she say to that?"

I elongated my neck, arched my eyebrows and dropped my jaw as I imagined Mrs. Elrod had done. "'It's obvious to me that you young women have a power over Benjamin that keeps him coming back. Who am I to stand in the way of such powerful mojo?' I got her mojo, all right."

Gloria made an appropriately contemptuous sound.

"I told Mrs. Elrod my idea about an evening ceremony followed by dinner."

"What did she think?"

"She was surprisingly helpful. She said she could make some restaurant recommendations and even some phone calls if I liked. Then she said we needed to get details worked out since time was short. Here we are."

"Yep, here we are."

"Gloria, she knows the position she's putting me in. Even after I came to her, she's going to insist I do all the bending. I turn down invitations to Sunday dinner at her home, but where does she want to meet?"

Gloria had come with me because I needed an ally. Mrs. Elrod didn't radiate warmth toward me, and Gloria didn't care for Benjamin. At least there was parity.

After we left the car, my friend reached for my hand as if I were five years old, needing help crossing a major intersection. I held on and decided the best strategy would be to say a prayer and hope they opened the door quickly, so we wouldn't have to wait on the porch too long. If I looked hard, I could see Carolyn's bloodstained hands. Mrs. Elrod opened the door as soon as we got on the first step. Thank God.

"Mrs. Elrod, this is my maid of honor, Gloria Wellborn. Gloria, this is Benjamin's mom."

"Hello, Gloria, nice to meet you. Come on in. Let's go to the kitchen and see what we can accomplish."

"What a beautiful home, Mrs. Elrod," Gloria said.

"Thank you, my husband and I had it remodeled a few years ago. We're happy with the results."

I was sure they were. The sitting area held shades of green, yellow, and tan that complemented the blond wood in the kitchen. In the area immediately off the entrance hall, one couch and two love seats surrounded an oversized ottoman in front of the fireplace. A flat screen TV rested above the mantel. Adjacent to the right, Ficus trees abounded near a huge picture window.

"Where's Benjamin? Gloria asked.

"He took Roy to the library," Sharon said, joining us in the kitchen while Mrs. Elrod busied herself laying out snacks. "They'll be home by eight o'clock. It's just seven now. I'll bet by the time they get home, we can have some concrete ideas that Benny will agree to. He's not fussy about most things."

Gloria and I looked at each other. By "most things," she didn't mean me, did she? No, I was being overly sensitive.

"Don't look shocked, you two," Sharon said, taking us both by the elbow. "I'm not planning to pressure my way into the wedding. Even if you had asked me, I couldn't be a bridesmaid. School keeps me too busy, and you're getting married in the middle of the semester."

I hadn't deliberately meant to exclude Sharon. She was Roy's aunt just like I was, but, somehow, we never bonded. "Oh. Okay." Good information to have, I suppose. "You remember my friend, Gloria?"

"Of course I do." Sharon took my hand to look at the ring. She smiled. "Wow, this wedding is a turn of events no one could have predicted."

"Yeah, you're right about that," Gloria said.

I gave Gloria a look.

"Well, I gotta say. I've never seen Benjamin happier," Sharon said. "That means a lot to me."

"That means a lot to me, too. I love him," I said.

"My primary concern is how he feels about you."

I glanced at Gloria again, and then locked eyes with Sharon. I thought I recognized rudeness, but maybe it was her directness that bothered me. "Yeah, I guess it would be."

She guided me to a chair and sat between Gloria and me while we made wedding arrangements.

Mrs. Elrod had printed a list of five possible locations for the reception that could accommodate one hundred fifty people. She'd made a chart including what each place specialized in, and if an outsider caterer could be used or not. His mother was in her element. Based on her experience, I found myself deferring to what she would prefer. As long as I enjoyed a good, but relaxed dinner with friends, I could be flexible about everything else.

Roy and Benjamin came home. Benjamin's gaze seemed to test the waters as he peeked in the kitchen. With a tentative voice he asked, "How are we doing, ladies?"

Mrs. Elrod excused herself to put Roy to bed saying things were going without a hitch. Benjamin joined us at the table, and by ten o'clock the four of us had a master list of people and places to call.

Before we left, Sharon invited Gloria and me to Sunday dinner. "It's always served at three," she reminded us. "You're going to be family now and, as you can see, we don't bite. You really ought to reconsider. We need to get to know you." She and her mother were persistent women.

CHAPTER 23
Andrea

"Girl? What is this? Why are you throwing away these perfectly good flowers? Did you and Ben have a fight?" Distressed, BJ stood over the trash can in my kitchen.

I poured a second cup of coffee and offered more to BJ, but he declined. "No, those aren't from Benjamin, BJ, they're from Eugene. Since his open house, he's sent me flowers three times; twice at school and once here."

"Oh, poor thing; can't get a clue. And after all those years you two were apart. What's his problem?"

"I don't know. Well, I kind of do. You see this scar?" I pointed and leaned toward him.

"Yeah. What happened?"

I filled him in on the details, while BJ placed each rose on damp paper towels. "What! I know Benjamin was hot! Folks don't play that mess. Eugene's going to end up dead not respecting boundaries." He found the card and read it. "'For me.' I don't think so, my brother."

"Actually, the cards would be kind of cute if they weren't unwelcome. On the first card it said 'You are,' on the second card it said 'The one' and then this last one."

"Cute my ass, what are you going to do about him?"

"I'm getting hang-up calls. I'm thinking about calling the police."

"Have you told Benjamin?"

I closed my eyes and shook my head. "Nope." I sighed and sat down at the kitchen table. This was bad. If I told Benjamin, I'd never hear the end of it. As it stood now, I'd already kicked myself enough for misjudging Eugene. I didn't need anymore help from Benjamin in that regard.

"Tell Benjamin." BJ opened drawers and cabinets until he found a plastic bag for the flowers he'd salvaged. "He's got enough muscle to take on that hairy oak tree of a man. If he doesn't, he can get a few of his friends from the street crew to help pound the message home, if you get my drift."

"That's another reason why I haven't told Benjamin about the flowers or calls. I don't want that, BJ. No violence, no uproar, no mess. Can I get through one Christmas without a lot of drama for a change?"

"I hear you. Carolyn's drama did steal the joy from many a holiday. Well, as long as you aren't scared of Eugene or anything, it can probably wait a few days, but you definitely should tell Benjamin." BJ joined me at the table, placing the bagged flowers next to him. "Christmas is next week, you know, and these flowers are going to look right nifty on my coffee table until then."

I smiled.

"Had you realized Christmas is around the corner?" he asked. "I looked under that tree that you have all nicely decorated and there was nothing under it addressed to moi." He batted his long lashes at me. "An oversight, I hope."

"Did you notice there's nothing addressed to anybody under that tree? Roy is expecting Santa Clause to bring all the gifts this year."

"Oh, that explains it. Well, I know I'm on Santa's list. I'm nothing if I'm not good, ask anybody." We laughed.

I sipped from my cup while BJ whipped out his PDA. "Let's see," he said. "We've got your invitations ordered, and they will be back mid-January. That will give us plenty of time to get them addressed and mailed. Today, we'll pick out your three favorite gowns and your three favorite headpieces to narrow down your dress choices. We will have lunch, and in the afternoon, we'll go over to the sanctuary and see how we want it decorated. What did you all decide about music?"

"We still haven't decided about the songs, but I want you to sing at my wedding."

BJ's hand covered his heart. "Me? Really? My voice is in prime shape, but are you sure?"

Reaching for his hand, I said, "Yes, I love your voice, BJ."

"I am honored. I would love to sing at your wedding. Did you already clear this with Ben? I know he's got this unfriendly gay thing happening."

"Yeah, I'm sorry about that, BJ. I'm not even sure Ben's conscious of it. He and I need to sit and get that cleared up. But, once he hears you sing, he'll be fine with it."

"Girl, I never let attitudes like his bother me. If I stopped moving all the times I've run into people who had problems with my sexuality, I'd be a statue in the park. I'm not about a lifetime of pigeon shit. You hear what I'm saying?"

"I hear you." Suddenly, a wave of sadness blindsided me.

"Hey what's this?" BJ cupped my my chin, pulling it up so he could look in my eyes. "You miss them, don't you?"

I looked at him, my eyes wet with emotion. "My mom ... She's not here. Carolyn ...." I shook my head, and the tears flowed freely. "I know. It's going to be a lovely wedding, and Benjamin and I will have a wonderful life. But, my mom and my sister aren't here, BJ. We're—" I had to stop to let the knot in my throat dissolve. "We're planning this wedding without them, and I'm worried about Eugene on top of everything else."

BJ stood and pulled me into an embrace, patting my head to soothe me. After a few shaky breaths, I said, "It feels ... unfair. You know me, BJ, I don't believe in feeling sorry for myself, but it's like—what already? What does God want?"

"This is a big event, and your family isn't here. You have a zillion choices to make and Eugene is acting like a fool. It's a time for tears. Go ahead and cry. Use them up. That's what they are there for. I cried myself to sleep just last night."

I didn't believe him because I knew there was a joke hidden somewhere, but I eased out of his arms to better read his expression. "Why?"

"Mr. Works-for-the-Governor's office and has already started to worry about his boss being re-elected next November. This is creating stress that's affecting him in ways too painful to discuss."

"I'm sorry," imagining I knew the kinds of problems that would temporarily frustrate BJ, I had to giggle.

"Did Mrs. Elrod offer to pay for any of this, or will I have to cash in a few bonds?"

"That's sweet of you, BJ, but fortunately, that won't be necessary. I almost fell off my chair when Mrs. Elrod agreed to foot the bill for the reception. Benjamin and I will split the rest."

"Well, finish your coffee, bride-woman. We've got a full day ahead of us. Chop chop."

CHAPTER 24
Benjamin

Andrea called and asked me to meet her at Carolyn's grave. She went every month, while I had only been a couple of times. However, I couldn't say no to her direct requests.

Because I stopped to get flowers, it was after 4:30 when I got there. I laid my carnations next to Andrea's. Daisies were hard to come by in the winter, well, from the grocery store anyway.

I greeted Andrea with a kiss on her cheek, fully aware of the pending darkness, the cold, and the isolation. In fact, I looked over my shoulder because I heard something, but no one was there. "We're out a little late, aren't we?"

"We won't be long."

"What did Carolyn say when you told her you and I were getting married?"

Andrea looked at me with a curious expression. "How did you know I told her?"

"I know you. You'd want her blessing. Did she give it to you?"

"Sort of."

"What's that mean?"

"She said if we ever have a girl, we have to name her Carolyn."

"Yeah, right." I did a double take. "Did she?"

"Gotcha," Andrea winked. "You should talk to her and see what she tells you."

"I would, but I don't feel like trying to free my ankles from her angry clutches."

"I have the feeling that forgiveness is a huge topic of discussion where she is at the moment."

That was an opening for all kinds of philosophical discussions, but I didn't have the energy to take any on.

After a minute or two of silence, she asked, "Do you dream about her?"

"I do, periodically. What about you?"

"Sometimes. Are they happy dreams?"

"Sometimes." I pulled my skullcap over my ears. Working outside all day in winter weather kept me dressed warmly. "Are you ready to head out? The park closes at five, doesn't it?"

"We have a few minutes. If things had worked out differently and Carolyn was still with us, what do you think she'd say about us getting married?"

"Well, she loved you. She'd be glad for us."

Andrea responded with her eyebrows raised and a quick tilt of her chin. She stood with her hands behind her back in her black floppy winter hat and her black wool coat, obviously content to look at the headstone and think.

After a minute, I put my arm around her. "If Carolyn's okay with us getting married, chances are she didn't mind you coming to my mother's house last week and she won't mind you coming to Sunday dinner tomorrow."

Andrea sighed and put her arm around my waist. "A new year is coming. It's time for a change. It's time to make wrongs right, if we can, and move on."

"Carolyn told you that too?"

"No, it's just what Jesus would do."

We walked to the cars with her arm still around my waist, mine on her shoulder.

"Benjamin, I don't actually talk to Carolyn, I just think about her."

"I know that, Andrea."

"So, you think she'd come to the wedding and reception or just to the reception?"

"Are you kidding? Carolyn never shied away from any kind of controversy. Her worries about what people thought of her would all fit in an ant's pocket."

"An ant's pocket?" she laughed. "She would be at the ceremony, you're right."

Searching for a way not to dwell too much on the past, despite where we were, I asked about the wedding music. "Have you thought any more about the music for the wedding?"

"I was going to ask you about that. BJ has a wonderful voice. How about we ask him to sing at the wedding?"

"BJ? Does he sound more like Tina or Whitney?"

Her smile acknowledged my facetiousness. "He sounds like Tina with a touch of Prince thrown in. You can listen to him first and see what you think."

"Tina and Prince. That's got to be a winning combination. I don't have anybody else in mind. We all think we can sing in my family, but I know for sure no one is up to a solo. BJ will be fine, if that's who you want."

"Okay, good. I thought you might protest that one. Do you have a problem with BJ being gay?"

Her cell phone rang before I explained that Sharon's horrific encounter with a pedophile had made me look at any kind of sexual deviance with concern, if not disgust. Of course, BJ would argue homosexuality wasn't deviate, but his natural state. Nevertheless, I was happy keeping it all at a distance. We moved apart so she could talk.

"Okay. Okay. Still nothing new? All right. Thanks for calling back."

"Who was that?" I asked when she'd hung up.

"Detective Peck, the one assigned to Carolyn's case. I check in regularly. He gets back to me eventually."

"There's that Andrea optimism I love. You think they are going to catch the crack head that killed her after all this time?"

"We don't know who killed her. Maybe it wasn't a crack head."

"In the absence of other proof, what else is there to think?"

I opened the car door for Andrea. Carolyn's murder would always be a mystery Andrea would struggle with. It never affected me like that. If I let it, tiny seeds of guilt would begin to grow, and that wouldn't be a good thing. "Sunday dinner at my house tomorrow, right?"

"Right." Andrea's tone saluted, answering the call of duty.

"Thanks Andrea. You finally coming means a lot to me and Roy—to the whole family."

The next day the house brimmed over with people, just like it did every Sunday, except my ladylove graced us with her presence.

The topic of wedding music came up. Tim said we needed to go classic and be sure to include "Ribbon in the Sky" by Stevie Wonder. Mr. Elrod said that all we needed was some smooth jazz playing in the background. My mother said the Lord's Prayer sung would say it all. Roy said he hoped we would pick the theme from Barney. We'd make a decision later.

I looked around at the happy couples and smiled. My mom and Mr. Elrod, Tim and Maryann, Sharon and Cecil, yeah Cecil was here.

It was good to see him. He still hadn't invested in those teeth yet. They overlapped worse than the cards in my hand would when we got a Whist game going later. His bookstore, The Griot, was doing well, so it wasn't like he didn't have the funds. He had a tight web site, too, and did a booming Internet business in Black Literature.

I looked at him using his napkin to dabble at a glob of sweet potato pie that hadn't made it into Sharon's mouth. *Damn.* I shook my head at devotion like that. But, I was slowly gaining respect for him as a man and definitely as a businessman.

I took this opportunity to tell my family I had reenrolled at the University of Missouri and with their prayers and support, I'd have my degree in business by May.

"Nice going, Benny." Mr. Elrod patted me on my back. "I admire your determination."

Around eight o'clock, after Andrea and I had run our second Boston of the evening in Whist, Uncle Fred told me a friend of mine was at the door.

"Who?" I asked.

"He didn't give me his name. Just said he wanted to see you."

I closed the pocket doors between the sitting area and the hall so as not to disturb. I had no idea who it could be.

Eugene Sherwood stood under the porch light with the cold winter air turning his breath into spurts of white vapor—like a bull about to charge.

"I got something for the bride-to-be," he said. "Check it out." He handed me something small in his leather covered hand.

It didn't feel cool him showing up at my house like this, but my address wasn't a secret and obviously not hard to find. I opened the storm door and took it. I flipped open the velvet box and found a stunning pair of diamond earrings—the kind that dangled.

"What's up, man?" I was about five seconds from being pissed, but, after all, with Christmas around the corner, this was the season for love.

"I'm thanking Andrea," he said.

Okay, I thought. He had approached me directly so maybe I was getting mad for no reason. Maybe he was giving this to me and not to Andrea as a way of showing respect and with any luck, it was his way of saying goodbye to both of us forever.

"I'm thanking her for the other night," he continued. "She can get a little enthusiastic, but I like that in my women. That's how she ended up getting scratched like that."

"What?" I wasn't exactly sure what he meant, but something told me I had been right to want to kick his ass the moment I saw him standing there.

"Yeah, man, she begged for it. Took everything off, except that cheap-ass ring. She told me to call her house the next day because she figured you'd be there. We worked it out. She's slick all right, stays wet, as a matter-of-fact." He winked at me.

I could barely take it all in. Stepping out in front of him, I looked him dead in the eye. He was my height, but almost twice my size. I'm sure I smelled like beer, but he reeked of whiskey. My fist made contact with his jaw. His head jerked to the side, but this John Henry ass stood there grinning at me.

"Don't Ben." Sharon appeared from nowhere putting a restraining hand on my shoulder.

I shrugged her hand off only to feel his thick fingers grab me by my neck, squeezing it like a pillow during a nightmare. I jerked my arm up with enough force to make him let go, but that effort threw us both off balance. I righted myself, but he tripped over the doormat and went down like a felled Redwood. Sharon saw her opening and jumped in front of me.

"Stop it! He's drunk and somebody is going to get seriously hurt! Go back inside, Ben."

I stood over Eugene, proud of myself for not taking aim at his nuts. "Stay away from me, Eugene. Stay away from Andrea."

"Ben!" I looked at Sharon. She stared me inside, then followed me, shutting the door in his face.

"Is your hand okay?"

I shook out my hand and flexed it a couple times. "Yeah, thanks, I'm fine. He's drunk and he's mad because Andrea is with me and not with his grizzly ass. He's jealous."

"Go back in with the others."

I rubbed the back of my neck, waiting for the adrenaline rush to dissipate.

"Mama is going to come look for us in a minute," Sharon urged me on.

"Did you hear everything he said?" I asked.

"I think so."

"Poor SOB is infatuated with her, but that's no excuse for him lying like that."

"So, Andrea isn't capable of what he suggested?"

"No, no way. Absolutely not."

"All right. Let's just hope you're not getting played."

That night, I pretended everything was copasetic. I needed time to get my head straight. The next day, I was ready to speak with Andrea and see if we needed a game plan to deal with Eugene. I headed for her place. A black SUV sat parked in front of her house. I pulled up behind it, cursing because I knew it belonged to Eugene. I'd seen it last night. As soon as I turned off my ignition, he started his. He pulled off, burning rubber.

CHAPTER 25
Andrea

I stood inside my doorway as Benjamin drove up. Eugene took off before they got a chance to exchange words. *Good.* I didn't want any extra drama.

Benjamin's expression told me he had recognized Eugene. The explanation left my lips before the screen door closed behind him. "Eugene is being annoying. He rang my doorbell, and I tried to ignore it, but, of course, he saw my car. He banged on my door, started calling me with his cell phone …"

Benjamin took what I held. "What's this?"

"He left this in the planter. I was going to put it straight into the trash like I've been doing his flowers."

"What flowers? He's been sending you flowers? When were you going to tell me about all this?"

The disappointment in his voice reflected the hurt in his eyes. Right then, I knew I should have told him earlier and was disappointed in myself for not doing so. "I didn't want to tell you until after Christmas. Eugene's been calling, sending flowers, and now this."

He held the box up. "This is what? Like a sex tape?" He looked at me in that intense way he has, his eyes darting to all parts of my face, waiting for an answer.

"I have no idea."

He took the tape out of its box and walked to the VCR.

"Benjamin, this is just one more thing he's doing to be annoying. I don't want to watch it."

"I'm a big boy. I can handle it. I want to see it."

"Why?" I persisted.

He ignored me and put the tape in.

I shot him a venomous look when he patted the cushion next to him. "Come here, Andrea. Sit with me a second. Where is this? Where were you when he filmed this?"

I chose to remain standing. The bedroom I had escaped to at Eugene's new house appeared on screen. He was going at it for all it was worth behind a bent over brown-skinned woman with crinkly hair and large breasts. It could be described both ways.

"That's not me," I said.

Benjamin looked at me. His eyes slowly undressed me as if to compare images. "Sure looks like you. You don't know where this is?"

"It's Eugene's new house, but the woman's face is buried in the pillow. It's not me."

"You have a sweater that color, don't you?"

I didn't bother to answer him since nothing I said seemed to register.

He stopped the tape, but I kept staring at the blank screen in shock. What was that I'd just watched? I sank to the couch, feeling faint.

"Do you think that bastard put something in your drink? Did he drug you, and then take advantage of you? That seems like something right up his alley." In a voice filled with conviction, he said, "I will break his neck."

I shifted my focus to Benjamin. "No, that didn't happen, Benjamin. I wasn't drugged," my voice gained confidence. "He must have hired someone who looks like me. That's the only thing—" Benjamin appeared to stop listening, so I stopped talking.

"Eugene came around yesterday and gave me some diamond earrings as a thank you gift for you."

"What? You mean he came to your house yesterday? He's a disturbed man, Benjamin. That's all I can say. I'm going to get a restraining order."

"Andrea, he said that you wanted to be with him. He said you told him to call here and talk to me so I wouldn't get suspicious."

"That's a lie! He's lying!" Moments passed while we both looked at each other.

He broke eye contact first and clicked the tape back on. When he saw what he was looking for, he froze the frame. The person in the video had a ring on her left hand just like my engagement ring.

"Bu-Benjamin, he can go to a jewelry store and buy a ring just like you did."

A new scene appeared with an overhead shot of me on top of Eugene. I heard myself gasp in real time. I inhaled like somebody had thrown ice water while the heat of embarrassment climbed into my checks. I recognized this scene. I had lived it.

Eugene and I changed positions. Now there was no doubt about my identity. I jumped up and pushed stop on the VCR. "Oh my God! Benjamin! I didn't know—" By now I was talking to Benjamin's back. "Benjamin!" I called. "Wait!"

He was halfway to his car when he shouted, "Fornication is a bad thing. Yeah, right. And to think I fell for that. To think I defended you yesterday. You're a real piece of work, lady."

I closed the door shaking, struggling to breathe. Was I losing my mind? I collapsed on the couch and let my tears take over. *No, no, no. Eugene must have staged the whole thing, props and all. Unless ... unless he had made a tape of us having sex when we were together.* My heart froze. Could Eugene be that despicable? Summoning courage, I watched the tape a second time, noting the details.

The first couple of minutes the camera angle from the side showed the guest bedroom I'd slept in. Eugene and the naked woman owned the screen. Her left hand was barely visible. The glare off the diamond and her breasts swaying in time to Eugene's thrusts transfixed the eye.

The tape kept going, but the camera angle and setting changed to an overhead shot in Eugene's apartment bedroom. A tiny camera must have been attached inside one of the light fixtures in the ceiling fan. *Lying bastard!* Eugene had said there was a short in his ceiling fan, and that's why it worked intermittently. I was on top of Eugene for less than a minute. When we switched positions, my hair spread out on the pillow. Even with my face distorted in passion, people could pick me out of a line up.

The side angle returned with more of the opening footage, the roundness of the look-a-like engagement ring stood out.

The two different scenes confirmed my theory. Eugene spliced the tape. *He must hate me, but not as much as I hate him at the moment. I could kill him.* I ejected the tape and threw it into the fireplace knowing there was at least one more video tape out there, the tape Eugene had copied from and inserted to make this one. Feeling sick to my stomach, I got wood from the patio and stared the fire.

In an angry haze, I went to the police station to request a temporary restraining order against Eugene. A judge read my petition, asked me questions and issued one. I would have a court hearing within fifteen days to seek a more permanent solution.

CHAPTER 26
Benjamin

I have been caught in an indiscretion or two. I know the cardinal rule. Deny, deny, deny. At the brunch a couple of months ago, Andrea had admitted how lost she was. She had said she was angry and confused. With Eugene reentering her life, she probably just fell for the okey-doke. After months of religiously enforced celibacy, maybe she was embarrassed to tell me the truth.

The next evening we had a family event at my brother Tim's church. He and Maryann had signed up for clean up crew afterwards, but Sharon and I insisted he take the kids and a very pregnant wife home. Sharon and I got to work.

"What's the matter?" Sharon asked, studying me while she tied on an apron. "Did you talk to Andrea about Eugene showing up at the house?"

"Yeah, in a manner of speaking. Roy, do you see those puppets in that basket on the other side of the room?" I asked.

"Can I play with them, Daddy?"

"Yes, play with them at one of the tables over there."

I watched Roy dump the whole box of Bible character puppets out on a table while I handed Sharon leftovers to be dealt with. "Yesterday Eugene brought a sex tape to Andrea's house."

"What did you say? A sex tape?"

"It shows Eugene and someone who looks like Andrea and who happens to be wearing a ring like the one I gave her, going at it pretty good."

"Oh, no way!"

"She says it's not her. But it looks like her."

"If it walks like a duck and quacks like a duck …"

I raised my eyebrows in resignation. "That's what I'm thinking."

"Then again, there are creative camera angles. Have you seen some of that stuff they try to pass off as real on the Internet? People can put anything together these days with the right software." She turned to the job at hand. "Where do you think they keep the SOS pads?"

"They're not under the sink? Try that top cabinet. I find it hard to believe Eugene would go through so much trouble. Getting a ring like Andrea's? Hiring someone? He even had a blue sweater like hers on the bed."

"Oh yeah. I found the pads. Who knows what burr is up his ass? People do crazy shit all the time. You were so sure about her character yesterday. Why would Andrea lie?"

"You mean besides the fact that she's caught? Maybe she's confused. Being celibate—"

"What?" Sharon stopped mid-scrub.

"We were waiting until after the wedding."

She looked like she was going to burst into laughter any second, but went back to cleaning the Dutch oven. "You probably have enough pent-up energy to power half the city."

"Something like that."

"So anyway, she's not having sex with you, but she's getting busy with Eugene? Maybe she's another Carolyn."

I took the pan to dry it. "How so?"

"You know, starting out with good intentions." She did a rough imitation of Carolyn. "I'm giving up crack. Benjamin, I promise." And, then her imitation of Andrea—"I'm giving up sex, Benjamin, until after we're married." Her voice went back to normal. "Could be those Young women love their pleasures too much. Maybe you should try dating someone with a different last name?"

"Funny. I thought you liked Andrea?"

"I like her fine, you're the one accusing her of infidelity."

I didn't have a response for that. I wiped some more tables down in silence, blocking pictures from my mind. I heard Roy play with the puppets.

"Bible girl," Roy said, "this is Aunt Andi. Aunt Andi will play with you. She knows games and she makes good oatmeal raisin cookies, and she'll take you to the park even if it's cold outside."

"Roy is sure crazy about her," Sharon said after a few minutes. "

"They're incredible together. Watching them is like watching one of those sappy Chicken Soup stories come to life."

"Yep, they've always had that special bond." I shook my head. "I don't know anymore, Sharon, about the tape. Now, I'm confused."

"Well, if your scenario is the correct one, and that is her, what are you going to do?"

"I don't know. I guess, if she admits it, I could consider forgiving her."

"Are you sure you love her enough to let bygones be bygones?"

It would be easy for me to glibly say yes, of course I love her like that, but in reality, "Good question," was the more honest answer.

She turned off the kitchen light and looked at me. "Christmas is in a week. You two will probably make amends by then. I mean, if your love is strong enough, no one should be able to come between you two, right?"

CHAPTER 27
Andrea

I'd seen Roy twice since the video tape, but it had been five long days and no flowers from Benjamin. No "I love you" balloons tied to my door. I got no late night phone calls from him saying he couldn't stop thinking about me and how sorry he was for doubting me. *If he hadn't rushed off so quickly, I could have explained everything to him.*

I wanted to tell him how the tape came to be, but pride wouldn't let me call him first. Random bursts of energy inspired me to touch up the pale lemon paint in the den, thoroughly clean the tile in the bathroom, and bake dozens of oatmeal raisin cookies. But when I wasn't busy, I mostly traipsed through the house doing nothing. Why hadn't he called by now?

Yesterday I didn't bother getting dressed. I hadn't wanted to be alone, but I hadn't felt like going anywhere either. BJ and Gloria offered to give up their plans to come keep me company, but I told them it wasn't necessary. I called Brother Ward, my Bible study teacher, and we talked for almost two hours. I told him everything about how I had kept what really had happened at Eugene's house a secret, how I was sure Eugene had been following me even before that and his gift sending afterwards.

I wanted to stop there, but I figured getting everything off my chest would help me feel better. When I told him that some of the footage on the video tape wasn't fake, that Eugene had filmed us having sex, my face generated the warmth of a space heater, I was that flushed with embarrassment.

He said that marriage required trust, and just as I expected Benjamin to trust me, I needed to be trustworthy and not withhold information from the man that I loved.

Brother Ward said I had to talk honestly with Benjamin. Ask for his forgiveness and pray for a chance to make a new start. And, after I did that, God would take it from there.

The advice was sound. When we hung up, I called Benjamin, but he wasn't home, and he wasn't answering his cell phone.

I would shower, dress, and take the cookies I'd baked to the senior citizen home. I figured there were enough cookies left to make a presentable gift; I had eaten quite a few because I needed something to feel right. Going to the home would be a perfect use of my time. I wouldn't be sitting around moping all day like yesterday.

I stood in the shower, smelling like the soap made from goat's milk that my secret pal at school had given me. *Good thoughts, good thoughts.* I tried to conjure them up, but questions kept coming instead.

I turned off the shower, no wiser than when I started out. The big question remained. How to admit there were some scenes of me on the tape without pushing Benjamin farther away?

CHAPTER 28
Benjamin

By noon on Christmas Eve, every album or CD worthy of the title "Holiday" lined up awaiting playtime. Pans banged in the kitchen, and low conversing voices periodically exploded into raucous laughter. The smells alone had me drooling. Last minute shoppers like me secretly wrapped packages, and the rest of the family enjoyed their free time doing whatever made them feel happy or most useful. Yep, nothing like Christmas with a broken heart.

Lonely me, adrift on a sea of holiday happiness, but I couldn't bring myself to call Andrea. Just as I was about to take one more shot at putting Roy's racetrack together, Sharon and Marissa walked through the front door.

"Surprise! Look who's back for Christmas!" Sharon led the way with fanfare.

After I peeled Roy off Marissa, I was able to get a good look. She was definitely eye candy. Her hair, cut now so it turned under at her jaw line, swung with her every move. She took off her sweater coat to reveal a red lacy top and those spandex type bell-bottom pants that barely covered her belly button, which captivated my attention. Marissa had discovered a floral perfume called Sung that a former girl-friend of mine used to wear. It added to Marissa's allure. She had matured into a poised, confident young woman.

When she asked me what was new, I told her about my engagement, not sharing that it might be temporary. Did I imagine the fleeting look of sadness that crossed her face?

I asked her if she'd met anybody interesting. She shook her head no. The guys were probably on her like a pig on slop. I remembered my days of sweating the pretty ones unmercifully.

"Roy has grown so much, Ben."

"Yep, he has. How's his Spanish? Can you tell yet?"

"Not bad. The more we talk, the more it comes back to him. Soon it will be like we were never apart. Little kids are good with languages."

"Your English is more precise," I complimented.

"I've been working hard. I had to take two remedial English classes, mostly for the writing, but the writing helps my speaking." Her face became pink." Ben, you're making me feel embarrassed. You are looking at me all the time."

"I am?" I knew I was guilty. Who knew a few months could make such a big difference? "Sorry, I was remembering that scared young girl I used to know and comparing her to the beautiful young woman you are now."

She smiled. "Thank you."

"It's really great to see you, but I had no idea you were coming."

"I know. Surprise! Your sister made all the arrangements. She sent me the ticket."

What was Sharon up to I wondered?

"Excuse me. I'm going to spend some time with your mother now," Marissa said.

"Okay, and I need to get back to my project."

After dinner, we got a Monopoly game started. Maryann, Tim's wife, owned Marvin Gardens, three railroads and Park Place within an hour.

I guess Uncle Fred thought because he'd been married four times, he had what it took to pull the ladies—even the eighteen year old variety. I sat back and watched my uncle in action.

He anticipated Marissa's every need. He brought her cokes, refilled her snack plate and even moved her iron token on the board so she wouldn't have to reach too far.

I took my hat off to confidence like that, especially considering he was stone-cold sober the whole time. Not that he was ugly or out of shape or anything. He wasn't. He was strong from all the years working the street crew, and he was a year or two younger than my mother, who was fifty-five. Many would say he was just hitting his stride, but an eighteen-year-old? That was some mighty wishful thinking on his part.

The Monopoly players had enough by ten. Everybody went home, intending to reconvene on Christmas Day.

Being with family all day made me miss Andrea with an intensity that caught me unaware. I craved her, and suddenly couldn't imagine why on earth I'd been avoiding her calls. Compelled to speak with her, disappointment jabbed at me when I got her answering machine. I started to hang up, but then I figured leaving a message was a good way to save face. "Tomorrow is Christmas, Andrea. I know you were looking forward to celebrating it with Roy. Come on over first thing in the morning. See you then."

She arrived at six the next morning. It was awkward, but we had a goal bigger than our issue at the moment. We both wanted to make sure this a special day for Roy.

Andrea and I sat in the kitchen sipping coffee. She said, "Benjamin, I think we can straighten this out." But that's as far as we got because Mr. Elrod came shuffling in, looking for his morning cup of java.

We charged the extra battery for the video camera to have something to do while we waited. We looked at the camera, then looked at each other and the strain returned. I was getting ready to ask her to take an early morning walk with me, but I heard Roy came down the stairs. The three of us filed out to greet him. "Merry Christmas!"

He'd stopped in Marissa's room and brought her down with him, his hand in hers.

When Marissa saw Andrea she told Roy, "Go on, see what Santa brought you." She pulled her robe tighter around her. "I want to get dressed first."

"No, come on," Roy insisted, pulling her hand. "We don't have to be dressed, do we Daddy?"

I shook my head no.

Andrea said, "Hi, I didn't know you were here." She threw me a questioning look. "Please stay, Marissa. Roy will have more fun the more people there are to share Christmas morning with. Don't go."

True. Roy thought of Marissa as his older sister. How much fun can Christmas morning be without your siblings?

Marissa hesitated until Andrea walked over and hooked her arm around Marissa's elbow, bringing her to the Christmas tree. "I'm sure Santa brought you something," she told Marissa. Andrea helped her look, and sure enough, there was something. Roy made a beeline for the racecar track on a low table in the corner.

"Daddy! My racetrack!"

Just as Marissa was holding up the black leather jacket I was surprised to learn I had bought her, we heard a camera click. My mother took pictures. That reminded me to get the video camera going so we wouldn't miss recording a second of the movie we would dub "Christmas Day Fun." I handed the job over to Mr. Elrod. Too many good and bad thoughts boxed in my head about videotapes.

Before long, my mom's egg and cheese casserole—minus the bacon this year on my behalf—spread good cheer. Sharon joined us about nine, followed by Uncle Fred and a couple of more aunts. More guests trickled in as the morning went on.

Over spiced eggnog, we talked football, crime, education, and the movies. Then we talked stock market, jobs, and the housing market. Then we argued which was best—chocolate or vanilla ice cream, chocolate or vanilla cake, or chocolate or vanilla women and why.

Every once and a while, Andrea would catch me looking at her, or I would turn to see her watching me. Our vibe was stronger than ever. She and I would be all right. Eugene had issues and that tape was bogus. I couldn't remember why I had been willing to believe him and not the woman I loved.

Right before lunch, I went upstairs to get more film. Marissa came out of the upstairs bathroom as I was going into my bedroom.

"Ben, can we talk a minute?"

"Sure, let's go back downstairs—"

"No, privately please. In your room?"

"In my room?" Something must be wrong. I bet I knew what it was. Uncle Fred was back again, refreshed and even more eager than he had been yesterday to make an impression on Marissa. "Okay." She sat on the bed and after not thinking for a second, I sat next to her. "Is it Uncle Fred? He doesn't mean any harm, honest Marissa, but I can talk to him."

"No, it's something else." She got up, closed the door, then came back and sat down.

"What's the matter?"

"This." Her lips were on mine faster than syrup goes on pancakes and just as sweet. She pushed her tongue against mine and that triggered an automatic response.

CHAPTER 29
Andrea

The expectation was I'd stay, have dinner, and be immersed in the family. I loved sharing Christmas day with Roy, but my head was killing me. I swallowed two Advil with the help of a Diet Coke and tried to figure out how to get through the rest of the day without Benjamin and me coming to some understanding about Eugene's tape.

On the other hand, he and I were being civil. His demeanor toward me wasn't cutthroat like it had been. I guessed it couldn't be or he wouldn't have invited me here today.

Timothy and Maryann had brought their karaoke radio. I laughed in spite of my headache when quiet, unassuming Mr. Elrod sang "What's Love Got to Do With It" complete with hip switching strolls across the floor and phantom hair shakes.

When I dried my eyes, I knew love had everything to do with it. At the end of the day, nothing else mattered. I needed to find Benjamin and convince him of that.

Coming to the top of the stairs, I could see the bathroom door ajar, but Benjamin's door was closed. I knocked on his door and opened it at the same time. "Benjamin?"

Benjamin and Marissa were melded together. For a minute, they looked like a mutant life form. I emitted a squealing sound. They broke apart and looked at me like I was the two-headed, four-armed monster.

I was cemented to the spot. *Oh, this must be a dream, that's why I can't move. But then, why can't I wake up?*

Both had their clothes on, but she was redder than Mrs. Sherwood's shingles rash, and he was breathing as if his air supply was in jeopardy. The outline on his pants leg made me think of polish sausage—grilled.

Finally, my legs decided to work. Images swam. I got my coat, jumped into my car and was half a block past the first stop sign before I realized I'd left my purse. *Shoot.*

I pulled to the curb and cried into the steering wheel. I'd left my purse, my fiancé, my nephew, my whole life back there. The pages of my life had come undone with no stapler in sight.

The car door flew open, and my head flew up. Benjamin, coatless and panting, slid in next to me, taking the key out of the ignition in one swift motion.

"Andrea, you don't need to drive when you're this upset. Nothing happened. I mean, the kiss, but … she said she wanted to talk to me and it just happened."

Thirty silent seconds passed.

"I'm calmer now," I said. "I left my purse. I think it's near the mantel next to that gold flowerpot."

"Your purse can wait. We need to talk about this."

"Forgive me, I don't know where to begin. What is Marissa doing here in the first place? Is that what you two did the whole time she lived with you? What would have happened if I hadn't interrupted?"

His hands floated up and down in the stay calm gesture. "Andrea, it was a kiss. There was nothing before it, and there would have been nothing after it. My body reacted. Physical reactions happen the mind can't control."

"Do you control where you put your lips?"

"She kissed me."

"How about your tongue? Do you have any say-so over it whatsoever?"

He shook his head and said nothing.

"It's payback, isn't it? You invited me here today so you could humiliate me. I admit it was me on the tape, not both times, but the second time was me. I swear Eugene did something to make it look recent. The fake ring, the sweater—props. They were all props,

Benjamin. Eugene wanted to hurt me, and he succeeded, but nothing compared to how you've hurt me today."

"No, Andrea, I'm sorry to disappoint you, but you're wrong. I didn't set out to humiliate you. That's ridiculous. Who has time for some soap opera stuff like that?"

"Obviously you do. You sent for Marissa after you saw the tape."

"No, I didn't. Sharon invited her. She probably thought Roy would get a kick out of seeing her again."

Could he sit there, looking innocent and lie to my face? "And if I ask Marissa about all of this, she'll tell me the same story?"

"Yes."

"Then let's go ask her now."

"I don't want to do that. She'd be mortified. She's a kid. She may have the body of a woman and a woman's desires, but she's a kid. It was only a kiss."

I nodded. He cared more about Marissa than he cared about me. "Okay. Give me my keys and get out. I'll pick up my purse tomorrow."

"Andrea?" He stared at me for a long second. "Whatever. Take your keys." He plopped them down in my waiting hand. "I'll bring you your purse later tonight." He slammed the car door harder than he needed to.

I put the car in reverse, turning around, gauging how close I could get to the small, dark sedan behind me. I didn't dawn on me at first, but then something clicked. The car behind me was small and gray. I got out, walked behind the vehicle to read the name. Camry. A dolphin gray Camry, the right model, year and color.

"Benjamin!"

"What?" he yelled back.

"Come here, please!"

"What? Did you hit it?" He asked upon his return, staring at the car like I was staring at it. "What's the matter?"

"Do you know whose car this is?"

"I think it's Cecil's. Why?"

"Because one of the women who lives on the street where Carolyn was killed saw a Camry this year and color that night she was killed. Doesn't this look like a 1992 or 1991?"

He looked at it again and shrugged. "But, what are you saying? You think Cecil had something to do with Carolyn's murder? That's even more ridiculous than this soap opera gimmick you accused me of. Who haven't you blamed for the murder, Andrea?"

I could see I'd get no sympathy, let alone empathy here. Rolling my eyes, I got back in my car.

"Oh, so I'm dismissed again?" Benjamin shouted. "Wait a second, will you?"

No, I would not. I drove away, engine gunning.

CHAPTER 30
Benjamin

I watched Andrea leave in her huff. When I got back to the house, I found Sharon alone in a corner of the kitchen, icing cupcakes.

She looked up as I approached. "What was all that commotion?"

I almost didn't know where to begin. "Man, when it rains it pours. I'm selling T-shirts if you're interested."

She laughed. "What happened? Can't be that bad."

"It's pretty bad. Marissa kissed me. Andrea saw it. Disaster followed. Did she come downstairs yet?"

"Marissa? I haven't seen her." She licked some icing off her thumb and examined me. "Did you kiss her back?"

"Yes, and I know why I did. She's an attractive girl—woman. What I don't know is why she kissed me."

Sharon shrugged. "She's got a crush on you. Why is that so hard to figure out?"

"Do me a favor. Go upstairs and make sure she's all right?"

"Boy, that must have been some kiss. Here." She handed me the knife to continue with the cupcakes. While I made intricate chocolate designs on my second cupcake, I replayed and examined the events of the day to try and see what had led to them. The truth peaked like my latest swirl. Marissa as a consolation prize—that's what Sharon had offered me. When Sharon got back, I was ready for her.

"She's fine," Sharon said. "She was in the guestroom thinking you were upset with her. She'll be down in a few minutes."

"Thanks. Sharon. Is that the real reason you brought her here? To see if you could stir something up between us?"

"Pardon me?" Sharon scoffed. "How did you come up with that bizarre notion? Too much sugar is a bad thing, Benny. Give me my knife back."

"Marissa and I lived together almost three years, and she never laid a lip on me. Andrea and I are going through a rough spell, and all of a sudden Marissa's here because you arranged it. That leather jacket from me was a nice touch. What's going on?"

Sharon tried to convince me frosting techniques enthralled her. I waited her out.

"All right." She put down her knife and folded her arms. "Marissa took excellent care of Roy. I thought maybe you needed one more chance to be sure you didn't want her. When did caring about you and my nephew become a crime?"

"Good intentions are fine, Sharon. But this is my future. Mine, Roy's, and the woman I choose to marry. My life is not an episode on *As the World Turns* that you can write and direct."

Her shoulders dropped. Maybe I'd said too much, her motives were pure after all. I tilted her chin up.

"Hey, let me come up with the pudding-headed schemes to ruin my own life from now on. As it is, I'm going to have to try and explain why I didn't push Marissa away immediately. My reason's got to be a doozy, or Andrea won't be buying it." That got a smile again.

"Yeah, right. You need me, you just don't know it. Look how it turned out. You know you want Andrea despite the tape, so that's a good thing."

"Yeah, well, if you're so good, help me figure out what I say to Marissa."

"That's easy. You apologize to her, even though she kissed you first. Say you're sorry. Say her beauty temporarily overwhelmed you, and you hope she can forgive you. Take her guilt away. She'll be fine."

"Good, now what about Andrea?"

Just then, a rumbling of concerned voices gained momentum, spread out from the sitting area and found us in the kitchen. *What now?*

I ran to see what the ruckus was. The backs of family and friends crowded around the window. My mother held the phone asking to speak to the police.

My mouth went dry. "Where's Roy?" I asked my uncle.

"He's with Marissa over there," he pointed. I scanned and found him huddled in her arms sitting on the stairs in the hall with my niece and nephew.

"What happened?" I asked.

"Somebody drove up on the lawn," Mr. Elrod said, coming back inside. "Thought I was going to have to get my gun, but it's just somebody drunk asking for Andrea—too much holiday cheer."

Just great. It's got to be Eugene. He's lost his damn mind. I might be tempted to get that gun myself if the police weren't coming.

"It's Eugene." Sharon held back the curtain, confirming my suspicions. Under her breath I heard her say, "Asshole could have killed somebody."

Sharon caught my arm before I went outside. "Ben, you need a restraining order against him."

"Andrea said—" I began.

"If the kids had been playing out there, someone would be dead or seriously hurt. I don't want Roy exposed to his crap. Eugene Sherwood needs to be put in check."

"I'm on it," I said.

"Good. I'm going out of town a couple of days for some residency interviews. I can't worry about this."

CHAPTER 31
Andrea

Gloria looked at me with a sad face. "I'm not going to say I told you so. You know why not?"

"Thank you for bringing me my purse, Gloria, and it's good of you to spare my feelings. You must not be feeling well," I teased.

"Because that would be lowbrow and petty and as downtrodden as you look right now, I know you don't need to hear it."

"I'm not that downtrodden. Can I get you anything?" We were at my place. I'd changed from my Christmas day finery into blue jeans and a sweatshirt. I had my wineglass in hand.

"No, I'm fine, thanks." Gloria had on an expensive black pants suit, accessorized perfectly. She'd interrupted her Christmas celebration for me.

I toasted the air. "Merry Christmas! Gloria, guess what I saw—I mean what else I saw?" She already knew about the kiss. I had explained that when I had called and asked her to go get my purse from Benjamin's house.

"What else? You're having a lottery winning kind of day. Tell all."

"I saw a Camry like the one Mrs. Tuddle described. It's Cecil's!"

"Get out! Cecil's car?" She sank down on my couch to consider this. "Cecil Chambers," she repeated, biting her lower lip in thought.

I sat on the coffee table in front of her, sipping wine.

"Andi, thought you said you asked Ben about cars back in the summer?"

"I did, but I was casual about it on purpose. I didn't want him to think I suspected him or his family."

"You never asked him if he knew someone who drove an early 90s dark-colored Camry?"

"No, I never phrased it that way."

Gloria crossed her legs and let the top one swing a few seconds. "Carolyn and Cecil, what was up between them?"

"I don't think there was anything between them. She knew him. You know he's Sharon's boyfriend."

"Yeah, he owns that bookstore—The Griot?"

"His family owns it."

"Access to cash then. Does he get high?"

"Seems pretty straight-laced to me. More of a health nut than someone who does recreational drugs, but I don't know him that well."

I watched her twist her mouth in continued thought. "Maybe it was a love affair gone bad?"

"I sat next to Gloria on the couch and put my feet on the coffee table. "Between him and Carolyn? No way. The way he fawns over Sharon? Little chance of that. Besides, I would've known about it."

"We have to look at the circle of people around Cecil," Gloria said.

"Yeah, you're right. Who would Cecil lend his car to?" *Sharon, of course.*

"What about his family and friends?"

I emptied my glass and set it on a coaster. "He's got a grandfather retired to Lake Carlyle. Friends?" I shook my head. "I don't know. That's the black hole that will prevent us from getting anywhere, unless we just ask him. 'Hey Cecil, who do you let borrow your car?' Think that would work?"

No doubt reading my expression, she said, "Don't get discouraged, Andi. What's Sharon's alibi for the night Carolyn was murdered?"

"I don't know. How can I find out what she did ten months ago?"

"Good point. And I'm sure Detective Peck and company didn't bother to question her."

"I'm sure he didn't either—no reason to."

Gloria looked at me, her bright-eyed enthusiasm newly ignited. "We still have the popcorn clue."

"Yeah, you mean find the popcorn bag and get a fingerprint? After all this time? It would take a miracle."

"Or, some really good detectives?"

"You mean … us?"

"Why not? You've given Peck his chance. We backed off like he requested, now we have to get involved again."

"Popcorn? I don't know, Gloria. Everybody eats popcorn. And what about the neighborhood being dangerous?"

"Oh, come on. It's Christmas Day. Even the bad guys are at their mama's cribs getting their eat on. Besides, I don't want you stewing about Benjamin. Let's shake something and see what falls loose."

She was probably right. Still, I resisted because Peck's picture of electricity-deprived hooligans had scared me. "But, BJ's in Jefferson City. We had more luck when there were three Angels instead of two."

"Stop fretting. We can do this. Come on."

"We could talk to Mrs. Freelon again," I relented. "Take her some oatmeal raisin cookies and see if Dale Edward is back, even though the police already spoke with him. He might remember something more for us."

"Now you're thinking."

Christmas lights blazed and blinked on a few houses. Mrs. Freelon's was one of them. Otherwise, things seemed quiet on the block.

"Hold these." I gave Gloria the cookie tin on the way up Mrs. Freelon's steps as I pulled out my phone.

"Who are you calling?"

"Detective Peck. It just occurred to me that no one knows where we are. I'm going to leave him a message, just in case … you know, something happens."

"Let me leave it." Gloria gave me the tin and took the phone. "Detective Peck, this is Gloria Wellborn, a friend of Carolyn Young. You might recall Ms. Young was the woman murdered on Vernon Avenue ten months ago. Her case is still open. Her sister, Andrea, and I are here following up on some leads. Holler back when you get a chance."

She handed me the phone and flashed her "that's how it's done" smile.

Unable to locate the doorbell near Mrs. Freelon's door, we knocked and waited.

"The lot is cleaner than it was." I gestured toward the empty lot next to Mrs. Freelon's house.

"Yeah, maybe the city sponsored a clean up your crack neighborhood campaign since we've been here last."

Just as we were about to knock a second time, we could hear a slow advance coming toward the door.

"Who is it?"

"It's Gloria and Andrea, Mrs. Freelon. We spoke with you this summer," Gloria reminded her.

Mrs. Freelon cracked open her door, a puzzled and wary look crossed her face. "This summer? What y'all want?"

"We wanted to thank you. We talked to Mrs. Tuddle like you suggested, and she gave us some helpful information about that night my sister was murdered."

She opened the door all the way now. She had on a housecoat, her wig was on crooked, and this time I noticed she walked with a cane. I held out the tin. "I brought you some cookies."

"Oh, thank you." Her smile went straight from her lips to her eyes. She took the tin. "I remember you, but where is that nice young man that was with you before?"

"He's out of town," Gloria said.

"Y'all out visiting on Christmas Day? That's nice. Wish I could get out and about. Well, don't stand there. Come on in, it's cold out there.

Take off your coats and sit a spell. Since I can't get out, I'm glad for the company."

Perfect lead in. "Did Dale Edward come back yet?" The dim light in the living room could not conceal the shabbiness of her furniture, but there was not a rug fringe out of place, and her wood floors sparkled.

"Yes, yes he did. He's out running the streets now. "'Spect to see him some time in the morning. All Dale Edward knows is party this, party that." Mrs. Freelon lowered herself in an armchair with a plop and a sigh. "That's all he wants to do with his life. That and play those computer games all day long."

"How old is he?" Gloria asked while I savored the smell of greens and corn bread and told my stomach not to growl.

"Dale Edward just turned twenty-three last month. What kind of cookies are these? I can eat one or two, but I gotta watch my sugar."

"Those are oatmeal raisin," I said.

"Oatmeal raisin. Might save 'em for breakfast in the morning." She set the tin on an end table. It shared the space with a small Christmas tree with twinkling lights.

"We were hoping to talk to Dale Edward. See what he saw, if anything, the day Carolyn was murdered," I said.

"Oh, well, leave me something with your phone number on it so I can give to him. I can't keep up with him. I wish he'd find something to do with his life other than run the streets, but he's a good boy. He put my Christmas lights up for me outside."

"He did a nice job," Gloria said and I agreed.

"He keeps the kitchen spic and span. Even helps me with that old nasty lot over there." She tilted her head.

"What do you mean? He picks up trash off the lot?" Gloria asked. The sun began to rise in Gloria's face, but I didn't know why. Did she think Dale Edward would remember picking up a popcorn bag and even if he did, February to December was a longtime ago. Any trace of it would be far gone by now.

Mrs. Freelon massaged her left knee like it was sore. "I'd do it, don't nobody want to put up with all that trash right next door, but with this leg, I can't be bending down. I told Dale Edward to get up all that trash and to be careful. He showed me a needle he found in that grass one time." She shook her head. "These drugs has been the *ruination* of a whole generation." She pursed her lips in disgust. "Umph umph umph."

"How often is the trash picked up?" I asked.

"You mean by the city? They come and empty the Dumpster once a week."

Anything found on the lot in February would be long gone. I envisioned mountains of slimy trash some place. I could almost smell it. I hoped Gloria didn't think either of us were up to taking that on.

"You looking for something on that lot?" Mrs. Freelon asked.

"A popcorn bag."

A popcorn bag? Umph, Well, seeing as how Dale Edward just got back last week, and he's been gone since last Easter, that trash you talking bout might still be sitting out there in the can, believe it or not."

Gloria and I spoke at the same time, "What can?"

The trashcan on the side of the house. Metal can."

"We didn't see a can out there."

"It's further up in the gangway. It sits there til it's full enough to dump."

"Full enough to dump," I repeated, half way out of my chair. "Mrs. Freelon, could we take a look?" Even while I asked, I knew it sounded ridiculous. Trash left in a can over ten months? That would be the miracle we'd been seeking.

"Y'all gonna get out there as cold as it is, sorting through trash?"

"Yes, ma'am. It could be a link to her sister's murder."

"Well, I got one pair of Platex gloves I can let you borrow. I seen 'em do this kind of job on TV on those cops shows. You can't touch nothing directly. It will mess up the evidence and the court will throw it out."

"Good point, Mrs. Freelon," Gloria said. "Andi, call Detective Peck and tell him I said to come out and look through the can for us."

"It's Christmas Day, Gloria. We can see if we can find it, then call him." The three of us were standing, plotting.

"Uh-uh." Gloria shook her head. "He's liable to say we planted it ourselves or something. I'll call him. Give me your phone." She took it, pushed redial, then listened and pushed buttons, no doubt activating his emergency beeper.

"The police is coming out?" Mrs. Freelon let out a gleeful cackle. "I was sitting here feeling a little sorry for myself because my days are so boring even if it is Jesus's birthday." She shuffled on her bad hip toward the kitchen. She came right back. "Take these gloves, but don't start 'til I get back. I'm a go fix my face case this 'tective wants to interview me."

Detective Peck called back in three minutes. He made me tell him three times why I had called. I was trying to think of how to rephrase it the fourth time when Gloria snatched the phone. She reminded him he was the lead investigator on a cold murder case, and unless he wanted the media to hear our desperate Christmas Day story, he would get here within the next twenty minutes.

Gloria handed me my phone back. "You are too nice sometimes, Andi. All that time he wasted talking, Peck's butt could have been here."

Twenty-five minutes later, Peck arrived and we showed him the trashcan. "Ladies, all I can say is that this better be damn good." He glared at both of us. "Where's the third party in this popcorn bag seeking trio?"

"I'm up here, 'tective." Mrs. Freelon leaned over her porch and waved. "Ask me anything you want to know."

Detective Peck jumped, obviously startled at the unexpected voice from above. Gloria and I tried not to laugh at his reaction. We knew he had been referring to BJ.

"Hold this," he handed Gloria his flashlight, giving her a steely-eyed stare in the process. "I'm going to dump it. Stand back, might be rats, roaches, or all the above. Don't touch anything."

"Here 'tective," Mrs. Freelon's voice reigned down once again. "Take one of my old canes case you need to push that mess around to see what's what." Mrs. Freelon leaned over her porch and lowered it down.

Winston Peck accepted the cane with a thank you.

Crap spilled forth. Ripe baby diapers were on top, soon to share the spotlight with beer and wine bottles, scrunched pizza boxes, and water bugs two inches long scurried as fast as fat water bugs can scurry. More fast food wrappers, newspapers, plastic bags from Walgreens, empty cigarette packages, used condoms, what looked like elementary school math papers, but no popcorn bag.

"We had to look," I said, more disappointed than I realized I would be.

"Yeah, we did," Gloria said.

Detective Peck didn't say anything as he began to rapidly replace the items in the can. We watched silently, knowing we had to wait until he was finished and listen to him fuss. When he got to the plastic bag, he stood straight up, untied the bag and looked inside.

"Bingo ladies. Looks like we've hit pay dirt."

I walked up to him to look at what he pulled out of the bag. There it was, our microwave popcorn bag. It looked like gold to me. I grinned at him.

"Thank you, Jesus," Gloria said.

Mrs. Freelon clapped. Gloria and I watched him put it in an evidence bag.

"How long does it take to process for fingerprints?" I asked. If Carolyn's were on it, we were definitely on the right track.

"Three days to two weeks. Depends on what they are up against and how difficult it is to process. Being in this plastic bag probably helped preserve any usable prints."

I took a deep breath. "Okay, well, I'll wait to hear from you."

He nodded.

I walked back up the porch steps and returned the borrowed cane to Mrs. Freelon who was still standing there, watching us.

"That popcorn bag was sho nuf in that can. My Lord. You and your friends are welcome to stay and have Christmas dinner with me."

"Thank you, Mrs. Freelon. That is such a wonderful invitation. Let me check with them."

When I came back down, Gloria was saying goodnight.

"Mrs. Freelon has invited us to join her for Christmas dinner."

"Mrs. Freelon," Detective Peck said, "I would love to stay, but I have a previous engagement. Thank you for your help tonight. Good citizens like you make our job easier." If he wore a hat, I'm sure he would have tipped it.

Mrs. Freelon's smile put the half-moon to shame. I hope Peck appreciated her freshly rouged cheeks.

"Ladies." He nodded at Gloria and me, then left.

"Those greens were smelling good, Mrs. Freelon. What else are we having?" Gloria asked.

"Child, I got some fried chicken, macaroni and cheese, coleslaw, and some lemon meringue pie for dessert."

Gloria and I raced each other up the stairs.

Mrs. Freelon refused to let us lift a hand to help her get the food on the table. In fact, she insisted we have a glass of her "special occasion" spirits. She put ice in our glasses, then poured from the Chivas Regal bottle and told us to relax. I said a silent prayer of thanks.

CHAPTER 32
The Killer

"Oh, what the fuck is this?" Beady eyes looked into the barrel of a handgun. Big, thick hands flew up in surrender without hesitation.

"You thought I was going to let you get away with some shit like that?"

He stepped back from the front door. "Wait just a second. Calm the hell down. I—I was having a little fun is all." Sweat glistened on his brow in a thin sheen. Fear rose off him like steam on a paved road in the middle of summer.

"Move another step, if you think I'm not serious."

Immediately Eugene Sherwood froze. Hands still in front of him, he had the nerve to call on the Almighty.

"A little fun, right. I noticed it's always at someone else's expense. Why is that?"

He slowly lowered his hands. "What do you want? We can work something out."

"What do I want? You mean like an apology or money or something? Maybe respect?"

"Whatever it takes."

"That's funny. It's also the classic example of too little, too late. Eat shit and die."

"Don't do this, please. This is my life you're talking about."

The first shot penetrated Eugene's thick belly. His expression of pain was gratifying to watch. Eugene tried to stem the blood with a hand and a horrified look. Neither helped. The red spreading across his white shirt created a colorful, butterfly design. Two final shots to the head finished the deed.

BETWEEN TEARS

He tottered for a moment before he fell face forward onto the blue, gold and white Mediterranean tiles that I understood he had specially ordered. His eyes popped open. They blinked periodically. He wasn't dead, not yet, just clearly unable to move. He would die soon, though. No matter.

CHAPTER 33
Andrea

I pulled on my coat and was getting ready to put on my hat when the phone rang, interrupting my plan to see a movie. Anything to get out of the house. I hadn't heard from Benjamin since the Marissa kiss, two days ago. My guess was, he'd dropped by my house like he said he would Christmas evening, although Gloria had already brought me my purse. I'd been out with Gloria rescuing the popcorn bag. He hadn't left word. The ball was still in his court, but maybe I should call and let him explain. After all, I expected him to extend the same courtesy.

The ringing continued. My heart beat faster because hope is eternal. Maybe it was him. "Hello," I said, my voice ending on a high note of expectation.

"Andi, this is Joanna Sherwood."

"Oh, hello Mrs. Sherwood." I fought back the urge to give her a full report of her son's shameful behavior. If I told her what a jackass he was, would she make him stop ruining my life?

"Hello dear. Listen, I have something dreadful to tell you."

I lowered myself to the couch and let my coat slip from my shoulders while I waited for her to go on.

"It's about Eugene," she said.

"What's happened?"

"Somebody shot him yesterday. He's dead."

"Eugene's dead?" *Impossible. He was just here.* I looked at my TV, expecting to see him moan and say, "Oh yeah, baby."

"Yes," her soft voice broke with hurt.

"Oh." It took several seconds for me to go on. "I'm very sorry, Mrs. Sherwood."

"Thank you."

"How did it happen?"

"It seems someone shot him when he opened his front door. At least that's what the police have come up with so far. I found his body in the foyer."

"Oh dear God." What an unsettling image. I could envision her on her hands and knees, bloody from his wounds, wanting to help her son, but not being able to see. My heart went out to her.

"I know. My Eugene is gone."

"I'm sorry Mrs. Sherwood. What do you need help with? I'll be happy to—"

"No, no. My neighbor is here helping me. We'll take care of everything."

"Okay."

"The police are investigating. I gave them your name."

"My name?"

"Yes, they wanted the names of his friends, particularly those who had visited recently or would know to look for him here and not at his apartment."

"Oh, I see."

I was still absorbing it all when she said, "I just though you should know. Goodbye."

I don't remember if I said goodbye to her or not. Eugene, the person who was making my life a living hell, was dead. Was I a suspect? Yes. The restraining order pointed to the disharmony between us. The police were probably on their way here right now.

The operator implored me to hang up if I wanted to make a call. I clicked, so I could get a dial tone and then I called Benjamin's cell phone. I left a message: "Benjamin, Eugene is dead. I need to see you."

As I sat on my couch, the living room walls began to close in. The flight instinct took over. I gathered my hat and coat. I would sit through a movie or maybe walk around the mall. I needed to be somewhere else.

CHAPTER 34
Benjamin

"Someone killed the bastard. I'm not surprised." At one o'clock in the morning, the lamp in Andrea's living room cast a shadowy quiet.

"Eugene came looking for you Christmas Day," I told Andrea.

She covered her mouth in shock, but her eyes raged under furrowed eyebrows as she sat on the couch next to me. "What?"

"Drove up on the lawn drunk. The police arrested him."

"Oh no." She shook her head at the horror of it. "The police are going to want an alibi from both of us."

I leaned forward, elbows on my knees while she sat back on the couch with her arms folded. "I know. When things settled down Christmas Day, I came over to apologize again for what happened with Marissa and to tell you about Eugene, but you weren't around. Then, I figured you could use a day or two to be less emotional about it."

"I wanted to tell you about that videotape," she said.

"What about it?"

"You saw the real me sandwiched in between footage of someone who looked like me. I wasn't the first person on the tape and that wasn't this ring you saw."

"I figured it was something like that. Eugene relied on shock value and it worked. Someone who would do that—well, that's the kind of thing that gets people killed."

Andrea's whole body sighed. "Benjamin—you didn't … Oh, never mind. My nerves are fried. Of course you didn't. I'm sorry, I'm glad the tape isn't an issue between us any more. This murder is enough to cope with."

"Where's the tape?"

"I burned it."

We let that thought float through the room for a silent minute. I wondered if Benjamin was thinking about the original being out there somewhere and was just being too kind to mention it. There was no point in me bringing it up if he didn't.

"You weren't home Christmas evening," I said.

"Gloria and I went back over to Vernon Avenue. Guess what?"

"What?"

"We found the popcorn bag."

"Which popcorn bag is this?"

She got up, her white terrycloth robe scraping the floor. She went into the den and came back with a piece of paper.

"Carolyn had undigested popcorn in her stomach," Andrea explained.

"How do you know?"

"The medical examiner's report says so. You want to read it?" She handed it to me.

I considered a moment before I shook my head no. "I'll pass," I said giving it back to her. "I'd rather remember Carolyn my way."

She frowned at me a moment. "Mrs. Tuddle, the neighbor who spotted the Camry like Cecil's, said she could tell the driver was eating something."

"Because it could have been Cecil's car, you are thinking that Cecil's prints will be on the popcorn bag? Am I following you?"

She nodded.

"When you want two and two to add up, I guess it does."

"Yeah, well," she shrugged, "it could be a stretch, but maybe something will fall into place. Mrs. Freelon told us about Dale Edward cleaning the lot and that's how we found the popcorn bag."

"Dale who? And why didn't the police gather all that stuff from the crime scene? Anything around the body would have been potential evidence."

"Dale Edward Freelon is the grandson of the lady who lives next door to where Carolyn's body was found. The bag had probably blown in front of their building or whatever. We need a break. If Carolyn's prints are on it, we would know we're on the right track."

"You and Gloria have been trying to dig up something the whole time?"

"On and off; BJ helped twice."

"You never talked to me about it. How come?"

"Because any time I bring up Carolyn's murder, you say drugs killed her, Benjamin. Just now, you wouldn't read the medical report."

Despite the slight resistance I detected, I pulled her into my arms. "She's your sister and you have to try to do everything you can. I understand and admire loyalty like that. It's not that I'm not interested, I just need to deal with Carolyn's death differently from how you do, that's all." I kissed her forehead as she rested against my chest. After a few minutes, I said, "It's getting late and I'm tired. Are we straight?"

"Is Marissa gone?"

"Yes. Andrea, you are the only woman I want to be with, you know that." She looked up at me. My lips lingered, teased a breath away from hers before they found their target. She kissed me with a passion that made me weak.

"You smell good, Benjamin. You showered after work?"

"Yeah. I knew I was coming over here," I said, not welcoming the interruption. My lips got back to work.

"Mmm," she hummed into the side of my neck, adding thrills.

"I should go, right?" The huskiness in my voice made it tough to get words out.

Andrea looked at me with bedroom eyes, nodded and patted my chest. "You better."

"I don't want to." My lips found hers again for several intense seconds, head angles changed. Lost in the feel and taste of her, I reached for her belt.

She pushed at my chest again. "Good night, Benjamin." She gathered her robe closed.

I took her hand and placed it where I expressed the most need. "I don't know how you can do it—send the man you claim to love off in the middle of the night like this."

She snatched her hand away like I'd stuck it in a flame. "You know why. We agreed to wait—"

"Yeah, yeah. I know. I'll see you later."

CHAPTER 35
Andrea

I pushed my covers away and turned off my alarm before it sounded. My hands traveled from my breasts down. Heat still surged through my body; the after-effects of the sexually provocative dream Benjamin's hardness had inspired.

I wanted Benjamin, but we'd come this far. We could wait and we should wait. I sat on the side of my bed and said my mantras for the morning. Colossians 12 "Everything is permissible for me"—*but not everything is beneficial.* "Everything is permissible for me"—*but I will not be mastered by anything.* 1 Corinthians 7:9 "But if they cannot control themselves, they should marry, for it is better to marry than to burn with passion."

I made coffee and checked the Internet. A paper local to Mrs. Sherwood carried the story.

Murder probe crosses state lines

By Oscar White

Gazette Staff Writer

The probe into the killing of Eugene Sherwood is leading investigators into another state.

On Saturday, Sheriff Carl Haines, with the Summerville County Police Department, said he is continuing to track down leads with the cooperation of the St. Louis City Police Department in Missouri.

Eugene Sherwood was the son of the now deceased Robert Sherwood and his widow, Joanna Sherwood, both longtime residents of Summerville County. Eugene Sherwood grew up in Summerville, but had been living in St. Louis for the last sixteen years, pursuing a career in education as a high school history teacher. He was home visiting his mother and supervising the final construction phase on his new home when he was shot three times.

Haines said that police are still investigating all possible motives, and that no prime suspect or suspects have been identified despite Mrs. Sherwood's earlier statement that she believed her son was killed by family members who were plotting to regain ownership of the fifty-two acre spread currently owned by Mrs. Sherwood.

Haines confirmed the findings of the autopsy that was performed Saturday morning in Summerville by the tri-county medical examiner, Davida Sutton. The death from three gunshot wounds has been ruled a homicide. The time of death was approximately 7 P. M. on December 26th. No weapon was found at the scene.

Mrs. Sherwood discovered the body of her son, lying across the doorway of his house. Eugene Sherwood was forty-one. Funeral arrangements have not been finalized.

The article, as gruesome as it was, had a nice hometown feel to it, or maybe it was the English teacher in me surfacing. I was glad to read that Mrs. Sherwood "liked" someone else for the crime. I must be watching too much T.V.; I was stealing their police lingo. Land owner-ship was a serious matter. Eugene and I had talked about the money that could be made by developing that land, with the housing market seemingly in a constant growth spurt. I hoped this Sheriff Haines had investigated Mrs. Sherwood's lead thoroughly.

I was on my way to church when Gloria called.

"Girl, have you heard?"

"Eugene is dead," I said.

"How'd you find out?"

"His mother called me."

"And you didn't call me? I was talking to Michael and he mentioned that he was going to be working the investigation in conjunction with the Kentucky police."

"Okay, thanks. Now I know who to contact. I was thinking of going to the police station since I know they want to talk to me about Eugene."

"Yeah, Michael is who you can contact. Who's your lawyer?"

"Lawyer? You think I need one?"

"For a murder investigation? Damn skippy you need a lawyer. I've got Demetria's number right here."

"Mimi? Has it been that long?" Mimi and Carolyn had been close friends. It was at Mimi's wedding reception when Carolyn had breast-fed Roy and the nosy table neighbor hadn't thought it was proper etiquette.

"Yeah, Mimi is all grown up and doing her thing. I hear she passed the bar exam her first time out. I can ask Michael for some names if you don't want to work with a novice, but she's with a good law firm downtown."

"Ughh!" I screamed, pulling at my hair. "Benjamin will need a lawyer, too. This is an incredible, expensive mess."

"It's worth every dime unless there's something about being in a cell with Licky Lucy that's attractive to you."

"No, I can't say that there is. I have a strong motive and a weak alibi."

"Girlfriend, that's a doubly-bad combination."

"I was home the day it happened, and apparently Benjamin was out thinking things through. The police will think that one or both of us decided to confront Eugene and things got out of hand."

"That's why you have to do what you have to do. Get a pen and take this number down and call Mimi. You should meet with her before you talk to the police."

"Okay." I took the number and said goodbye to Gloria. Immediately, I called Mimi, while visions of her bridesmaids' tangerine dresses danced in my head. Her voice mail said I should leave a message. As I turned, I noticed activity out front through my window. "Wait Mimi, the police are coming now. I see Michael Wellborn and another guy I don't recognize. I'll tell them—"

"Andi," Mimi picked up. "Don't let them in unless they have a warrant. Do not go with them unless they arrest you."

"Arrest me?" *Oh God.*

"I'll see you in about thirty minutes."

"Okay." With shaking hands, I opened the front door.

"Miss Young, I'm Sheriff Haines from Summerville, Kentucky. I understand you already know this gentleman assigned to help me with the investigation into the homicide of Eugene Sherwood."

"Hello," I said. "Yes, I know Detective Wellborn." I greeted Michael with a slight nod.

"We'd like a few words with you," Sheriff Haines said.

"No. I've spoken to my attorney, and she advised me not to speak with you."

"A man is dead, your former boyfriend," Detective Haines said. "You could help us get to the bottom of this a lot sooner."

"No."

"We spoke to Eugene Sherwood's mother. She speaks highly of you. We are just trying to do our job, ma'am and give this mother some closure."

Michael spoke up. "Andrea, I'm sure you understand how his mother must feel."

Of course I did, and he knew it because I was sure he and Gloria had talked. I wanted people to come forth about Carolyn's murder and now the police needed information from me to solve Eugene's murder. Being innocent, what could it hurt? Mimi would be here soon, and I would be careful about what I said to them. "Come in."

Sheriff Haines was a well-pressed Southern version of Columbo. His slow, Kentucky drawl counterbalanced those quick, bright blue eyes of his. He was a tall man, in his late fifties, not attractive, not unattractive. If I were lost and I knew he was looking for me, I'd take comfort in that.

I'd known Detective Michael Wellborn most of my life. If his physical good looks—tall, finely chiseled features—were all that mattered, I would probably swoon.

I showed them in. They both shook their heads when I offered to take their coats. The kitchen table felt like the place to conduct business.

"Miss Young," Detective Haines said, "Eugene Sherwood was shot on December twenty-sixth. Can you account for your time that day?"

"I was here."

"Can anyone corroborate that?" Michael asked, taking notes.

"No, I'd talked to a couple of friends that morning, but I was alone all day."

"Your car stayed parked in front of your house the entire time?"

"Yeah."

Detective Haines crossed his arms and let his head tilt a few degrees while he studied my every reaction. "Your relationship to the deceased," Haines said, "describe it."

I cleared my throat, wet my lips and swallowed. "Okay. Well we, at one point in the past, over two years ago, we dated." My nervousness made it hard to get out a coherent sentence. "Recently, within the last couple of weeks, Eugene had been calling me, sending me flowers and giving me gifts and other things that were upsetting to me and to my fiancé. I had gotten a restraining order."

"Where did the flowers come from? Which florist?" Michael asked.

"I don't remember. They came in a white box with red tissue paper, but I don't remember from where."

"What other things did he give you?" Michael continued.

"Eugene brought earrings for me that I didn't actually see. He gave them to my fiancé, and Benjamin, my fiancé, threw them at him." I watched Michael take notes.

"When was this?" he asked.

"The Sunday before Christmas."

"Did you witness your fiancé and Mr. Sherwood with this earring incident?" Haines asked.

"No, Benjamin told me about it."

"Did Sherwood give you anything else besides the flowers and lost earrings?"

I took a deep breath. *Here we go.* "Yes. He gave me a sex tape."

"Of you and him, correct?" Michael asked.

"Yes and no."

"Yes and no? We found a box containing six different tapes at Mr. Sherwood's home." Haines explained. "Upon initial viewing of all six, we concluded there was a strong likeness to you, Miss Young." He pulled a brown envelope from his overcoat breast pocket. I brought a couple of them with me. Would you mind taking a look?"

I reached for the envelope slowly, waiting for reality to reappear. I opened the envelope and pulled out two VCR tapes. One was called "Making it Hot" and the other, "Teacher's Pet." *How original.*

"Maybe you could take a look at them," Michael urged, probably because I had been staring at the tapes and not moving. *Damn it.* I wanted the one I had burned to be the end of this.

"Do you have a VCR in your living room, maybe?" Sheriff Haines said pressing me on.

I stood. "Wait here."

"Sure, not a problem," Haines said.

I put "Making it Hot" in first. I saw Eugene's apartment on screen, the kitchen to be precise. I'd been there often enough once upon a time, what seemed like a previous life now. He appeared, backing away from the camera. I could hear him greeting me, and then I appeared on camera. He'd edited out our chitchat that had proceeded my top coming off.

From behind me, his hands covered my breasts. My bra came off and his hands slowly resumed their motion. The sensations made me moan on screen. His lips on my neck made my eyes flutter. When he unfastened my pants and reached inside, I pushed the eject button.

I sat down on my couch, practically hyperventilating. This tape might as well have been a match in an arsonist's tool kit. Humiliation engulfed me.

My greatest fears were realized. Eugene hadn't filmed me just one time. He had a collection. If Eugene had a camera in the bedroom, and in the kitchen, then he probably had them all through the house. I covered my face with my hands and tried to think of what to do.

We were never in love, but still. Eugene had taken something I thought was special, boxed it, labeled it, and had done Lord knows what with the tapes. That knowledge stung worse than pouring alcohol on an open wound.

Was God punishing me? Why did he let Eugene do this to me? But, I quickly corrected my wrong thinking. God hadn't done anything. This happening was an example of consequences that come from living outside His will. I was convinced of that.

Mimi burst in the door.

"Andrea? Where's the warrant?"

All I could do was point to the VCR. She turned the tape back on long enough to see the source of my dismay. She jerked it out of the VCR and grabbed the other one I had yet to view.

"That bastard."

Which bastard? Did she mean Eugene or one of my guests? Throwing her coat unceremoniously on the chair, she stomped off toward the kitchen. She didn't need to go far—my guests were right there, probably on their way to see who had come in.

"That's it, gentlemen. My client has nothing more to say to you." She shoved the tapes at Haines. "You may leave now and take your crap with you."

Michael and Haines headed toward the door, one beige and one gray raincoat flapping.

I called after them. "Eugene made them without my knowledge or consent. How can I go about getting them destroyed or sealed forever or whatever I have to do?"

"Right now, they are considered a primary motive for Mr. Sherwood's murder. There's nothing you can do. Someone will be back today with a warrant."

CHAPTER 36
Andrea

"Mimi, are they going to arrest me?"

"If they had enough evidence, you wouldn't be here now. What did you tell them?"

I filled her in.

"Where is the tape Eugene gave you?"

I looked at the fireplace. "I burned it."

"Do you own a handgun?"

"No." I wrapped myself in my arms and tucked my legs under me, facing her.

"Have you ever owned a handgun? Do you know how to use one?"

"No."

"When was the last time you were at Eugene's home?"

"The new one you mean? Almost a month ago. I haven't been to his apartment in two years." I told her about the attempted kiss and scratch and the two times he'd shown up at Benjamin's home. "Can I get you something, Mimi? A coke, tea?"

"Yeah, sure. I'll take a coke." We relocated to the kitchen.

I set two diet cokes on the table, then added ice cubes to the glasses.

"The police will be back to search. What do they think they'll find?"

"Anything that connects you to Eugene. A gun for example, bloody clothes. You got any of that stuff?"

"Nope."

"That's good. I'll lay odds those cops were snooping around while you watched the tape."

With that, I rested my head on my arms on the table, like a bored student wanting the school day to be over.

"It's going to be okay, Andi." She patted my arm. "Hold it together, girl. You've got a strong constitution."

"I want Benjamin here. Is that okay?" I asked.

"Sure, call him."

Mimi waited as long as she could, but when the police hadn't returned with the search warrant after a couple of hours, she had to leave. It was okay because Benjamin had come.

They showed up at two in the afternoon, placing the search warrant in my hand.

"Do you have any weapons in the house, ma'am?"

"No."

"Who else is home with you now?"

"Just us."

"Any pets we should be aware of?"

"Not a one."

"This will go faster if you're out of the home. You can wait in your car or go next door or something. Otherwise, I'll have to stand guard with you in one room and that will make this take longer."

I looked at the police officer like he was nuts, but it made sense.

"Where should go?" Benjamin asked.

"Nowhere. Let's just wait. I don't feel like going anywhere. We can sit in your car. I've got something to tell you.

I had originally planned to find a better way to break this news to Benjamin, but being emotionally exhausted prevented that. He started the car to keep us warm as I began. "The police were here earlier. There are more tapes. Not spliced, just me and Eugene ... Raw."

I watched Benjamin sigh and rub his chin a few times. I took a deep breath, put my fingers over my lips and waited. If he walked out on me this time, I wouldn't blame him. This was a lot to deal with.

Finally he said, "The police found a boxful, you said? Was he a sex addict or addicted to porn or what?"

I thought those were rhetorical questions, but I pondered a minute, in case they weren't. Eugene and I had enjoyed an active sex life, but I wouldn't say the levels reached addiction, but then again, I didn't know if Eugene saw other women. I suspected he did, especially when we first dated and when we were breaking up. In the months we were together, however, I never came across anything, not even a *Playboy* magazine.

"Not as far as I know," I concluded, "but we weren't together all that long," I added in my defense. "You're upset."

"That doesn't come close to what I'm feeling." His face creased and distorted, like he was in pain.

"I wish he hadn't made them," he said, "but he did and I can't change that. Hey, couples do that sort of thing nowadays for fun. The only reason I probably never made one is that I could never afford a video camera." He forced a laugh. I loved him for trying to find the humor in all of this.

He touched my chin. "I'm furious because he betrayed you like that. That was foul."

"Suppose they do get sent around? They could end up on the Internet. I'm a teacher. I could be asked to resign, I think. And, that's on top of living through the embarrassment of it all."

"Oh, honey, don't even think like that." He gathered me in his arms. "They can't very well fire you for having a sex life. You just can't let them trace the profits back to your web site."

I yanked myself free, then I saw that mischievous twinkle in his eyes, but I swatted him anyway.

"I'm sorry, I shouldn't joke at a time like this, but …" I understood, he had to grab onto something, or get sucked hopelessly into the mire. Benjamin had a constitution as strong as mine. We could get through this.

CHAPTER 37
Benjamin

There's nothing like coming home to a cruiser and an unmarked police car in front of your house. Fortunately, I didn't have to run through a list of awful possibilities in my mind; I knew exactly why they were here.

On my way in, a young cop passed me by carrying two handguns, each in its own evidence bag. She called out to Detective Wellborn. *There go Mr. Elrod's guns.* When I moved back home, he had shown me the closet where he kept them locked in the basement. He kept the ammunition in a separate place.

My mother sat next to someone I figured must be Gloria's cousin. There was a strong family resemblance. He stood.

"Benjamin Dunn, I'm Detective Michael Wellborn. We need to speak with you at the police station. You come with us now willingly or I can arrest you for suspicion of murder."

"What's going on here?" My mother looked like an angry bear about to attack to protect her cub. "Don't talk to them, Benjamin."

"Mama, I've never been to Kentucky in my life. I just want this over."

"You're going to talk to the police without speaking to a lawyer first? How wise is that, Ben? This is a murder investigation."

"I'll be all right. Tell Roy I'll be home soon."

"I'm going to call Dean. He'll be at the police station by the time you get there," my mother assured me. "Listen to him." Dean Whitby was an attorney who stopped by the gas station for coffee every morning.

Once the preliminaries were taken care of inside the interrogation room, someone named Sheriff Haines began. "Would you say that you have a rather explosive temper, Mr. Dunn?"

I glanced at Dean. His constipated look told me he disagreed with my willingness to cooperate.

"No, I would not say that. Why would you even ask me that?"

"Well, people pulling at your life have a habit of dying with a .38 automatic being the weapon of choice."

I paused before I responded, trying to process what he meant. "Okay, you're telling me Eugene was killed with a .38. I'm with you so far."

"And so was Carolyn Young. That's interesting, by the way, how long have you been involved with sisters?"

Dean spoke up. "Wait a minute. I thought we were talking about Eugene Sherwood. What does Carolyn Young's death have to do with this?"

"You'll see," Wellborn said.

"I never knew anything about Carolyn's death beyond that she was shot near a crack house." Who I was involved with was none of his business, so I ignored his comment about sisters.

"She was shot three times," Haines explained.

"Okay, and?" Being slow to get to the point must be this guy's specialty.

"Eugene Sherwood was shot three times," he said.

Rubbing my eyebrows, I tried to keep that gruesome image of Carolyn from flooding my thoughts, but I couldn't stop it. This Sheriff Haines knew how to ply his trade.

"Three shots, same parts of the anatomy, and with the same type of gun." Detective Wellborn felt the need to summarize it for me in case I had a learning deficit.

"When will the ballistics tests come back from the guns you took from my mother's home? That will prove the guns I had access to were not involved in either case. I didn't kill Eugene, and there is no way in hell I could have shot Carolyn."

"Yet someone wanted them both dead," Haines said.

"It wasn't me."

"You didn't mind that Mr. Sherwood was set to distribute sex videos with your fiancée playing the starring role?"

"I didn't know about that until recently. Yeah, I would have wanted to stop that, but I didn't know about it."

"What about Mr. Sherwood's disruptive visits to your home? When a man violates the sanctity of another man's home, especially if he does it in pursuit of a man's woman, it's understandable there'll be retribution of some sort."

I didn't answer, but Haines kept looking at me—waiting me out.

"My client and I have had just about enough of your postulating."

This whole thing was preposterous, and I wanted to help them see they are wasting their time. "I'm all right, Dean."

"I understand Carolyn Young's drug habit drove you away, but you returned after her murder."

"That's true, but I didn't kill her."

Sheriff Haines turned pages in his folder as if he were perusing through *Popular Mechanics*. "Uh-huh. Well, perhaps you and Andrea, working together, cleared the path, shall we say, to happiness?"

"Man, you are so far off base it's laughable."

"Then why aren't you laughing, Mr. Dunn?" He paused so I could feel the "gotcha" effect. "With Carolyn and her messy drug business out of the way, you come back home a righteous hero to your son, and your love for Carolyn's sister grows faster than grass after a good rain. Let's start at the beginning again, shall we?"

I recounted everything that had happened since Andrea had accepted that invitation to Eugene's open house.

Halfway through my recitation, somebody came and got Detective Wellborn, who had been largely silent. Haines wanted me to tell it from the beginning a third time. This time, when Dean Whitby spoke up, I was glad.

"Sheriff, Mr. Dunn has been answering questions a long time. He's cooperated fully, there's nothing more to learn."

Haines reluctantly agreed I could leave.

On the way out, Dean and I walked past another interrogation room. The door was ajar briefly before someone inside closed it. I'd had time to see Andrea face-to-face with Michael Wellborn.

I turned to Dean. "They're questioning Andrea again?"

"I'll wait for her then." I extended my hand to shake goodbye.

He made a cautionary gesture. "I'm not sure that's wise. If you hang around here, there's nothing to stop them from trying to question you further. You're tired, your fiancée is here. They might convince you I don't have to be with you for them to clarify a few things. You could end up making things more difficult for yourself and Ms. Young. You've had enough for tonight. There's no telling how long they plan to keep her here. My advice—go home, talk to her tomorrow."

I nodded. I was beat. More than that, I felt lightheaded from all the questions still twirling in my mind. I'd go home and talk to Andrea in the morning. There was nothing I could do, and I was sure Andrea could hold her own.

CHAPTER 38
Benjamin

Andrea and I talked briefly the next morning and agreed to wait until after Bible class to go over what happened yesterday. I wanted to blow off class, but Andrea was insistent. She said we needed every tool at our mental and emotional disposal we could gather. I couldn't argue with her.

The ice cream shop was where we usually headed after class, but today its ambiance felt too virtuous. We had some heavy-duty topics to discuss. I remembered a little Italian restaurant right around the corner from the ice cream place. We could have some appetizers, a drink and talk.

Andrea scooted over on the red vinyl seat, leaving me a space to sit next to her. She continuously ran her fingers through her hair, her signature sign of distress. She didn't seem to notice or care when I sat across from her, rather than cozying up next to her like I normally do.

There were about five other tables occupied in a restaurant that held maybe twenty tables total. Low candles on the red-checkered tablecloths provided most of the lighting. The waiter asked if we wanted to order something to drink. We both decided on white wine and thanked him.

"What did you think of the lesson tonight?" Andrea asked.

"I think the point was, there is often something we can learn from even the most annoying people. It's about brotherly love and the spirit of acceptance."

"Speaking of annoying people, I can tell that Sheriff Haines is at the top of your list."

"He's occupying the number one spot with Detective Wellborn running a close second," I said, grateful that she had gotten to what we needed to discuss.

"And what did you learn?" she asked.

"That Eugene and Carolyn received similar wounds with the same kind of gun, and he thinks I might have something to do with both of the murders."

Her reaction looked more like a double recoil than a couple of nods. "No way could the gun thing be a coincidence. Then, to hear Michael insinuate that you and I wanted Carolyn dead so you could come back and we could be together cut me to the core, Benjamin. It really did."

One look into her troubled eyes and I knew I had to say something to keep her morale up. "The police are making some crazy connections, that's all. I don't know where they get the nerve to come with such bull-shit to our faces."

The waiter brought our drinks. Neither of us had an appetite; we declined anything further. We drank and said nothing for a couple of minutes.

"The police seem to think we were in love the whole time you and Carolyn were together," she said. Our eyes locked a moment. Neither one of us wanted to go there.

"There's something else," I said. Andrea stiffened. "Yesterday, the police took a couple of Mr. Elrod's .38's to do some comparison testing. They won't match anything, and that's the bottom line. The police have zilch; they're trying to pull a rabbit out of the hat. They've got no solid evidence."

"And they never will, not against us. I just hate that they are spending all this time speculating about what we didn't do. It's preventing them from getting at the truth." Her tears streamed down her face.

I handed her my napkin. "Don't cry, Andrea."

"I can't help it. When I talked to the medical examiner, she said Carolyn didn't suffer, that it was over in seconds. I don't know, probably she was high and feeling no pain anyway, but what if she saw her killer? She must have been so afraid." She wiped her eyes and blew her nose.

"She was in rapid decline, just inches from earning her living on the street." She shook her head, took a deep breath and let it out. "By then, I had run out of words and tricks. I had no more cajolements, no more patience and God help me, no more hope. You always say how I'm an optimist, I'm not always. I had nothing to give her, Benjamin, when she needed me most. That's why I've been looking for her killer, because if I could have just hung in there with her a little longer—"

"You hung in there longer than anybody did. She was twenty-five when she died. That meant you stuck by her through eight long years of on and off drug use. I bailed after three."

"Yeah, but she wasn't your sister."

"Even if she had been, a drug addiction is a setup for constant heart-break and disappointment. You did good by Carolyn. Don't think for a moment you didn't."

"Maybe that's what's really bothering me. I can't get over what Michael Wellborn said to me. He and I grew up together. How could anyone ever think I would kill Carolyn, especially him?"

"Statistically speaking, someone close to the victim is quite often the murderer, so friends and family are the most likely suspects. Don't take it personally."

She took another sip of her drink. "But, I know," she said, trying to pull herself together, "getting emotional about it doesn't help. I have to put aside the brainless police theories about our involvement, and focus on the investigation of Carolyn's death. I think somebody shot her because she was Carolyn Young, and not because she was in the wrong place at the wrong time. Who would want her and Eugene dead?"

I shook my head. "Like I said, Andrea. I think the police are grab-bing at straws. Carolyn's death could be drug-related and nothing more. I'm not sure you should take what the police said to heart. .38s are everywhere, and how are Eugene and Carolyn connected? I don't get it, do you?"

"No, but I will. I'll figure it out if it's the last thing I do."

CHAPTER 39
Andrea

Detective Peck called. "We've got the report on the fingerprints from the popcorn bag."

At the rate my life was going, I knew better than to expect good news. "Was anything usable?"

"Yes, we were able to identify Carolyn's print."

Finally progress. Praise the Lord. I could tell he had something else to say. "What else?"

"Cecil Chamber's print showed up on the bag."

"Both of their prints were on the popcorn bag? His car was there and he was there, too?" I was out of my chair on my feet now. "Oh my God! Now what happens, Detective Peck?"

"Now we get a warrant to search his place, search his car, and see what we come up with."

"That's the best news I've had in—was Christmas just last week?" It hardly seemed possible because so much had happened. I massaged my neck as I explained, "I'm going through something else now. Did you know that my ex-boyfriend was murdered?"

"Say what? Where was this?"

"It happened in Kentucky, but the police there and here consider me and Benjamin Dunn suspects. He was Carolyn's old boyfriend and is now my fiancé." I listened, waiting for the typical reaction to that information. Detective Peck curtailed his thoughts or at least the words that went with them.

"Congratulations. And about you being part of the investigation, we have to check everything out, you know. Did you kill anybody?" His tone was light, like he already knew the right answer.

"Of course not."

"Then you don't have anything to worry about. Like I've been saying, can't make a case without evidence."

"Right. Tell that to the innocent folks on death row. The cops working Eugene's case think there could be a connection between Carolyn's and my ex-boyfriend's murders." I pushed my hair back on one side. "I'm surprised they haven't consulted you."

"I'm not. It's not uncommon for the left hand not to know what the right hand is doing in city bureaucracy. What's the detective's name working the case?"

"Michael Wellborn and the guy from Kentucky is Carl Haines."

"Oh yeah, I know Wellborn. I'll make it a priority to get with him and see what's up."

"Okay, thank you Detective."

"I'll be in touch. Happy New Year."

"The same to you."

I hung up, needing to tell someone about the fingerprints, but it was New Year's Eve and BJ and Gloria were unavailable. Benjamin and I were going to have a candlelit dinner here when he got off work. Somehow I didn't think he would be as excited as I was.

CHAPTER 40
Andrea

Benjamin didn't know what to make of the news, but he was sure there was some logical explanation for why Carolyn's and Cecil's prints would be on the same microwave popcorn bag, although he couldn't think of one.

A few days later, Detective Peck showed up at my door while I was in the middle of paying bills. I stuck my pen behind my ear and let him in. "What's the matter? You're here. I usually have to send up flares to get your attention."

His smile could disarm. I was sure it did when he put his mind to it.

"The phone has its uses, but it has its limitations also," he said.

"You're scaring me. What happened?"

"The gun used to kill Eugene Sherwood showed up."

"Whoa." I walked into the living room and felt for the chair before lowering myself into it. "Seriously? Where?"

"It belongs to Cecil Chambers, or I should say it belongs to someone in his family. We found it at his bookstore."

"Cecil's bookstore?"

"Yep."

"My God. His car at the scene, his prints on the popcorn bag and now he has the gun that killed Eugene? Something's not tracking. When I found out he had a car like Mrs. Tuddle described, I expected a tie to Carolyn's murder, not Eugene's. I'm confused. What reason would Cecil have to shoot Eugene?"

"I don't know yet, but I thought you'd want to hear about this sooner rather than later."

"What did Cecil say?"

"He's pleading the fifth."

Standing, I paced back in forth in front of the fireplace mantel. I handed him a picture of Carolyn and Roy. "This is my sister, by the way."

"Wow, that's a nice picture. Holding her son like that, you can tell she loved him very much." He placed it back on the mantel.

"So Michael and Detective Haines weren't just pulling rabbits out of the air? There really is a link between the two murders?"

Detective Peck adjusted the winter scarf around his neck. "That would be my guess, yes."

"It seems obvious to me, and if there is a connection, it has to be Sharon."

"Sharon Dunn?" Detective Peck was still standing.

"Have a seat," I said.

He took off his coat and sat down on the couch. I sat next to him. "Yes, Sharon Dunn, Cecil's girlfriend."

"Take it easy. Don't jump to conclusions. Why couldn't your fiancé be the link, or it could have been something personal between Cecil and Eugene, or you could be the common link. You never know. Sit tight and let us do our job."

Too excited to sit tight even for a second, I stood with my hands in front of me to help plead my case. "But you always say that, Detective. Maybe you should check out Sharon's place. Sure, it's possible that Eugene and Cecil had a beef, but for a strong enough motive to kill someone? I don't know. I'm laying odds it's got something to do with Sharon."

"And maybe, Ms. Young, you should come down and fill out an application for the police academy."

"That's not fair. I'm only making suggestions, not telling you how to do your job. If I'm a pest, I have a right to be. I just want answers, and I thought we were supposed to be on the same page about that."

He stood, nodding in slight concession. "Yeah, well. We're doing the best we can."

"Thanks for coming to tell me in person. I appreciate it."

"Not a problem. Good night."

I called Benjamin with news of the latest development. He kept repeating, "Cecil had the gun that killed Eugene?" and I kept saying, "Yes."

He said, "I don't get it. I feel like I walked into a movie an hour late, because I have no idea what's going on. Maybe the police made a mistake."

"Anything is possible, I suppose," I said. "Cecil isn't saying anything."

He sighed as if he was exhaling his dying breath. "Okay, I'll see what I can find out and let you know."

CHAPTER 41
Andrea

The following week, the phone rang, jarring me out of a sound sleep. I'd taken to going to bed early these days. To stay awake meant I had to confront my conundrum. Two murders, one motive? What motive? Whose motive?

Not only that, the wedding was right around the corner, and I didn't think I would be able to marry Benjamin until I had some closure on Carolyn's case. I loved him and he loved me, but Carolyn's murder and how it connected to Eugene's occupied most of my thoughts.

I answered the phone on the third ring. It was Gloria. "Andi."

"Yeah?"

"I woke you, sorry, but I got news, girl. Tonya, someone I know who used to work with Michael, just told me the story going around the station about Sharon."

"About Sharon?" I sat up wide-awake. "What did Tonya say?"

"Okay, hold onto to something. Apparently, they've questioned her a few times. Sharon is claiming Eugene assaulted her and Cecil shot him after the fact."

I mouthed Gloria's words to myself, unable to get meaning out of them. "Assaulted her? Where? When?"

"I don't know, but there's a definite buzz about it."

"Okay, okay." My mind was reeling. "Does Benjamin know? Let me call him."

"Later."

Mrs. Elrod picked up sounding alert despite the time. It was midnight.

Benjamin came to the phone, listened, then said in a tight voice, "Sharon already called. I'm on my way over to the police station now."

"I'm up. I can meet you there."

"No, don't come, Andrea. My mother is going. Thanks, but we've got it covered."

"All right." Exclusion hurt a minute, but when I thought about it, I realized I only wanted to be there in the way people watched accident clean-ups, to glean details and to gawk, which wasn't very nice of me. He wanted to be there to support his sister.

Sleep wasn't an option, I made coffee and corrected five periods of English essays instead. That's what I did until it was time to get ready for work. Benjamin still hadn't called. I got dressed and braved rush hour traffic, which was always a nightmare. I listened to Tom Joyner, a morning disk jockey I liked, desperate for a laugh or at least a pleasant distraction.

Two blocks away from school, Benjamin finally called. I was so hyped, I needed to pull over so I wouldn't endanger other commuters.

"Andrea, I don't even know where to start," Benjamin said, sounding dejected.

"What? What's is it?"

"We've been here, what? Six hours and we can't get any clarity. We're getting everything secondhand, and all I know is that Sharon says she was sexually assaulted." He'd almost whispered the last words, like saying them louder would hurt too much.

Even though soft, they were a direct blow to my stomach. "What? Sharon said Eugene raped her? Is that what you said?"

"That's all we know so far. I have to talk to Sharon, but they won't let me. Her attorney said that's why Cecil shot him. That's why he killed the prick, because he'd-r—because he assaulted her."

I heard a loud banging sound and figured Benjamin had kicked something out of rage.

"You know what, Andrea? If Cecil hadn't, then I would have killed him."

A wave of nausea gripped me. My mouth went completely dry even while I felt the dampness of sweat on my brow. I couldn't speak.

"Forget my little movie analogy before. I've crossed directly into the Twilight Zone now."

"Me too. I'm so sorry, Benjamin."

"Yeah. I gotta go. They're going to run some DNA tests to corroborate what Sharon is saying."

"DNA tests?"

"Yeah, I guess on the sheets or evidence found at Eugene's house. Gotta go." He hung up.

I let the phone slide down from my ear, afraid to think of all the ramifications, but unable to stop myself. The only reason Sharon would be anywhere near Eugene must be because of me, and that animal had hurt her. I wanted to go to Benjamin, but I knew he probably didn't want to see me now.

Weaving back into traffic, I planned to get a sub and leave work as soon as I could. My head just wasn't in it today. I didn't doubt Eugene was capable of rape, but like Benjamin, I wondered how Eugene had managed to suck Cecil and Sharon into his warped corner of the world.

CHAPTER 42
Benjamin

My mother and I had been the only people sitting in the police station reception area. Not meant to welcome long-term visitors, the chairs were hard plastic. We had toughed it out all night, watching police come and go through the buzzer controlled doors.

"Mom, I'm going home now."

She lowered her magazine that I had bought from the newsstand across the street. She looked up with a resolve that made me know she wasn't going with me, but I needed to get Roy to daycare to keep some semblance of normalcy in his life at least.

"All right, Ben," she said. "Yeah," she checked her watch, "go on and get Roy off to daycare. I'm going to wait right here, shouldn't be much longer. I'll call Rudy when I need a ride.

I kissed my mother bye and left. I put the key in the ignition, but couldn't start the car right away. My head lulled back, hitting the headrest. I closed my eyes a minute. What was Sharon doing at Eugene's house in Kentucky? It had to be because of him coming around the house. *Because she liked to fix things in my life for me.* This was my fault. If I understood correctly, then this was my fault. I banged the steering wheel. The horn blast couldn't compete against the screams inside my head.

At home, Mr. Elrod and Roy were finishing breakfast. He looked at me with understanding eyes. I managed to stay upbeat for Roy's sake. I even grabbed the last pancake, smeared some strawberry jelly on it, then washed it down with caffeine.

I took Roy to daycare. Not in any shape to work, I called in sick.

When I got back home, Mom and Mr. Elrod had just pulled up, both of them looked like somebody had died.

Hurrying to their side I asked, "What happened?" I looked back and forth between his mournful eyes and my mother's swollen red ones. "Somebody please, tell me something."

Mr. Elrod just shook his head. "Let's sit a minute." I followed them into the kitchen barely able to keep from badgering them to hurry up and say something."

Mr. Elrod rubbed his jaw, then his chin. "They found Eugene Sherwood's semen on the sheet from his bedroom that they took the day he was murdered. They also found hair and even blood that could match Sharon's. They'll take a couple of weeks to get the results."

My mother's face was almost unrecognizable now. She smacked the kitchen table like she was squashing a bug. "If it wasn't for that Andrea, none of this would be happening. You know that, don't you? That girl, her whole family is nothing but poison!"

I put my hands on the sides of my head to keep it from spinning off into space. It wasn't bad enough that I had to deal with what I just heard, now I needed to defend Andrea.

"Now Millie," Mr. Elrod began.

"Don't now Millie me, Rudy. Don't you dare!"

"Mom, why blame Andrea?"

"Why not blame her? He was her ex-boyfriend. It's got something to do with Andrea. Trust me."

I didn't have the desire or the strength to argue. "Where's Sharon?"

"They let her go," Mr. Elrod answered. "She wouldn't come home with us."

Wiping at her tears, my mother said, "She won't let me comfort her, Ben, she hugged me, said I shouldn't worry, that she was okay, then she walked out the door. She's been through so much ...so much."

Mr. Elrod's pulled my mother into his arms while she cried. "What happens now?" he asked.

We get to the bottom of this," I said. "I'm going to talk to Sharon."

The doorbell rang.

Mom broke free of Mr. Elrod's arms and ran for the front door. "Maybe it's Sharon. Maybe she changed her mind." We all ended up there. It's wasn't Sharon, it was Andrea.

My mother sighed, shook her head and walked away with Mr. Elrod.

I opened the door, but instead of letting Andrea in, I went out.

"I had to come, Benjamin. Do you know any more than you did when you called?"

"No, they still have to match DNA and that will take time. I was just on my way over to Sharon's."

"Oh …" she tugged back her hat and looked down. "I saw how your mother looked at me. Does she hate me?"

Hesitating, I wondered if she could take the truth and decided she could. "For now, but it's just her protective reaction and the need to lash out at someone. She doesn't mean it."

She nodded, looked up, biting her lower lip. "What about you, Benjamin. Do you blame me?"

I put both hands on her shoulders and dipped down so she could read the honesty in my eyes. "How could you be responsible for what Eugene Sherwood did? No, I don't blame you, Andrea. I mean, I feel bad too, but at the end of the day, people make their own choices, and we are helpless to control that. Eugene was a sick man."

She let out a choking sound and gripped my arms like she needed to hold on to them or fall. "I'm so glad you said that. I feel so awful. If I had known Eugene … if I had handled it better … been truthful about him from the beginning …"

"You were dealing with a stone cold nut case. You couldn't know."

"Yeah but, I just feel so guilty … like I brought the plague or something worse into your lives."

Squeezing her shoulders, I reassured her. "Don't feel that way. What happened wasn't your fault."

"Thank you. What—what about Roy?" she asked.

"I took him to daycare."

"Would it be helpful if I picked him up today? Maybe he can spend the night with me."

"Good idea. I imagine there will be a lot of sadness here tonight, and Roy doesn't need that. I'll pick him up first thing in the morning."

"Okay, tell your mom I'll get him. Will you call me later?"

"If I get a chance. If not, I'll see you tomorrow morning." I kissed her forehead.

"Benjamin, tell Sharon I'm sorry."

CHAPTER 43
Andrea

Gloria let me into her place before I could use the gold door-knocker. Her tiny, pleasantly cluttered condo was the haven I needed. The walls in the living room were periwinkle blue. Carolyn had picked the color; and Carolyn, Gloria, BJ, and I had painted it. The gray carpet and the white furniture reflected a cool atmosphere despite the tropical temperatures Gloria was happiest with.

"Girl, you look like you need some cheesecake," Gloria said. I ditched my coat and hat as I followed her into her stark white kitchen with touches of blue.

"I must really look bad if you're going to feed me cheesecake."

"Well, we'll start of with a nice cup of coffee and you can bring me up to speed."

"Okay, I told you about how Carolyn and Eugene were killed by the same method and how the police suggested Benjamin and I conspired to end her life because our wild passion for each other could not be denied one more minute.

"Yeah, that's just too whack."

"Oh, it gets better." A Wandering Jew framed the window in the kitchen, which, from the tenth story, overlooked a main thoroughfare. I looked at the cars below, while Gloria rinsed out the coffee carafe to start a fresh pot. I turned to her. "Cecil's print on the popcorn bag led to the police searching his home and the bookstore."

"Yes, I know," Gloria said, "the gun that murdered Eugene was found at his bookstore. Then the police expanded their investigation to include Sharon. Okay, I know the history; get to the current event. What's the deal with Sharon now?"

"You're not going to believe this."

"Spill the beans, child," she said, drying her hands.

"Sharon is saying Eugene raped her."

"Oh-my-God!" Gloria said, each syllable claiming its own space.

"That's what I said."

She brought two cups of coffee to the table, but the coffee would take a few minutes to brew.

"You mean Eugene totally snapped and went after Sharon?"

"I don't know how it happened. Benjamin doesn't have the first-hand version yet. Gloria?"

"What?"

"I have another question. Please tell me how I'm going to get married in the middle of all this?" It was a relief to give voice to that knot in my stomach.

"See, there was a time when hearing those words would make me do a happy dance, but now you've gone and convinced me you're in love with this man."

That wasn't an answer. The knot stayed. I'd have to figure it out on my own.

"To be honest, Andi, I don't know. If Sharon was raped like she said, Benjamin is going to have to blame you on some level. You brought him, unintentionally, of course, but you brought Eugene into their lives. There may not be anyplace you and Ben can go from there."

I sighed, rested an elbow on her table, holding my head. Good old Gloria. I could depend on her for the truth, no matter how ugly. "On the one hand it's like a nightmare I can't wake up from, but on the other, it's good we're making progress solving Carolyn's murder. Did I mention I've scheduled my nervous breakdown for next Thursday?"

"Oh, don't do that."

"I don't know, Gloria. Benjamin was so sweet just now. He said I wasn't to blame. And, of course I love him. But …"

"Come on." She collected the empty coffee cups. "We can't stay here. You need to clear your mind for a while."

"Where are we going?"

"There's a new restaurant on Fourth Street. Lunch is still going on, or we can go to Steinberg's."

I debated a second. It took energy to say yes. It was much easier to continue to mope. I called on all reserves. "I can pick? Let me think. The frenzy of the lunch hour crowd, or fresh air whizzing past me as I glide with grace across the ice."

"Grace who? And make that fresh, freezing air whizzing past."

I laughed at her grace joke.

Minutes later, the tan roof of her Chrysler convertible came down. Thirty-three degrees-so what? We giggled like we used to when we were kids. Back then, the sheer joy of life was all it took to make us happy. This was as close as we could come to that now.

"No murders, no wedding. Just us, and just ice. This will be fun, Andi."

CHAPTER 44
Benjamin

I took the stairs two at a time to get to Sharon's apartment; I couldn't wait for the elevator. My apprehension spilled over into my rapid knocks on her door. I heard the lock release, so I let myself in, "Hello?" Her towel-wrapped body disappeared into the bathroom.

"Yeah, be right out."

I filled my mind with the details of her room layout. Mindless reverie was the pin that held the hand grenade closed. Her bed, draped in her favorite color, purple, was directly opposite the door.

The three large pictures on the wall stood out on white walls. The radio played Metallica. I turned it off because there wasn't much a rock band could do for me.

A minute later, she came out in a red silk robe, smelling like Ivory soap, but she looked like hell. All I could do was take her into my arms.

"What happened?"

"I finally told the police about the rape. I'm glad it's out. I only kept it a secret because Cecil and I agreed it was best."

After the word rape, her lips moved, but I hadn't heard a thing. That hand grenade exploded in my mind. I thought I had prepared myself for this. Obviously, I was wrong. "Rape? So, it's true?"

"What does that mean? If I said he raped me, he raped me."

"No, I'm sorry. I didn't it mean it that way. It came out wrong. I believe you, Sharon."

"I had to come home and scrub the filth off again, Benny. The way the police made me relive it, it's like it happened all over again."

An elevator dropped ten stories straight down with me on. I had to sit down or fall over.

"I went to talk to Eugene at his place in Kentucky. I had just inter-viewed at Vanderbilt for my residency and Paducah was a couple of hours away. I planned to make him understand he needed to get it together, get over Andrea and leave us the hell alone."

That should have been my job, my brain screamed.

"I underestimated him, Ben. Both times I'd seen Eugene, he'd been drunk. I knew he was big, but I thought he was more into mind games instead of brawn. He came across like a giant teddy bear, essentially harmless I thought. I was wrong."

I shook my head and moaned, but I didn't dare blink or tears would fall.

"It started as soon as he closed the door behind me. He was too strong. I couldn't make him stop. I tried." She reached for a tissue box. "You'd think there would be no more tears left, but they keep coming."

"Sharon, Sharon." I could hear the despair in my own voice. "You went there to help me. I should have been the one to confront him." Sharon had ended up abused once again because the man she had a right to depend on let her down. At that moment, I didn't think I was fit to walk the earth. What kind of weak man was I? "Oh God." I fought to think straight. "Why didn't you call me instead of Cecil?"

"I don't know. Subconsciously, I probably knew Cecil had a gun and I wanted Eugene dead."

"Cecil killed him?"

"Yes." She didn't blink or flinch.

"Good riddance," I said.

"My thoughts exactly."

She looked at me and hugged me. "Don't cry, Benny. And don't blame yourself. You warned me about staying out of your affairs. I did what I had to do."

I wiped my eyes and nodded. That was nice of her, but I'd take this guilt to the grave. She was so … so stoic. Too much in control, and it bothered me. But if that's what she needed to do to get through this … so be it. "Have you talked to Dr. Fields? That's his name, right? Your psychiatrist?"

"Yes, I've spoken to him."

"You're going to be all right?"

"I'll be all right. This may slow me up a bit, but nothing is going to stop me. I'm used to bouncing back."

CHAPTER 45
Andrea

BJ had invited Benjamin and me to a fundraiser for his significant other's boss, the Governor. I got to meet the guy BJ had been gaga over for almost a year now. He was as tall as BJ, which meant he was around six feet. BJ was slim, but this guy didn't turn down too many steak dinners, he was beefed up but just on the right side of fat. He had alert, light brown eyes that seemed to sum up people and situations quickly.

Mr. Governor's office had a name. It was Donald Alteg. I don't know why I had always pictured him as a white guy. Maybe that was because he had such a large discretionary income and could set BJ up with his apartment and other accoutrements. *Guess I'll have to stop making assumptions.*

They were not "out." I sat between the happy couple the whole evening, making me privy to those unmistakable come-hither looks that passed slyly between them. I liked that BJ had one partner and was happy.

Benjamin had decided not to come. He'd told me he wasn't up to it. He needed to stay close to home while his family healed from the effects of what had happened to Sharon.

While Donald mingled, BJ and I chatted.

"Raped. That's a damn shame. Cecil knew exactly what to do with that gun. I predicted that Eugene would end up dead not respecting boundaries, didn't I?"

"Yes, you did. I feel bad because she went there to talk to him because of me."

"That was unfortunate. I hope Benny doesn't blame you."

"I think he does on some level, but he's been extraordinarily kind about not pushing my face in it." I took a sip of my champagne.

BJ patted my hand. "You got yourself a good man. Did you know that people who are sexually abused once are more likely to be abused a second time?"

"No, I didn't know that." I frowned, hating to think that were true. "You know, sometimes I wonder if the abuse she suffered explains her. There's something about Sharon I can't put my finger on."

"Like what?"

"Her directness with people. She always has an agenda, and if you can't help her achieve it, you need to get out of her way. She's very protective of Benjamin and Roy, too."

"Andi, where did you say Benjamin was tonight? Spending time with family?"

"Yeah, why?"

"Part of the family is here. Isn't that Sharon at the table behind you?"

I turned, waved and smiled, caught like a cat with a canary in its mouth. Sharon sat about eight feet away from us at the next table.

"Hello, Andrea," Sharon said as she sauntered over to us. Her short black hair, cut into one of those wispy, carefree styles, looked great. Her purple gown showed off her equally stunning figure. She was thin and busty and had the confidence with her body of people who workout regularly. Her dark brown skin and makeup were flawless. Most of the people gave her a second look, probably thinking she was a model or African royalty.

Already standing at her approach, BJ offered her his chair. "Who does your hair?" he asked.

"I can't reveal all of my secrets, now can I? Some things people should wonder about." She looked at me when she said that. What had I just said? Had she overheard something?

After I introduced her to BJ, I said, "I didn't know you had political leanings, Sharon." I tried my best to carry on with imaginary canary feathers still tickling my tongue.

She gave me a lazy smile. "I'm apolitical, but someone I know had an extra ticket. This is a nice break for me."

"Benjamin told me what happened. I'm very sorry, Sharon. Eugene and I, well I thought I knew him. I made a grievous mistake about him. I'm so sorry. I hope you will be all right and that things work out for Cecil."

"Thank you. Cecil and I will be fine. I appreciate your concern, but I'd better get back. Nice to meet you, BJ. Oh, I hear you have a beautiful voice. I can't wait to hear you sing at the wedding."

"Thank you. I'm looking forward to it."

BJ turned to look at her behind as she sashayed away.

The band began to play a slow tune, popular two decades ago. BJ pulled me close on the dance floor. "Nicely packaged, but a little scary. How could she be out on the town all fancied up, recovering from a three-week-old rape, while her boyfriend is locked up for killing the guy who did it?"

"Don't know, but people are entitled to grieve in whatever way works for them, BJ."

"That's true, I shouldn't judge. But, what do you think? Did she hear us talking? She's pissed about something, if you ask me."

"She did look peeved, didn't she?"

CHAPTER 46
Andrea

I stopped by to pick up Benjamin, because it was Bible study night. The wind was high, threatening to elope with my black winter hat. Busily competing against this intention, I didn't realize Benjamin's car wasn't out front, until I had rung the doorbell. Sharon answered.

"I'm sorry," I told her, holding my hat on with one hand and bringing my palm to my forehead with the other in disbelief. "Now I remember Benjamin telling me that someone from work had extra tickets to the circus tonight and that he was going to take Roy."

"It's all right," Sharon said, leaning into the partially opened door. "Listen, I know you have your lesson to go to, but there's something I need to talk with you about. I thought this might be a good time, since no one else is home."

I looked at my watch. I couldn't spare the time or I'd be late, but Sharon had never asked to talk to me before. I said okay. The mouth-watering smell of what had to be pot roast led me through the hall and sitting area into the kitchen, where I could see she'd been studying. I assumed that's where we would talk. Hat in hand, my coat was halfway off when the verbal attack began.

"What you can't put your finger on is my ability to take charge of a situation. Weak, sniffling people like you stand around catching flies in their mouths wondering what the hell is going on. I make things happen the way I want them to happen." She turned and walked back toward the couches leaving me alone in the kitchen.

"What?" It felt like I had walked into a movie theater an hour late. Years of dealing with Carolyn, or maybe it came from teaching hormonal teenagers, but for whatever reason, I didn't let outbursts like hers get to me. Calmly, I looked around and saw that she had been studying before I got there. I noticed her rotation schedule on top of a pile of books; certain times had been highlighted. On some paper she had doodled four stick figures, one of them was horizontal. *Hmm.*

Thirty seconds later I followed her. "If something I said offended you, Sharon, I apologize. Ever since Carolyn's death, my friends and I have been trying to figure out who did it. Cecil's prints near Carolyn's crime scene, the gun and now the sheet have us asking questions. I may have strayed off topic a bit."

"Yes, Carolyn's investigation. Maybe I should cut to the chase for you. Would it help you to know I killed both of them?"

"What? What's the matter with you?" I circled her, not getting too close, like you don't get too close to a rabid animal, but I was close enough to see her eyes. They were wide with evil veiled in innocence. "Why would you say something that depraved?"

"The matter with me? What was the matter with them? Do you really believe there was something else good those two parasites were meant to contribute?" She walked over to the CD player and pushed some buttons. Obviously, what this evening missed was a score comprised of melodic rock music.

I blinked. "You're not funny. I'm leaving." If this was her way of teaching me a lesson, it was effective.

"Fine. I'll tell my brother you stopped by. They shoot horses long before they are allowed to wallow in their own shit like Carolyn was doing near the end."

I gasped. Eugene was not the only one who didn't respect boundaries.

"And, Eugene was going to make your life a living hell. There's not a damn thing wrong with me. If anything, I have more gumption than you will ever comprehend. If I did do those things, that is." The force behind the "if" in her sentences could inflate a balloon.

I opened my mouth to speak once or twice, but nothing came out. Zombie-like, I remembered how to open my car door. The wind grabbed it and pushed it all the way open, but that was the least of my worries. Sharon watched me from behind the curtains. Was she laughing at my reaction? Was it the trauma of the rape making her act this way? I'd jumped to so many conclusions since this torment started, I couldn't make a mistake this time. This was Benjamin's sister. I needed to be careful, not overreact.

I turned the ignition because that was the next step required to continue living life as I had known it until now. I don't know how long I sat, stunned.

Could Benjamin's sister have killed two people? Would she have planted the gun at her boyfriend's place? Was Cecil so in love with Sharon that he'd take blame for her murders?

CHAPTER 47

Andrea

"Andrea, it sounds like she was pulling your leg."

"That's what I thought at first, or that it was a carry over from her ordeal with Eugene, but once I had made it home, I believed her." Benjamin and I were standing in the middle of my living room, having this discussion. He barely had time to take off his coat before I started in on him like Sharon had started in on me.

"Sharon is known for her deadpan expressions; it's hard to read her sometimes."

I hung up his coat and turned to him. "Deadpan or not, she convinced me. What sort of person says something like that in jest?"

He shrugged, apparently not as concerned as I was.

"What she said about making things happen got me thinking. Could she have put the vial and the pipe in Carolyn's gym bag?"

"What? Where did that idea come from?"

"I'm putting the pieces together, now that I have an idea of what the puzzle might look like. Tell me what happened that day you found that pipe in Carolyn's bag."

"Jesus, Andrea. Like I don't have enough on my mind these days?"

"Well, your sister just added a whopping helping to my plate, too."

A dismissive sound of air tumbled over his lips. "Do you mind if I sit down first?"

I moved out of his way.

"Do you remember what happened the day you found the gym bag?" I asked.

"Yeah, I'll never forget it. Roy and I were hanging out. I was studying when Sharon stopped by. The house was a mess. Sharon came over ranting about how the place looked and how I was letting Carolyn pull me down to her level. She spent some time with Roy and left after I promised her I would pull it together."

"And later you found the bag?"

"Yeah, I looked around and Sharon was right. Things had gotten out of hand; the apartment was in bad shape. I had cleaned the bathroom and discovered the shower curtain had become its own science lab. Of course, I couldn't find quarters for the washer and dryer. I checked Carolyn's bag for change and there the stuff was."

"Her bag was in the closet?"

"Umm, I don't think so … maybe. I know I had checked coat pockets and under cushions for loose change first. I think it was—actually it was right in the doorway to Roy's room."

"So Sharon had access to it or she got it and left it there for you to see. While she checked on Roy, she could have slipped into your bedroom and put that stuff in the bag, then left it for you to find."

"But, Carolyn could have put those things in her bag, too. Isn't that the more likely scenario? I mean, seriously, Andrea. There are endless possibilities. Can we stick with the more logical ones?"

"Carolyn swore she didn't put the things in the bag. Sharon's trying to spin me like a top. She's a manipulator. I wouldn't put it past her to do something like that because she knew you wouldn't stay with Carolyn if she were doing hard drugs again."

"She was an addict! I didn't want her on any drugs. And why would Sharon frame Carolyn?"

"Benjamin, I know you didn't want Carolyn smoking weed, but you didn't leave her when she did. Sharon saw this, and I think she did something about it because she loves and wants to protect you maybe? You two are awfully close." That was one possible motive.

"Yeah. She's my sister, but it's Roy she dotes on."

"Well, okay, so she wants to make sure Roy is safe because no one made sure she was safe when she was his age."

"Wow. Didn't know you had a degree in psychology, too. When are you getting your own radio show?"

I closed my eyes a second as if that would make me immune to his sarcasm. "Why don't we go talk to Sharon together and see what she says." He hesitated. Would he let me in their heretofore exclusive world? A place where outsiders didn't normally tread?

"Sure, we'll talk to her together. But we'll give it a day. She's suffering, even if you don't realize it. You can't accuse her of this now with all she's been through."

If I couldn't, then Detective Peck could. I called him after Benjamin left. His voice mail said he was on leave for a few days, and told me who to contact instead. That was okay. Maybe the wiser thing to do was to see what happened after we spoke with Sharon. Besides, if I was wrong, I would have upset Benjamin and Sharon needlessly, and I wasn't sure how close I was to finally crossing the line with him in my quest to solve Carolyn's murder.

He loved his sister, I got that. It was just that I loved mine too.

CHAPTER 48
Andrea

In the elevator on the way up to Sharon's room, Benjamin said, "I know this is hard because we're talking about Carolyn, but if you can keep accusations to a minimum … at least start out civilly, that'd be helpful."

I looked at him, kept my arms folded, but didn't answer. I didn't want to make any promises I couldn't keep.

"Ah, visitors to my humble abode. Come on in and take a load off." Sharon stepped back to let us in.

Benjamin located a folding chair, and I sat uncomfortably on the twin bed. Sharon's apartment was small, practically sterile and lacking in any innovative décor except for the pictures that filled the wall just inside the door. They were family shots, blown up larger than usual and done in black and white. *Who's the photographer,* I wondered. The pictures were riveting, but I didn't trust myself to speak.

"You like my pictures?" she asked. "That's canvas stretched across a frame. Roy looks so sweet there, doesn't he? That was his first Christmas."

"Nice."

Sitting in her desk chair, back to her computer, she asked, "So, which is the good cop and which is the bad cop again?" Her index finger slowly wagged between us as if it had sonar.

"Andrea needed to ask you again about what you said to her."

"Oh that. You pissed me off at the fundraiser. Andrea, I didn't shoot your sister, and I apologize for letting you think that I would do such a thing. What would I have gained? It didn't bring Ben home right away. Euthanasia would have been a good motive, but I wouldn't have ventured into the heart of the ghetto in search of her favorite crack house to find her. Now, I suppose you want to know about Eugene?"

"Tell us," Benjamin said.

"I don't think so."

His face contorted like he smelled something distasteful. "What?"

"Cecil and I will handle that. In fact, I don't even remember what I said to you, Andrea, about the day Eugene died. I'm not going to talk about what went on there any more than I absolutely have to. Legal issues."

"Sharon …" Benjamin began.

"It's okay," she said, hand up as if to stop a round of applause. "I'm not asking for your gratitude. And don't feel like you have to comfort me."

"What do you know about how the pipe and the vial got into Carolyn's gym bag?" I asked.

"What do you mean?" she asked

"Benjamin found drug paraphernalia in Carolyn's gym bag."

"I don't know anything about that bag. What I knew is that once Carolyn started smoking pot, it was only a matter of time before she started using crack again. Look at the statistics. Somebody should have done something. Well, somebody did, but it wasn't me."

"How did you know where she died?"

"I'm busy, but I do have time to read the newspaper, Andrea."

She swiveled back around in her chair and picked up a textbook. "That's it folks. That's all she wrote. You can both go if you're done, or you can stay and watch me study. Whatever floats your boat."

Benjamin tugged on my hand to leave, but I snatched it back. I swung Sharon's chair around and got in her face. "Cecil's car was there. The police found a popcorn bag with his prints near where Carolyn died. How do you explain that?"

"I don't have to explain. A fluke? A slip in fate? Anyone can drive on Vernon Avenue. Anyone can like popcorn, Andrea."

"No, you're involved somehow. I'm not going to let it go. I'm going to be all over you like a bad rash."

A sly smile shaped her lips. "Bad rash, huh? You know what? I've got the cure. I think it's here on page 343." She held up her book.

I flung the door open on my way out. I think Benjamin was able to dodge it. Unfortunately for him, he would not be able to dodge the ride home.

We didn't exchange one word all the way back to the car. I imagined Benjamin was trying to figure out who he would support. His sister, whom he loved dearly, or me, the woman he was going to pledge to love for the rest of his life. I understood what he was going through, because, ironically I was going through something similar. Who would I ultimately put first? Carolyn or him—the man I wanted to spend the rest of my life with?

"She killed Carolyn," I said after we had driven three blocks and pulled onto Highway 40.

He maneuvered into traffic, eyes focused on the road. "Andrea? You and BJ gossiping about her pissed her off. What she said was payback. She told you that and apologized."

"As soon as she said it, part of me knew she was telling the truth. She can try to backtrack all she wants now, it's too late."

Benjamin groaned. "I don't know what to say to you except maybe you and I should get away for a weekend, because the stress of you trying to find Carolyn's murderer is starting to get to you. I would mention PMS, but I know you're liable to hit me if I go there. Besides, why would a medical student use a gun? Why didn't she offer Carolyn some bad crack or something like that?"

"Maybe you should ask her, but a gun is anonymous and it's quick, dirty and lethal."

"Well, but a well-placed needle has got to be all those things too, wouldn't you think?"

I looked in my lap and shook my head. "I don't have the answers. All I have is more questions. For example, how can I live married to you, knowing Sharon may have killed my sister and Eugene?"

Now he glanced at me. "What are you saying? Do you hear your-self? Are you going to hold our wedding hostage because of this … this need to have a place to hang your guilt and grief for Carolyn?"

"It's not that. Well, it is that, but I'm not crazy. Where there's smoke there's fire. Something is going on here. Sharon is not telling us everything she knows."

Benjamin changed lanes twice before he spoke. "What am I sup-posed to do, Andrea? Just tell me that. What do you want me to do? My sister was raped by your crazy-ass ex-boyfriend who you invited into our lives when you went to see him."

"Oh, so you do blame me after all? You lied before!"

"Well damn it, you're giving me no support through this!" He was as angry as I'd ever seen him. The veins in his neck and forehead popped. "Instead, you tell me Sharon killed two people when Cecil already confessed to killing Eugene and you have no proof about Carolyn. All you have is a smart-ass remark someone made in anger and your suspicions predicated by your guilt."

Yep, that summed it up. We didn't say another word all the way home. Where would this leave us? Gloria's words ran through my mind. "Andi, there may not be anyplace you and Ben can go from there."

Was she right?

CHAPTER 49
Benjamin

What I could read in Andrea's eyes was true. I only saw one side of Sharon. She and I were close and besides that, she was the only girl in a family of two brothers raised without a father. Even if we weren't especially close, I developed the habit of protecting her and believing in her a long time ago because of what she'd gone through.

Cecil could tell me what I needed to know to let us put this thing to rest for the sake of my pending marriage. I'd learned he'd posted bond to the tune of 75,000 bucks, the required ten percent of his bail.

I had to wait until his bookstore closed, but I was more than willing to do that. While I waited, I got hit on by two nice looking ladies who ranged in age from twenty to fifty. It made me smile and appreciate Andrea all the more. Having someone I loved who was exclusively mine was all I was trying to accomplish with getting married.

"So, what's up, man?" Cecil asked after the last customer left. We shook hands, and then our fists alternately pounded on top of each other's before we hugged. He looked the same as always, dreads below his shoulders pulled back into a ponytail this time, same crooked teeth and smile.

"Let me buy you some dinner or something, Cecil. I want to talk to you about Sharon."

"I'm not hungry, but we can get a drink a few blocks away. You want to follow me?"

I followed his Camry to a joint downtown with the word "Stages" lit up in blue lights in the window. The R&B music met us across the street. Inside, the clack of pool balls made me turn to scan the whole place, difficult to do in the dim light. It wasn't too crowded, but I would still leave smelling like cigarette smoke. We slid into the black bar chairs and ordered a couple of beers.

"I need to know what the real deal is, man," I said, after a muscular, no-nonsense barkeep set our brews in front of us. We thanked her.

Cecil wet his fingertips on the sweat of the mug. "Sharon went to see if she could get Eugene to cease and desist. She didn't like him showing up at your mother's crib like that." He took a gulp of the foaming beverage, then set it down.

"He raped her. She called me. I took my gun and shot him. The police are thinking that because I had to drive three hours to do it, that there's more to the story. But, let me ask you, if it was Andrea, wouldn't you have done the same thing?"

Shamefully, I almost smiled with relief. Cecil killed Eugene. Andrea needed to hear this. But, in the next second pain sliced through my misplaced joy; the full effect of what Sharon had gone through hit me again. "No doubt. Sharon has been through something like that once in her life. I'm glad somebody was able to stand up for her this time to at least avenge her, if not protect her."

"I know that, man. I know about what happened to her when she was a kid. That's part of the reason I did what I did."

I squeezed his arm so he would know I appreciated what he had done.

"I love Sharon, it's that simple. Whatever it takes. I mean, I've had my eye on her every since she was on the pom squad in high school, man."

Cecil's bookstore was right down the street from the deli my mom ran. Sharon had often spent time there when she was in high school.

"That was ten years ago. She's the woman I'm going to marry one day. I should have cut his sack off, but it was too late."

"What do you mean too late?"

"Oh, uh. Too late because it was over. The rape was over. So I did the next best thing and took his life." He looked down at his beer. "My pops is upset, though. He had to hock a lot of shit to help me make bail. I hate to see him suffer because of me."

"I know that's right. Sometimes we forget the ripple effects of the things we have to do." I recalled Andrea mentioning that when I first got back. I took out my checkbook and wrote a check for a thousand dollars.

"Whose idea was it not to go to the police?"

"Sharon's. She said a murder trial would be too onerous. We knew the shooting was justified, but the courts may not believe us—so, why not avoid going to trial if we could."

"Then why did you keep the gun, Cecil?"

"Yeah, I blew it. I was supposed to get rid of it. Sharon was royally pissed, but then I would have had to explain to my grandfather, I call him pops, that his gun had gone missing—it was registered to him."

"I see." I didn't yet, but I was working on it. "How's your grandfather holding up?"

Cecil nodded. "He's doing the best he can."

I gave him the check.

"Thanks, man, appreciate this," he said, folding the check and putting it in his shirt pocket.

"It was your grandfather's gun? You don't own one yourself?"

"Uh—no. Not anymore." He checked his watch. "Say, listen. Thanks for the beer—"

"Wait a minute." Suddenly, he was in a hurry to leave. We hadn't been here ten minutes. "Let me ask you this. Do you think Sharon had anything to do with Carolyn's murder?"

"Carolyn's murder?" The pool players shouted in disbelief and triumph, like I would depending on Cecil's answer. "Naw, man. How'd you come up with a question like that? That's your sister. Don't you know her?"

"She told Andrea she had. I'm trying to figure out what would make Sharon say those things. Any ideas?"

He looked at me with renewed interest. "What kinds of things did she say?"

"I don't remember exactly. How did a popcorn bag with your prints on it show up on Vernon?"

He shrugged. "I don't hang out that way. I'm stumped." He scratched his neck and sniffed, but never broke eye contact.

"In late February last year, did you lend Sharon your car?"

"You're talking almost a year ago. I don't remember. She borrows it a lot. That Eclipse she's driving has seen better days." He stood up and drained his mug. "I'm out."

I stood with him. "Yeah, okay man, no problem. Thanks for your time and thanks for being there for Sharon."

"Don't mention it. Hey, I'll see you at your wedding next month, if not before then."

"Definitely." Well, maybe, if there was a wedding. I sat down and finished my beer, thinking about Cecil's reluctance to talk and his inability to remember details. I left tired. Inside my car, I sat thinking one word—quicksand.

CHAPTER 50
Andrea

"Hi, Andi." Gloria hugged me as she traded the frigid outside air for the warmth inside my house.

"Hi, Gloria. Thanks for checking on me." She and BJ had front row seats when it came to the Andrea and Benjamin saga. I inhaled the soft scent of lavender in my friend's embrace. Her hands came to rest on my shoulders. She looked at me with dark, serious eyes.

"You've been crying, haven't you?" Gloria knew me well.

"Just a little."

"Have you heard from Benjamin?"

"Yeah, he called last night to tell me he talked to Cecil. Cecil admitted he killed Eugene because of what he did to Sharon and now Benjamin thinks everything should be explained to my satisfaction. It isn't because I owe it to Carolyn to see this through to the end."

I walked toward the kitchen. Gloria fell in step beside me.

She draped her white, puffed-up down ski jacket on the back of my red farm chair, then she helped herself to a diet soft drink from the fridge. She popped it open, looking around the kitchen, dropping her gaze to the white half-shutter at the window over the sink, and then she spotted the cookie tins. "Uh-oh. You've been baking. Your favorite stress reliever. I should have known."

I pushed my hair back and acknowledged my guilt with a weak smile.

"Three tins, Andi? Girl, be careful. You want to fit into that wedding dress if you decide to use it." She set her can on the counter and opened one tin inhaling the buttery oatmeal raisin goodness. "I better not," she said, replacing the lid, "but they sure look and smell good."

"They're not all for me."

"Who are they for?" We pulled out chairs at the table and sat across from each other."

"Mrs. Sherwood."

"You're going to mail them to her?"

"Or ..."

"Go there?"

"Well, she's by herself and blind. I told her I wouldn't forget her. Her son was ... unkind, especially in the end, but that doesn't have anything to do with her. She's always been wonderful to me. Besides, Romans 12 verse 10 says, 'Be devoted to one another in brotherly love. Honor one another above yourselves.'"

Gloria looked at me with a worried expression. "A change of pace might be what you need. You must feel like a mouse and Benjamin and Sharon are giant cats batting you back and forth. But, I've got to say, visiting yet another crime scene is not my idea of fun, even though his mother may be nice and that scripture appropriate. How about a Chicago shopping weekend instead?"

"That's an idea. I'll think about it. Are you hungry, Gloria? I made chili yesterday. It's always better the second day."

"No thanks, I've got my nails and hair in less than an hour, and then I'm going out this evening."

"Good. Anybody I know?"

"Yeah, Winston Peck," she said smiling.

"Get out!" He wouldn't be able to forget about Carolyn's case as long as he was seeing Gloria. That was a good thing, and if they hit it off, it would be gravy. Gloria deserved someone great in her life.

"He's an interesting man, Andi. I might have to do a discreet search of his house for camera equipment. Can't be too sure these days."

Gloria went on talking about Winston Peck, but my mind had hit a speed bump. Mrs. Sherwood had said there was camera equipment in her guest bedroom closet. Would the police have searched Mrs. Sherwood's house? Yes, they would have, based on proximity alone, or to look for a murder weapon.

237

"… so, with my history with men, I figure what do I have to— Andi? Are you listening?"

"What? Sorry. I was having a Eugene flashback. Did Michael ever mention if the Kentucky police found anything in Mrs. Sherwood's house?"

"No, but you know he doesn't tell me everything. What are you thinking about?"

"Nothing. I don't know." I shook my head to dismiss the subject, but something was percolating in the back of my brain, I just wasn't sure what.

Gloria looked at her watch and finished off her coke. "Okay, well, have you talked to your Bible class teacher? He's seen you through a lot worse than this."

Brother Ward had seen me through the death of my mother, the loss of Roy when Benjamin took him, Carolyn's drug use and death, and now … *I suppose he could see me through the death of a relationship, should it come to that.* "Not yet, I'll probably give him a call."

"You should do that." Her jacket swished through the air as she put it back on. "And don't forget, you've got me and BJ, and the gym is also your friend for stress relief."

I stood and smiled at her less than subtle hint. She smiled too.

"You're going to be alright, aren't you, Andi?" she asked, her smile replaced by unfettered seriousness.

"You know me. I'm nothing, if not resilient. I'll be fine."

CHAPTER 51
Benjamin

I woke up with Andrea on my mind. We hadn't seen each other in four days; not since we had gone to visit Sharon at her apartment. I threw back my bedcovers, picked up the phone and punched in her number. I told myself to keep it together, even though I knew the sound of her voice could still make me stutter like a nervous schoolboy. "You know what today is?" I knew she did, but it was my opening line anyway.

"Of course I know," Andrea said.

"Okay. I thought you might want to go to the cemetery today. I'll go with you." I picked up a dirty sock and dusted the blue ceramic lamp beside my bed while I pretended everything was fine.

Her response didn't come right away, but finally I heard, "All right."

I scored two points as my multipurpose sock made it into my wicker hamper. "I'll bring Roy, too. Say about one?"

"Okay."

I had written a short poem and had been helping Roy learn it for the past week. He'd recite it today at his mother's grave on the first anniversary of her death.

My mom and Mr. Elrod were ready on time. I'd asked them to join us. Andrea would appreciate them coming.

At the cemetery, Gloria and BJ getting out of the car with Andrea didn't surprise me, but I had called them to be sure. When Tim, Maryann, and the kids pulled up in their red family van, Andrea's eyes shimmered. She mouthed, "Thank you."

Tim led us in prayer, and then he asked Roy to recite his poem. Roy looked around at everyone and smiled before he let go of my hand. I don't think he understood the seriousness of the moment; he was busy enjoying the snowflakes that landed on his eyelashes. He carried a bouquet of yellow daisies in his mitten-covered hands as he stepped front and center.

> *I know you're looking down on me*
> *Making sure I'm okay*
> *I know a mother's love is like that*
> *It never goes away*
> *I miss you now Mommy*
> *I'll miss you as I grow*
> *These flowers are for you*
> *Because I love you so*

When Roy finished there were not enough tissues in St. Louis to catch the tears. Roy placed the flowers near his mother's headstone and returned to my side. Tim asked people who wanted to remember Carolyn to come say a few words.

Andrea went first. "So much potential, so much of your inner beauty the world will never get to see. I will always love you, Carolyn. I miss you."

Gloria went next. "Girlfriend, I can't even get my laugh on like I used to. It's not the same since you've been gone. I hope you are at peace."

BJ was crying so hard he couldn't speak, and then it was my turn.

"Carolyn," I looked down at the frozen ground a second, "I'm sorry I hurt you. You know that was never my intention. You will always be a part of me. I see you in our son every day. Rest in peace."

Tim led us in a standard hymn called "In the Garden." In twenty minutes, our memorial service for Carolyn was over. I felt good, freer for some reason.

We gathered at BJ's place. It was my first visit there. I wondered why he kept his fridge stocked with a vegetable and a cold cut platter, then it dawned on me that he had planned for us to come over. That was gracious of him. I hadn't thought that far ahead.

After we filled our plates, we congregated in his living room. The fireplace was inviting and the view of the Gateway Arch exceptional. Everybody, including the kids, seemed to feel at ease, especially after BJ poured out one small jar of his marble collection.

BJ passed around a couple of photo albums full of pictures of the four of them: Carolyn, Andrea, Gloria, and himself. Most of them I had never seen, particularly those of them in grade school and high school.

I studied Carolyn's high school graduation picture. The corners of her eyes crinkled with excitement, her smile wide. It was as if her energy could barely be contained in her body. I had forgotten how vibrant Carolyn had been, not to mention beautiful.

When my family left, I was surprised I didn't feel like an outcast among Gloria, BJ, and Andrea. It wasn't like the four of us had known each other all our lives, but it felt like Carolyn had written me a pass, admitting me to their inner circle. I didn't even freak when BJ patted my knee.

Later that night, when Andrea and I were alone at her place, I noticed a round glass vase filled with yellow and white daisies on the coffee table. "Why do you think that was Carolyn's favorite flower?" I asked.

"I asked her that once. She told me because they weren't afraid to run wild, and neither was she."

We laughed. "Some people follow a path and some people make a new one," I said. "Carolyn was into making new ones. If she'd lived, she would have done something special. I mean, besides Roy. Her time was gone way too soon."

Andrea nodded. Unintentionally, I had brought her sadness to the surface again. Her tears threatened, but she sniffed and turned away. I reached to comfort her, but I stopped, not sure what I should do. I was afraid she was going to ask me to leave any second.

"It's nippy out there," I said. "Some hot chocolate would be great, if you have any."

"It is cold," she agreed. I followed her into the kitchen and watched as she poured milk into a pan to heat. "It had to be twenty degrees at Carolyn's grave, but I actually felt warm. It was all that love people were sending out for my sister."

I leaned, my back against the sink, watching her as she worked around me, returning the milk, and then opening a cabinet to take down the chocolate. She was careful not to get too close or make extended eye contact.

"Roy did good, didn't he?" I commented.

She gave me her full attention then. "Oh, Roy is a natural. He is redoubtable, that's what he is."

"Redoubtable? How long have you been waiting to work that into a conversation?" I teased.

She laughed. "Years. I just meant Roy was awesome." Her eyes twinkled with pride and mirth, the tears gone. We sat at the table.

"He's a future actor," I said.

"Or politician."

"There's a difference?" When the laughter faded, rather than notice the elephant in the room, we sat tapping with our fingers and smiling forced smiles. After a few minutes though, we were sipping from our cups. The tension lessened as we soaked up the bittersweet warmth.

"Have you thought anymore about what Cecil told me?" I asked.

"Yes." She looked at me, pursed her lips and slowly nodded while she let the cup rotate in her hands. "What else did Cecil say?"

"Other than he shot Eugene?" I frowned, I hadn't expected questions. "Nothing really."

She nodded, apparently still in thought.

"What he said was important," I said. "We should keep the facts in mind." I got up and set my cup in the sink.

She brought her cup to the counter and stood in front of me. "Are you keeping the facts in mind, Benjamin? May I review them for you?"

She barely took a breath before she began her teacher-like rundown. I knew I was supposed to shut up and listen.

"Fact one. My sister and my ex-boyfriend, Carolyn and Eugene, are dead. What did they have in common besides me? You, Benjamin and your sister, Sharon." Her pointing index finger stopped a millimeter short of my chest.

"How were they killed? Fact Two. Both were killed with a .38."

I grabbed her poking fingers and pressed her hand to my heart. "Hold on a second, Andrea. I get where you're going with this, but nothing you say is going to convince me my sister is a killer. You have a lot of nerve really. You've never once said Carolyn was an unfit mother, yet you want me to believe Sharon killed someone?"

She pulled her pointing finger back as if the electric nature of my response had shocked her. "If I haven't said it before, then let me be clear. Carolyn, at one point in her life, was a drug addict and yes, she started smoking weed again, which possibly meant it was a matter of time before she was back to her crack addict ways so yes, Roy was in jeopardy."

She folded her arms. "When you took Roy, she got straight again before she nose-dived and could not make a recovery. I don't know, we'll never know if she could have stopped with the weed and been the mother Roy needed. As Roy's father, you did what you thought you needed to do, and I'm okay with that. Now, may I continue?"

I gestured for her to go on. "Knock yourself out."

She put her hands on her hips this time. "Fact Three. We don't know for sure where Sharon was when Carolyn was killed, but we do know her boyfriend's car and her boyfriend's prints showed up on Vernon Avenue." She was on a roll now, counting her facts off on her hand as she went.

"Fact Four. Sharon's boyfriend, a man who would jump at the chance to bathe in a bucket of her spit, claims to have killed Eugene after the gun turns up in his bookstore. A gun she could have borrowed at any time."

Cecil had it bad for Sharon, no doubt about that. But the gun business was pure fantasy on Andrea's part.

"Fact five. She has motive. What she endured as a little girl of four, I'm convinced has done something to her mind. She needs to protect Roy because no one protected her from a pedophile. She's taken on that role for Roy in some sick way." She dropped her hands and sighed. "And I'm the one denying the facts? I don't think so." She made a face that had more lines than Wal-Mart on Christmas Eve.

I put both hands on my hips. I needed a Superman stance to stay on my feet. "Are you saying Cecil is so whipped that he's going to risk giving up twenty years of his life in a Kentucky prison?"

"If the shoe fits. Besides, he won't do twenty years. Not if he has a competent attorney. They've already played the rape card or Cecil would be charged with murder now instead of manslaughter. Sharon knows something more about Carolyn's murder. It wouldn't surprise me if Cecil knows more than he's saying, too."

I searched her eyes, hoping mine didn't give away my suspicions about Cecil. "What ties Sharon to Carolyn's murder? There's nothing."

She dropped her gaze before looking at me again. "I can't make any concrete connections. No witnesses, no weapon."

I stood a minute, dredging for something new to say. Unable to find it, I went to get my coat.

"Benjamin?"

I stopped, but didn't turn around.

"Thank you for what you did today for Carolyn. That was lovely. The poem, and everyone coming. It meant a lot to me."

Walking on, I grabbed my coat and opened the door. She was right behind me, and I didn't want to leave it like this. I turned and buried my hands in her hair. My lips brushed one cheek, then the other, and then they made a trail to her mouth. I tasted chocolate and a hint of turkey, but there was something else—a hesitancy on her part that had never been there before. "Do you love me?"

"I do love you, Benjamin," she whispered.

"I love you, too, Andrea. Remember that." I turned up my collar against the snow and went home.

CHAPTER 52
Andrea

Four inches of snow had fallen overnight, and this morning, more flakes wanted to whitewash everything, but I couldn't let that happen. Sharon had to be stopped. She'd taken enough from me. She couldn't have Benjamin and Roy.

I took one hundred fifty wedding invitations, secured them in a lidded container and set Mrs. Sherwood's cookies on top of it. I carried the load to the backseat of my car. Optimistically, the post office was a stop on my list of things to do today, but something else was more pressing.

Streets had been plowed, but the snow kept drowning out the effect of the salt and sand. I traveled at a snail's pace, which was probably a good thing, since my brain was rife with questions.

All I knew is that I needed some kind of proof of Sharon's involvement in Carolyn's murder, and I'd have to search her apartment to find it. My plan was to go to the gym, wait for her, then take her key off the rack where many of the gym patrons left their keys while they worked out. Once I had them, I could get a copy made and return them without her being the wiser.

She'd said she came to the gym a minimum of three days a week. I didn't know which days for sure, but I was prepared to wait. If she didn't come today, I'd come back until I found her there. I'd seen her class schedule that day at her house, so that helped me know the hours she probably wouldn't be here. I parked between cars near the edge of the gym lot, with an eye on the only entrance.

Desperate times called for desperate measures, but I promised myself: if I didn't find anything in Sharon's apartment, I'd let it drop.

I'd write off what she'd said to me as the words of a wounded soul and nothing more. Benjamin and I would get married and live happily ever after.

Three hours into my wait, I'd gained increased respect for stake out work. Sheesh! I was going nuts from boredom, but then … there she was in her purple cloth coat going inside. Good. Luck was on my side. Maybe that was a good sign. Still, my heart exploded behind my ribs as I tried not to look too shifty-eyed, refusing to make direct eye contact with anyone. I got out of my car and followed at a discreet distance.

As soon as she was on the treadmill, which faced away from the key rack, I found the set of keys with the Griot Bookstore symbol—a plastic yellow book-dangling from them. The hardware store was ten minutes away. I could get the keys made and be back in half an hour, as long as my luck held. It did.

On the way home with my copies of Sharon's keys, I mailed Mrs. Sherwood's cookies, but decided to hold on to the invitations one more day.

After checking to make sure she was not home the next day, I let myself into Sharon's apartment. With shaky fingers, I stood perfectly still listening, but there were no security alarm beeps. I hadn't noticed an alarm panel when Benjamin and I were here before, but I needed to be careful.

Her apartment was immaculate, just as it had been the night Benjamin and I visited. I knew leaving it in such pristine condition would be a challenge.

Removing my coat and hat, I got to work, allowing myself thirty minutes as I had done yesterday. Not knowing what I hoped to find, I began by checking her bookshelves, her drawers, even her hamper to no avail.

The top of the closet held neatly lined storage boxes. In one box I found toys; a teddy bear, a mechanical Ferris wheel, a fire truck, and at the bottom of the collection, a necklace. Sharon was stocking up for her nieces and nephews, no doubt. I was about to replace the top when the necklace, loose at the bottom of the box, caught my eye a second time. It was a silver chain with a daisy pendant attached. The pendant had six tiny silver petals with a garnet stone in the center. I was certain I'd seen it before, but now was not the time to ponder where. I still hadn't found anything useful. Compelled, I slipped the necklace on and extended my search to her bedroom.

Sweating, I looked under her bed and mattress, trying not to disturb her spread any more than I had to. I looked under the bottom of each of her drawers, then pulled the whole chest away from the wall and looked to see if anything was behind it. Nothing. I turned over her Parson Chair. Nothing. Time was ticking.

I caught an image of myself in the dresser mirror and wondered if I had lost my mind. The frantic woman staring back at me panted, and her forehead glistened liked she'd smacked around a few tennis balls with Venus. Regardless, I touched the necklace and remembered it had been a present from my mom to Carolyn on her sixteenth birthday. How could I have forgotten that, and what was Sharon doing with it?

Back in the living room, I sat on her desk chair and slowly pivoted, taking everything in. The apartment was not that big. My eyes settled on the three canvas pictures stretched over a frame. Roy's picture in particular beckoned me. I pulled it away from the wall and looked behind it. A video tape had been secured to it. Why had Sharon hidden a video tape? Was this of me and Eugene? Was it of her and Cecil? Was it a tape of Roy's first Christmas? I could be of anything really, but if it was of Eugene and me, I didn't trust her to have it. I'd take it with me.

I headed to her tiny galley kitchen to look for a plastic bag for the tape and any kind of proof that Sharon had shot Carolyn. Six cabinets and three drawers later, I'd found nothing of interest, except a plastic bag. I looked in her refrigerator, and behind it before I gave up and returned to the living room. I was out of time.

Putting on my hat and coat, I looked around her apartment again with what I hoped was an objective eye. *That's it.* I shook my head in despair. I'd leave with the tape and the necklace, but nothing that tied Sharon to Carolyn's murder.

Back in my car again, part of me knew I should feel ashamed for this futile escapade; but, actually, I was proud of myself for doing everything I could do to solve my sister's murder. Gloria would give me a pat on the back and I felt sure Carolyn would, too. Benjamin, well Benjamin was another matter, but even he might understand I'd done what I needed to do and was finally at peace.

CHAPTER 53
Andrea

At home with my meager booty, I pulled back my key from the lock, disturbed. The lack of resistance told me the deadbolt was already disengaged. With my adrenaline flowing this morning, had I forgotten to lock my front door? I proceeded cautiously, frowning when I couldn't identify the clump, clump, clump sound I heard. My shoulders, hunched in apprehension, relaxed when I saw Benjamin emerge from the basement.

"Hey," he said, "what are you doing home this time of day?" His black work boots were heavy-duty, hence the noise on the uncarpeted basement stairs. He wore a black turtleneck under his orange work overalls and carried my snow shovel in his hand.

"Shouldn't I ask you that? You work for the street crews. In snowy weather like this, I thought they would need every extra hand."

"I switched shifts with somebody earlier this week. I'll go in later." He walked the ten feet to where I stood, rested the shovel near the door, and helped remove my coat. He hung it in the closet, taking my hat as well. I kept the bag with the video tape inside.

"I didn't see your car." I said.

"Sharon had to borrow it this morning. A friend dropped me off."

"Oh."

"I see you're wearing Carolyn's necklace. Be right back, wanted to get some wood for a fire."

"Benjamin," I yelled to him on the patio. "I'm glad you're here. We have to talk."

He came back in carrying the logs. "That's exactly why I'm here. I wanted to have a nice dinner waiting for you when you got home." He set the logs on the hearth with a clunk, then turned to me. "We're in danger of losing each other, Andrea, and I'm willing to do everything I can to stop that from happening."

My breathing sped up, keeping pace with the butterfly race in stomach. "I don't want that to happen either." After he lit the fire, he sat next to me on the couch, placing an arm around my shoulder. He pointed at my lap. "What's in the bag?"

Shifting to face him, it was time to come clean. "I have a confession."

Benjamin narrowed his eyes and tucked in his chin as if I'd told him aliens were coming to dinner. "I'm not going to like this, am I?"

Lifting the pendant from my breast, I said, "I took this from Sharon's apartment."

He glanced at the necklace, then into my eyes with incredulity. "You did what?"

"I was looking for proof to connect Sharon to Carolyn's murder, and I didn't find it."

"Andrea!" he growled, pushing up to get off the couch.

I grabbed his arm. "Wait, please hear me out."

His angry eyes danced across my face, but he remained seated.

"I was desperate, Benjamin. I broke into Sharon's apartment and all she had that spoke of Carolyn in any way was this necklace. The only other thing I found was a video tape and took that because I was afraid it might be of Eugene and me, and I wanted to destroy it."

"You broke into her apartment? That's where I'm stuck. I can't get past your first sentence. You broke into her apartment? How?"

I told him my means of entry while he shook his head in disgust.

"Okay, so you stole a necklace and a video tape from my sister. Now what?"

"I had to, Benjamin. I had to do everything I could on Carolyn's behalf, but I'm finished now."

"I sure hope you're finished. I love you, but I can't take one more accusation so I really, really need to be able to believe you, Andrea. You're sure you're ready to let it go. You promise?"

"I promise."

"You promise as in are finally going to mail the wedding invitations?"

"I promise, Benjamin and I meant to do that today anyway."

We exchanged a kiss and then he held up the tape. "And what about this?"

"Will you watch it with me? If it's me and Eugene I plan to toss it into that fire. If it's something else, would you help me return it?"

"No, we'll return it together. You'll need to tell Sharon what you did and apologize. The necklace, too. You can't just take it from her. How do you know Carolyn didn't give it her?"

"Okay, I guess that's fair. Put the tape in."

Both of us sat in shock and watched the overhead shot that appeared on the screen. Sharon's perky breasts moved up and down as she panted, her arched back helping to highlight them. Nothing about it said rape. Benjamin watched, shaking his head. Sharon wasn't resisting. Eugene's face buried between her legs made me think her orgasm was real.

He flipped Sharon over. She said something inaudible, but from then on the brutality increased. She begged him to stop, but that seemed to increase his ferociousness. It became too brutal to watch.

Visibly shaken, Benjamin pounded the power button to turn the VCR off. "What the hell? That bastard! Jesus Christ! Is this what you needed to see? Are you satisfied now, Andrea?"

"Why would Sharon have a tape of this?" I asked.

"It's—" he ran his head across his head, "it's—I guess it's her proof of the rape."

"Yeah …" I wanted to ask him if the first part looked consensual, but he'd just seen the same tape I had and this obviously hadn't occured to him. My perspective must be tainted.

"We've got to give this back to her. I'm sure her attorney will want it for Cecil's trial," Benjamin said.

Benjamin's Nextel work phone rang. He put up a finger to excuse himself.

The speakerphone was so loud I heard the guy on the other end say, "We're calling everybody in early, Dunn. The weather's turning to shit. How soon can you be here?"

Benjamin's gaze zig-zagged across my face while his hand reached out to push back my hair. "I'm not sure. Hold on a second. Andrea, can I take your car?"

"Of course."

He told his boss he'd be there as soon as he could.

"Wonder how much snow we'll get?" I asked.

"Plenty for a day off from school tomorrow, I know that much."

He kissed me once and then the warmth of his lips tingled my throat and neck. Reluctantly, we parted, but I held on as long as I could, planning never again to be the first to let go.

CHAPTER 54
Andrea

Pressing my forehead against the cool windowpane, I watched Benjamin leave in the heavy snow. Stretched past exhaustion, all I wanted was a nice cup of tea. After setting the kettle on, I sat at my kitchen table to think.

I wasn't sure why Eugene had been a threat to Sharon or for that matter, why Carolyn had been. I suspected it had something to do with her warped version of love, like I mentioned to Benjamin when he'd asked me what I thought her motive could be. When I looked at the puzzle, that explanation was on the only piece that fit.

Sharon was savvy enough to know that Eugene would push a record button and I didn't think she would have minded. It allowed her to set him up for a rape charge, just on the off chance her plans failed and she was caught. Being so far from home, I'm sure she felt out of her element and had a plan B to fall back on.

The kettle sang sounding like a time out whistle, reminding me I'd have to find a way to disabuse myself of such negative thinking about Sharon. Cecil would pay for Eugene's murder and that tape had nothing to do with Carolyn, so I would let it go. A promise is a promise.

I poured hot water over my tea bag, dipped the bag a few times, then returned to my chair at the table. I took a sip and tried to lose my thoughts in the snowy scene outside my kitchen window.

I snapped alert when I heard a door opening. "Benjamin? What did you forget?"

"You bitch!" I heard Sharon yell. "You stole my tape!" With the directed swoop of a homing pigeon, she migrated to the kitchen and hovered over me.

"Who did you show my tape to? What are you going to do with it?" Her questions targeted me like bullets.

My wildly beating heart cascaded toward fear, but stopped at loathing. A cold uneasiness shimmied up my back, but I rolled my shoulders and picked up my tea to shake it off. "Hi Sharon. You didn't tell Cecil about the first time with Eugene, did you? The part where you and he are, shall we say, blissfully engaged? Were you afraid Cecil might push the eject button on that pedestal he has you sitting on? Were you afraid you couldn't sucker him into going to jail for the crime you committed if he knew what really happened?"

Arms folded and head cocked to the side, she looked at me with mild interest. "What are you talking about? Eugene caught me off-guard; I couldn't believe his gall. He threatened to hurt me if I didn't cooperate, and I don't care if you believe me or not. That he could play me like a violin with his tongue was embarrassing, but now you and I have something special in common."

What a putrid thought. "I saw you whisper something in Eugene's ear. What did you tell him? 'No matter what I say or do, don't stop?'"

A slow smile crawled across her lips. "Why would I do that? He practically tore me apart."

"Why didn't you just shoot him, Sharon?"

"What do you mean? Cecil shot him."

"No, you killed him, but for some reason you didn't do it before the sex and you didn't destroy that tape."

To appear calm, I took another sip of tea when, in reality, I was anything but. "I know you now, Sharon. By the way, we aren't allowed to shoot drug addicts because they piss us off. There are laws against that sort of thing."

Her eyes, glistening with venom again, zeroed in on the pendant. She straightened her head and dropped her arms to her sides. "And your point?"

Setting my cup down with a clunk, I said, "This is my point. You are a cold-blooded killer." For a second, I pitied Sharon. She'd come without a coat. Her blue cashmere sweater and black corduroy pants were stylish, but I envisioned her in a standard-issue convict uniform. "Sharon, I know you love Benjamin and Roy, but you have gone so far over the line, you may never find your way back."

"You ingrate. You fucking ingrate!" She banged the palms of her hands down on the table shaking it. "Eugene was an asshole. He was one of those sick fucks who get off on victimizing people, just like that piece of shit who molested me."

With her face scrunched up in a self-righteous gloat, she said, "And, let me tell you about your precious Carolyn. Carolyn was probably going to overdose or die of AIDS in the next year of her life, and you sit there on your fat ass, preaching to me about what this screwed up society deems acceptable?"

Hammer blows reshaping my cranium could not have hurt more, but I wouldn't give her the satisfaction of flinching.

"Some fucking Girl Scout you are, Andrea. I'm not giving up my career because of your moral certitude. You give me that damn tape, and then go straight to hell!" She swiped the teacup and sent it shattering against the wall. "Give me my tape!" she demanded, her spittle landing on my forehead.

I snatched open a napkin and wiped my forehead while taking note of the tea crying down my wall. I turned to stare into treacherous eyes that reflected the flavors of her madness.

In the next second, Sharon settled at the table like we were good friends, about to catch up on old times. "The tape proves nothing and neither does the necklace. You've had your fun, Scooby-Doo, now give the tape back like a good little would-be sister-in-law, and we'll call it a day."

I thought about pouring hot teakettle water on her and seeing if such a wicked witch would melt.

"Sharon, how did you get Carolyn's necklace?"

"Oh, you'd like to know that, wouldn't you?" She wore what was becoming her classic sly smile. "Here's a thought. You give me my tape first, and I'll tell you what you want to know after that."

My heart squeezed with anxiety. If I gave her the tape, Cecil would never know she was a liar. He'd do the time for the murder she'd committed … but, I reminded myself again; that had nothing to do with Carolyn. Maybe Cecil knew the truth and it didn't matter. People will go through a lot in the name of love.

"Oh, I think I hear the gears clacking in your little brain," she said in a singsong voice, but when she spoke again, her voice was flat. "You don't want to mess with me, Andrea. You really don't. I have access to my stepfather's guns."

The threat was already clear to me, but Sharon obviously wanted to make sure I understood. She frowned in pretend sadness. "Being distraught over your sister's death, then being a murder suspect yourself, while juggling a tenuous romantic relationship with my brother is enough to push anyone over the edge. One day, poof!" She illustrated the "poof" with her fingers springing open to make a cloud shape. "One day, poor thing just couldn't take it anymore and killed herself."

I looked around for a makeshift weapon, but in my heart, I knew I wasn't a head basher. If I played along, got her to talk, maybe she'd trip up and tell me something I could use against her.

"All right. The tape is in the VCR," I said.

"Let's get it."

She followed me into the living room. I turned on the VCR and reached to remove the tape.

"No," Sharon said, "I want to make sure that's the right one. Push play."

Five seconds was all she needed to see. She held out her hand for me to give it to her.

I held the tape close to my chest. "I'll give you your tape back, but only after you tell me everything."

She gazed at the tape, and then up at me. I knew she was debating whether or not she should try to force it from me. I narrowed my eyes and summoned by best, "bring it on" expression. "You'll have a knock-down drag out fight on your hands, so don't even try it. I'm as motivated to kick your ass as you are to try and kick mine and I have home court advantage."

She flopped onto the couch, slouching against the back of it. "Carolyn gave the necklace to me. Did you notice all the other stuff in the box? Those were things she asked me to send Roy. She was convinced I knew where they were."

I slowly took my spot in the armchair. *Of course.* I hadn't been able to put it together before. Carolyn loved teddy bears and Ferris wheels, and I guess she figured there wasn't a boy on the planet who wouldn't get a kick out of a big red truck.

Sharon shrugged her shoulders. "Since she was high all the time, I didn't bother to remind her that Roy was a little boy and probably shouldn't wear flower necklaces."

I rubbed my fingertips across the daisy pendant. Our mother had given Carolyn the necklace, and Carolyn wanted Roy to have it. Roy would have it.

"I'll give those things to Roy in time," Sharon continued. "I want Roy to be happy. Contrary to what you think about me, Andrea, I'm not without compassion."

I could refute that, but I wanted to make sure the noose was good and tight when she finished talking.

"What about Eugene?" I asked.

"What about him? Eugene didn't have to die, but he fucked up, literally, as you saw in living color." I still didn't believe her.

"Why did you involve Cecil?"

She sat up and forward. "Get this. Flat tire. Debris from the house construction. Talk about inconvenient. Good thing my life's work prepared me to cope with a dead body, so it wasn't that bad. I took care of the first gun with Carolyn, and I should have taken care of the second one too, but Cecil said he'd handle it." She let out a snort. "Men. God love them. They need to be taken care of like babies."

That's it. She'd just admitted to killing Eugene before Cecil got there. That's what I had been waiting to hear, but I needed more. "Go on."

"After I had to call Cecil, I needed a story to tell him. I kept the tape, on the off chance I needed to prove what happened. It was my fail safe. What he did to me is clear. Erasing the first part won't be a problem, depending on what my lawyer thinks." She smiled her Evilina smile. "But, far be it from me to tamper with evidence until my lawyer gives the go ahead." Her fingers tapped impatiently against both knees.

Taking a deep breath, I asked the hardest question I had ever asked anyone. "And the first gun? What did you do with the first gun?"

"It's at the bottom of the Mississippi River in a bag of rocks and haven't you heard enough? I hope you have, because I'm through talking." She stood.

She had shot Carolyn. My adrenalin soared. *My God.* I'd have to live with that knowledge the rest of my life, but there was still no way to prove it. I didn't even bother to wipe away the warm tears that dripped onto my shirt.

"Sharon?" Benjamin spoke, appearing from nowhere. His gaze ricocheted between Sharon and me. I looked back and forth between them. Sharon's face was a caricature of shock—eyes and mouth wide-open—and I'm sure mine wasn't far from that. His face was a blob of features distorted with pain.

"Oh my God. You—you heard everything?" Sharon stammered. She lunged over the coffee table at me. "Bitch! You set me up!" The vase burst. The flowers on the coffee table took wings. Sharon landed on me. I landed on the armchair. The chair toppled over with me in it. The tape sailed through the air.

Sharon untangled herself and got to the tape. She ran past Benjamin, who had bent down to help me.

"Go! I'm all right." I urged him to catch up with her, even though my legs faltered in the air like those of an upside-down insect.

As soon as I could, I gave chase. They were just beyond the patio, kneeling in the snow. The tape had ended up on the patio floor near my mother's glider. I snatched it up, and then I watched them.

"Sharon, it's all right," Benjamin said. "It's going to be okay."

"She stole my tape, but you can't stop loving me, Benny." Sharon's voice, an octave higher than normal, sounded like it belonged to a lost little girl. "I wasn't going to let them hurt Roy."

"I understand," Benjamin said.

She placed her open palms on both sides of her brother's face. "I have to finish medical school. I have to finish! Mama will be so embarrassed, Benny. The whole family—"

"The whole family will understand. It'll be all right. I promise." Benjamin caught her hands in his, and slowly they rose to their feet.

"But I'm smart. I can finish. What did I do wrong? Roy deserves the chance I never had. Don't you see? Why should his drug-addicted mother get the chance to fuck up his life like our father fucked up mine? Carolyn lost that right, Benny."

"It's okay, Sharon," Benjamin repeated.

"And Eugene, I was just going to talk to Eugene, I swear. And then that son of a bitch hurt me. He was a user, Benny. Just like that bastard our father handed me over to. Eugene deserved what he got. We couldn't have scum like that coming close, threatening Roy."

They held on to each other for dear life, then Benjamin's eyes met mine. I turned away, it hurt too much to look at her.

I put the tape behind some canned goods in my pantry and called Detective Peck. I'd give it to him and let the police handle it. Benjamin wrapped Sharon in a blanket. She sat motionless near the fireplace. Her face, a mask of chocolate porcelain, hid whatever she was thinking.

A towel soaked up water as I collected the pieces of the broken vase. Benjamin helped clean up. He looked as desolate as I felt. The strewn daises supplied an appropriate epitaph for this evening's events.

"It seems inadequate to say, but I'm so sorry, Andrea. She's not well. She's ... troubled."

"Yes, she is. You heard all of it then?"

"Most of it. I came in just as the cup hit the wall or the shit hit the fan, however you want to look at it. I—uh… I heard the part about the gun being in the river."

A sob caught in my throat. I wondered why Benjamin was taking it so well. When I made eye contact, I saw it hadn't sunk in. His eyes held that distant look of someone whose body was here, but his thoughts were a zillion miles away. "The police are coming."

"Yeah, I heard you make the call. Will they send an ambulance?"

I nodded. Finished cleaning, I stuck my hands in my pockets, raising and lowering my shoulders. What made you come back?"

"I spotted her or rather spotted my car in the rearview mirror. I thought she was going to confront you about what you'd done, and I wanted to be here for you."

"I'm glad you did."

The three of us sat in an atmosphere so heavy, words could not lift it. Fat flakes fell outside, and the fire crackled inside, while the clock ticked on the mantel. Ten minutes passed. It was surreal. I thought if someone could make an award-winning musical with AIDS as the topic, just think what a smart producer could do with this story.

Twenty minutes passed. How long could an ambulance take to get here even in the snow? And where was Peck?

Benjamin finally spoke to me. "I saw the invitations in the car. What are you going to do with them now?"

A siren squall filled the space I might have used to answer him. Paramedics shuffled through eight inches of snow to ascertain the nature of the emergency. Sharon didn't answer when they tried to get information from her, so Benjamin filled them in. When one guy said he'd be right back with the stretcher, she stood up. Benjamin put his coat around her shoulders. As she passed me, our eyes locked.

"You should mail the invitations," she said. "Roy deserves two good parents. Don't you get it? That's all I ever wanted."

Benjamin brought up the rear on their way to the ambulance. He halted in front of me and put my car keys in my hand, then folded his hands over mine. We exchanged soulful looks before he opened his arms, and I molded myself into him.

"It'll be a miracle if this doesn't destroy everything good in my life," he whispered as he rested his lips against my forehead, and then he was gone.

CHAPTER 55
Benjamin

Getting married in a couple of weeks was out of the question. Getting married at all would be the challenge.

It was my first time back in Andrea's home since Sharon's confession. Roy's and Andrea's cheerful voices floated into the living room from the kitchen. A game of Chutes and Ladders muted in the background; they might as well have been playing it on Mars. That's how disconnected I felt from everything around me.

Ghosts sat with me in the living room while I struggled to regain my life focus. Sharon in jail, the family learning of the murders, me trying to cope with the reality that my sister killed two people on Roy's behalf—every time I tried to take it all in … I just shook my head. My sister had murdered the mother of my child and Eugene Sherwood. *Unbelievable.*

I sucked in a deep breath, held it, then let it out as I looked around me. Sharon was only thirty minutes away in jail until they moved her to Kentucky, but the sister I knew had died in this very room. How much of me died with her that day was yet to be determined. With Sharon's murder trial for the death of Eugene pending, she planned to plead guilty to manslaughter. Her attorney shared that he anticipated she'd receive five years tops because her rape defense was viable. Chances were, she'd never be charged with Carolyn's murder. All the prosecution had was circumstantial evidence. It consisted of the confession Andrea and I had heard, which Sharon could deny, and the missing gun from Cecil's bookstore that now made its home in the sludge of the Mississippi River.

A low TV murmur from the den meant it was time for Roy's afternoon cartoons. I heard him settling in to watch. Massaging my brow, I looked at my backpack. I'd planned to study today, but I hadn't even unzipped it. There was a good chance I'd have to drop out anyway. I couldn't concentrate.

Andrea looked in on me. "Why don't I make a fire?"

"No, don't," I told her, glancing in her direction. No need to replicate every detail of that night.

She pulled her red sweater closed as if she were cold, but I think she just needed something to do with her hands. Now that the truth had been uncovered, she was free from the invisible chains that had been dragging her down. I picked them up as quickly as she had shed them, and tried not to resent her for them.

"Please, talk to me," she said.

Shaking my head, I looked away. "Talking won't change anything. Maybe time passing will help. That's what people keep telling me anyway."

"We need to talk. Otherwise, you leave me on the outside. We said we were going to get each other through this, remember?"

I removed books from my backpack, but Andrea didn't leave me to begin my work. "Sharon admitted to putting the drug crap in Carolyn's gym bag." I could barely look at her.

"She did?" Andrea asked.

"That set everything into motion. Everybody's life changed course. How can you stand to look at me, Andrea?"

"Sharon's not mentally stable. That's got nothing to do with you. My feelings for you have never depended on outside influences."

I had to chuckle at that. "Outside influences? That's one way to look at it. Let's be real. I love you, but maybe this is too much for us to recover from."

She came over and sat next to me, touching my face briefly before placing her hands in her lap. "I love you. That will never change."

"Is love enough though? Can you imagine what our lives would be like if I'd never met Carolyn?"

"No, Benjamin. Don't do that. What if I had spent more time with Carolyn while our mother was dying of cancer and afterward? What if I'd followed Carolyn to her Narcotics Anonymous meetings to make sure she went to them? Don't go there, Benjamin. The "what if" game is a maze with no exit. We can't hold ourselves responsible for what our sisters did. Besides, what would our lives be without Roy?"

I put my elbows on my knees and let my face rest in the cradle my hands made. Pent-up frustration broke through. I felt Andrea rubbing my back and moisture trickling into my hands before I realized I was crying. When I took the tissue from Andrea's outstretched hand, I saw concern in her furrowed brow.

"I let her down," I explained. "All these years … I should've seen something. It's so unfair, Andrea."

Andrea shifted on the couch. Looking closely at her, I detected a tinge of hurt. "I'm sorry," I said. "You must be thinking about Carolyn."

"Both Sharon and Carolyn represent wasted potential," she said softly. "The difference is, Sharon has her life and a chance to repair it."

"That's true. We have to think carefully about the next steps we take. Won't being around me and my family be too painful?" We paused to consider this.

"With God's help, I can get past it, Benjamin. We both can. Forgiveness. It's the only answer for both of us. We need to look at it for what it is, but refuse to let it dictate our lives."

My heart thumped. I wasn't dead inside after all.

"If we can overcome this, nothing will ever stand in our way. It just means letting our religion and our spirituality work for us. Pastor Tolley saved my sanity when you were gone with Roy and Carolyn was doing drugs again. Maybe we could talk to her?"

"That's a good idea."

Andrea slid closer to me. Her hand glided up and down my arm. Then she kissed my ear, the top of my head, and my cheek. I wasn't oblivious to her attention, but I wasn't in the mood to be the recipient of sympathetic overtures.

She turned my face to hers, placing her lips on mine with ever increasing sensuality. The smoldering look in her eyes encouraged me, hurling my mind full steam into the moment.

I pulled Andrea into my lap without letting our lips part. My hands explored the softness of her full breasts, and I knew this was what I needed. I knew I could find comfort here and know I was still alive.

Suddenly she stopped. "Wait."

I attempted to bury her words and thoughts under another kiss. "It's okay. We'll go into the bedroom, and Roy will be all right with his cartoons for awhile." Sympathetic attention or not, I'd take it.

"No, I thought of something else." She pulled back. I'm sure she could feel the full extent of my disappointment. "We can't get married in two weeks, but we will get married soon. When we do, we won't be doing Carolyn or Sharon a disservice because we're moving forward with our lives. We shouldn't feel guilty."

I nodded at her insightfulness. One of the images bothering me was my having the nerve to reach for happiness while leaving Sharon in the dust. How could I move on with my life, while Sharon sat in a hole-in-the-wall with memories of dead bodies and shattered dreams for company?

"We are blessed that we can focus on something this wonderful and positive in the midst of this … tragedy," she said.

"And you can do that? Just like that?" I asked, amazed.

"I can't, not alone. But if I rely on God's grace—if we rely on God's grace, we can do this."

Pushing back her hair, I looked at her with tremendous love and a newfound respect for the power of God and what her religion meant to her. I wanted what she had. I wanted, no needed, that same kind of grace. "Yes, we are blessed. I certainly am. If I ever lose you, Andrea—"

Her eyes smiled back at me. "Shhh," she placed her fingers on my lips, "you're not going to lose me. You're never going to lose me."

My old "can do" spirit emerged. Andrea was being strong for me, but she needed that strength reciprocated.

I closed my hands over both of hers and spoke from my heart. "We are going to take it a day at a time, and we're going to be all right, Andrea. I promise you."

CHAPTER 56
Andrea

Five months later, July became a month of celebration. Benjamin finished his college courses and would graduate, and we were getting married.

On our wedding day, shades of Easter-egg blue filled the sky. The temperature was in the 70s, rare for summer in the Midwest, but not unheard of for the changeable St. Louis weather.

I smiled at my finished image in the full-length mirror. My dress, made from ivory satin, had metallic accent thread embroidered into a loose floral pattern across the surface. It came with a tight fitting jacket with long sleeves that covered my arms and came across the top part of my shoulders. It was perfect for an early spring wedding and luckily, it wasn't uncomfortable to wear in the air-conditioning of summer.

My mother had kept a few of her mother's hats. I inherited a triangular shaped white satin one with a blusher length veil. Age had transformed the white into ivory, so its use was practically predestined. It matched not only the color, but the sophistication of my dress and looked good with my long frizzy curls. It felt right to reach through generations and bring "something old" to the present.

Changing angles in the mirror, I placed my hand where a necklace could have gone, but remained happy with my decision to go without. The diamond bracelet Mrs. Elrod had insisted I wear helped complete the look. It became my "something borrowed."

The wedding party gathered in readiness. Gloria looked great in her strapless satin blue dress. BJ escorted Mrs. Elrod to her seat, and then the soft strains of a jazz melody signaled Gloria to begin.

Suddenly, I sensed Carolyn's presence. I actually turned to speak to her before I realized she wasn't there, not in the flesh anyway.

Lacy, Tim's older daughter, was next. She walked throwing rose petals high in the air from her basket. The most precious, innocent laugh imaginable resounded as she stopped each time to watch the petals flutter to the carpet like heavy bubbles.

Next, a solemn Roy holding his ring bearer pillow with both hands and walking oh-so-slowly, made his way down the aisle. He wore a black tux with a blue cummerbund, as did his dad, and Tim. The crowd cooed their delight.

Then I heard the drummer kick it up a notch. That was my cue. I repositioned my rainbow of spring flowers across my right arm. The ribbon around them was my "something blue." Brother Ward took my left arm, and I began the most jubilant stroll I can remember.

Standing inside the doors of the sanctuary, I came to a standstill, totally amazed. I wanted to clap and cry at the same time. The church's stained glass windows, the candlelight, and the music created a wonderfully pious, yet romantic ambience. Gloria and Mrs. Elrod had been right. This moment was worth every hint of uneasiness that had gone before it.

Seeing our guests turn to look at me reminded me I couldn't stand there all day. I needed to walk forward. At the opposite end of the aisle, Benjamin waited for me. Handsome and stately as always, he was luminous now. If skipping down the aisle to get to his side quicker had been an option, I would have done it. Instead, I took my time and walked slowly ahead with Benjamin's grin as my guiding star.

When we stood in front of the pastor, Brother Ward answered the way he should to give me away. Benjamin took my hand and whispered, "You look like an angel." He helped me ascend three steps to stand in front of Pastor Tolley on the chancel. She gave us a warm smile and began her "We are gathered here today" introduction.

After that, BJ sang "For You" standing below the platform behind us. Benjamin and I turned to watch him. His melodious voice filled the sanctuary with a love affirming spirit.

The ceremony continued. Soon Benjamin and I were vowing to live our lives for each other. We exchanged rings, and then an enthusiastic kiss.

As we got into our limousine that we shared with most of the wedding party, Benjamin squeezed my hand and winked at me. I winked back. We'd done it. We were husband and wife.

Roy, sitting across from us twisted his face, trying his best, but failing to get out a wink. We all laughed.

Benjamin's mother had offered to let Roy stay with them while we had some time for ourselves, but both Benjamin and I agreed there had been too many changes in his young life. After the reception, he'd come home with us, and the three of us would begin our new life as a family.

CHAPTER 57
Benjamin

After Andrea and I tucked Roy into his new bedroom, I turned to my wife. "Mrs. Dunn, you are one beautiful bride, did I tell you that?"

"Yes, you did, Mr. Dunn. You whispered it to me right there at the altar and about a hundred times at the reception."

"Okay, because you should absolutely know how absolutely gorgeous you are in that dress." I drank in the sight of her. When I had seen her coming toward me down the aisle, my knees had gone weak. As she stood beside me in front of the pastor and I looked into her eyes, I knew the path to this day had been worth every heartache. Being married to her was my dream come true.

"Thank you." Andrea laughed. "But you know what? As splendid as this dress is, I'm about ready to come out of it."

"Music to my ears. Come here." Grinning, I slipped the sleeves from her soft shoulders and danced her into our bedroom. I weaved my arms around her waist from behind and nuzzled the crook of her neck.

"Mmm, that's nice," she almost purred before she wiggled out of my embrace and turned to face me, holding up one index finger. "Uhh, just give me one second. I need a couple of Advil."

I groaned. "Really?" She had to be as nervous as I was, hence the headache, but I refused to let my apprehension show. We'd waited so long for this night.

"Yeah, it's just the stress of the day," she said, running her fingers through her hair. "It's a good stress, but ..."

"How about this instead?" I asked, massaging her neck.

"Mmmm." She closed her eyes and breathed deeply, letting her head lull forward.

"Baby, I know how to take the tension away. Let me."

Her eyes flew open, and I saw anxiety in them.

"Andrea, you already have my heart and my soul. Our love is strong. We belong together. After what we've been through, there's nothing to be nervous about."

Our lips met, and I watched her eyes flutter close. A slow sizzling heat enveloped us, hot enough to melt any lingering doubts.

I knelt before her, tossed her shoes aside and then slid my hand up her thighs to take off her stockings. They weren't panty hose, but were stockings held up with one of those garter belts over her white lace underwear. I wasn't used to undoing garters and fumbled.

Andrea smiled down at me. "That tickles." Her playful gaze and lusty laugh confirmed she wasn't nervous anymore, and neither was I. Finally, I rolled the stockings down and off.

Taking Andrea's hand, I twirled her around so I could unzip her dress and watch it fall to the floor in a rustling mound. She stepped out of it and into my arms.

I kissed her forehead, her eyes, and then I took a second to visually devour her ample breasts that struggled to stay contained in her white lace half bra. I unhooked her bra, letting them spill free.

With the palms of my hands, I massaged already stiff nipples, teasing them until Andrea bit her lip and sighed in pleasure. I bent down and bathed them with my tongue and lips, savoring her shivers of delight.

Andrea's eager hands opened my shirt and tugged it free from my pants, brushing against my rock hard erection. The simple touch of her fingers made my heart and body throb.

She made a slow descent to her knees while the sexy intensity in her eyes mesmerized me. She unzipped my pants and reached inside, catching the moisture on the tip of my manhood gently spreading it around before kneeling to thrill me with her tongue. I sucked in air and held my breath. As good as I was feeling, I was about to explode. But, I couldn't go out like an inexperienced teenager—not our first time together.

"No," my voice sounded husky, "let me please you. I've been needing to do this for so long."

Andrea stood and took off her panties in one smooth motion, rotating and undulating her hips in a sensual move that twisted my gut in a good way. I yanked off the rest of my clothes, never taking my eyes off her.

Gathering her in my arms, I gently lowered us to the bed. "You're incredible," I whispered in her ear.

She stroked my face in reply, her eyes shimmering.

My lips explored the hollow spaces in her neck, the fullness of her breasts and the roundness of her stomach. She gasped and whispered my name.

My kisses trailed down from her stomach to the place I'd labeled "Sweet Juncture". Knees wide, she propped herself up on her elbows, watching me pleasure her, making me harder than a day old biscuit.

Flushed, she threw back her head. "That's it, that's it. Benjamin, it's so good," she murmured, strangling the sheets in the grip of her hands before dissolving into trembling ecstasy.

She reached for me, impatiently clawing me into her arms. We kissed, losing ourselves in the rapture, and then I guided myself into something close to heaven. I moved deeper and deeper. Her hips thrust against mine in our own private symphony. Every nerve in my body tingled to her touch. Our eyes locked in perfect communion. Waves of passion threatened to drown us.

Breathing hard, we basked in the sweaty afterglow. Our laughter tumbled out on ragged exhales, as our fingers and hearts intertwined. This moment was as magical and as everlasting as our wedding vows. The light of both left the pain of the past in the shadows while the promise of our future shone bright.

"Benjamin, I love you so much. I'll always love you."

"I love you, too, Andrea." Those words would never express what I really felt. I'd have to find ones that would, because this was the kind of love I'd be telling our grandkids about.

Burning with need, we found our rhythm once more. Afterwards, we rested, cocooned in each other's arms, and quietly exhilarated in the knowledge that we could relive the essence of this night every day of our lives for as long as we lived.

ABOUT THE AUTHOR

Pamela Ridley writes novels that combine faith, romance, and often murder. She's also the author of several short stories, poems, and children's plays where the topics range from lost treasure to alien encounters. A teacher by profession and a native of St. Louis, Missouri, she currently resides in Maryland.

Excerpt from

CAUGHT UP

BY

DEATRI KING BEY

Release Date: February 2005

THE CATALYST

Miami, June 15

"This is not up for discussion, Rosa. You're not moving to Chicago." Ernesto stalked across her bedroom to the window. They'd moved to Miami when she was twelve to protect her from Harriet's drunken fits and distance himself from David.

"But, Daddy."

"The Senior Vice President of Marketing position was vacated a few months ago. I've held it for you to fill after your graduation." He checked his Rolex. "In two hours, you graduate and take your rightful place as one of my Senior Vice Presidents. Someday Bolívar International will be yours."

Rosa twirled the tresses beside her ear between her fingers.

He crossed his arms over his chest. "Whatever you're calculating, forget it."

She released the hair. "Let's talk about this like the two rational adults we are." She motioned toward her beanbag chairs. "Please take a seat."

"I thought I told you to get rid of those things."

"That would be my fuzzy, pink dice chairs."

"This room is in need of serious redecorating," he grumbled as he situated his large frame onto the chair across from Rosa. "Order new furniture before you leave for Italy, so it will be here when you return."

"When I return, it will be to Chicago, not Miami," she stated calmly. "And thank you, but I won't be accepting the Vice President position at this time."

His expression matched hers, stoic. "Are you saying you need a longer vacation, maybe a year off? You've worked hard, you deserve it. I'll keep the temporary replacement until you're ready."

"No. I'm saying I'm moving to Chicago when I return from Italy and starting a computer networking firm with the hundred thousand dollar trust Mom gave me."

"I'll expand Bolívar International to include a computer networking unit. You'll be its Vice President."

"That won't work, Daddy. I'd still be working for you. Just as I have since I was nine. I want to be on my own. I want to build and run my own company. That's also why I'm not using the trust you've set up for me. I want to build my company from the ground up."

Ernesto had never been as proud of Rosa as he was at this moment. He could remember, many years ago, when he'd purchased the technology firm that grew into Bolívar International. At the time, he'd wanted to be free of David to prove to himself that he could be a success on his own. "I admire that you wish to do this on your own, but run your company here. Not Chicago. You can't save Harriet." *Just as I can't save David.* He couldn't pinpoint the exact time it happened, but he no longer envied David's fire. He didn't want David's type of power, which was rooted in the fear of others. Ernesto craved the power that was rooted in respect: the respect he received for being an industry leader, the respect he received for improving the community, and most importantly, the respect he received from his daughter for being her hero.

Rosa looked away. He leaned forward and weaved his hands through her long, bushy, black hair. "Your mother has to save herself."

She rested her caramel cheek on his shoulder. "I know I can't make her stop drinking. But I miss her. Perhaps I can encourage her to seek help. I have to try. Please don't stop me."

Weighed down by family burdens, he knew he couldn't cut ties with David—just as Rosa couldn't cut ties with Harriet. "All right, I didn't get this far without knowing how to negotiate. You may go to Chicago and babysit your mother, but I expect you to stay up on Bolívar International business. And you will continue attending the strategy and status meetings. I want you ready when it's time for me to turn over the reins."

"Yes, sir." She backed away with a salute.

He chuckled with his own salute to her. "Go get ready for your graduation, soldier."

Later that night, David staggered across the hotel room, slurring, "I'm so proud of Rosa. *Mi* Rosa." He stumbled over nothing and fell onto the bed. "Damn, Ernesto, we did it. We're gonna pull this shit off."

Ernesto continued watching David from the chaise lounge in the corner. Though Rosa was going against his wishes, he was proud of her. "You need to sleep it off if you want to have a real discussion about Rosa, Paige and the DEA."

"My ass ain't drunk. What the hell's goin' on? You been actin' funny all night." He rolled onto his back. "Rosa's gonna be the head of the largest fuckin' drug syndicate ever! They won't know what hit 'em."

Ernesto hopped up from the chaise lounge. "What are you talking about? When did we ever agree to something like that?"

"What the fuck?" David stood with his arms out to his sides. "So you sayin' you don't remember the original deal?" Accent thickening, he harrumphed. "And I'm the one who's drunk? Don't let your white ass get this shit twisted, amigo. Not now. Not after we've come this far. Now when does Rosa return?"

Ernesto reined in his anger. Rosa was his to protect, and he had no intention of relinquishing control. "Four, maybe five months."

"Shit! My girl will finally be at her rightful place, by my side. You hear me, Ernesto? Rosa is my baby! When she returns, she'll be all mine!"

"She's mine!" Ernesto glared down on David. "No blurring of power! I decide what we do with Rosa!"

The two stood toe-to-toe staring at each other. Ernesto had never noticed just how short David really was. Ernesto was as tall for a man as David was short. Looking back, Ernesto realized David's presence had made him seem bigger than life. Ernesto internally chuckled at himself for all of the years he'd chosen to stand in this little man's shadow.

David drew in several deep breaths, calming himself. In Spanish, he said, "This is a time to celebrate our daughter. We have time to discuss Rosa's future when she returns from Europe. Grab a seat." He motioned to the chaise lounge, then sat on the bed.

Guard up at an all-time high, Ernesto took his seat. This was one fight David wouldn't win. He'd protect Rosa at all costs.

"We need to talk about the DEA," David continued in Spanish. "I've made sure those bastards won't bother you again. I know you want out, but I need you're ass to continue laundering for me. I don't trust anyone else with my money. And that fucking Barry Paige." David nodded his head "I'm thinking about having his ass whacked."

Unsure how to handle this new change-of-subject tactic of David's, Ernesto half-listened while figuring out what to do to protect Rosa.

"Damn, damn, damn!" Ernesto stormed into his study with

Harriet close behind. He regretted allowing her to stay with them for the few days she'd be in Miami for Rosa's graduation. He wouldn't have agreed, but having Harriet close meant so much to Rosa.

"You're just angry because Rosa's decided to move to Chicago to be with me," Harriet taunted. "There was no way you could keep her away from me. You're losing control over her, and you can't stand it."

"I never kept Rosa from you. Your drinking did. Now leave me alone, so I can think."

She pursed her lips. "I saw David at the graduation ceremony. He's getting closer and closer to telling Rosa the truth every day. Wait until she finds out her precious daddy is nothing but a lackey for a drug dealer."

"Shut the hell up! David isn't telling Rosa shit." He thumped his chest. "I'm her father, that's the only truth she'll ever know."

Harriet's drunken laugh filled the room. "Not if David has anything to say about it, lackey."

2006 Publication Schedule

January

A Lover's Legacy
Veronica Parker
1-58571-167-5
$9.95

Love Lasts Forever
Dominiqua Douglas
1-58571-187-X
$9.95

Under the Cherry
  Moon
Christal Jordan-Mims
1-58571-169-1
$12.95

February

Second Chances at Love
Cheris Hodges
1-58571-188-8
$9.95

Enchanted Desire
Wanda Y. Thomas
1-58571-176-4
$9.95

Caught Up
Deatri King Bey
1-58571-178-0
$12.95

March

I'm Gonna Make You
  Love Me
Gwyneth Bolton
1-58571-181-0
$9.95

Through the Fire
Seressia Glass
1-58571-173-X
$9.95

Notes When Summer
  Ends
Beverly Lauderdale
1-58571-180-2
$12.95

April

Sin and Surrender
J.M. Jeffries
1-58571-189-6
$9.95

Unearthing Passions
Elaine Sims
1-58571-184-5
$9.95

Between Tears
Pamela Ridley
1-58571-179-9
$12.95

May

Misty Blue
Dyanne Davis
1-58571-186-1
$9.95

Ironic
Pamela Leigh Starr
1-58571-168-3
$9.95

Cricket's Serenade
Carolita Blythe
1-58571-183-7
$12.95

June

Cupid
Barbara Keaton
1-58571-174-8
$9.95

Havana Sunrise
Kymberly Hunt
1-58571-182-9
$9.95

2006 Publication Schedule (continued)

July

Love Me Carefully
A.C. Arthur
1-58571-177-2
$9.95

No Ordinary Love
Angela Weaver
1-58571-198-5
$9.95

Rehoboth Road
Anita Ballard-Jones
1-58571-196-9
$12.95

August

Scent of Rain
Annetta P. Lee
158571-199-3
$9.95

Love in High Gear
Charlotte Roy
158571-185-3
$9.95

Rise of the Phoenix
Kenneth Whetstone
1-58571-197-7
$12.95

September

The Business of Love
Cheris Hodges
1-58571-193-4
$9.95

Rock Star
Rosyln Hardy Holcomb
1-58571-200-0
$9.95

A Dead Man Speaks
Lisa Jones Johnson
1-58571-203-5
$12.95

October

Rivers of the Soul-Part 1
Leslie Esdaile
1-58571-223-X
$9.95

A Dangerous Woman
J.M. Jeffries
1-58571-195-0
$9.95

Sinful Intentions
Crystal Rhodes
1-58571-201-9
$12.95

November

Only You
Crystal Hubbard
1-58571-208-6
$9.95

Ebony Eyes
Kei Swanson
1-58571-194-2
$9.95

Still Waters Run Deep –
Part 2
Leslie Esdaile
1-58571-224-8
$9.95

December

Let's Get It On
Dyanne Davis
1-58571-210-8
$9.95

Nights Over Egypt
Barbara Keaton
1-58571-192-6
$9.95

A Perfect Place to Pray
I.L. Goodwin
1-58571-202-7
$12.95

Other Genesis Press, Inc. Titles

A Dangerous Deception	J.M. Jeffries	$8.95
A Dangerous Love	J.M. Jeffries	$8.95
A Dangerous Obsession	J.M. Jeffries	$8.95
A Drummer's Beat to Mend	Kei Swanson	$9.95
A Happy Life	Charlotte Harris	$9.95
A Heart's Awakening	Veronica Parker	$9.95
A Lark on the Wing	Phyliss Hamilton	$9.95
A Love of Her Own	Cheris F. Hodges	$9.95
A Love to Cherish	Beverly Clark	$8.95
A Risk of Rain	Dar Tomlinson	$8.95
A Twist of Fate	Beverly Clark	$8.95
A Will to Love	Angie Daniels	$9.95
Acquisitions	Kimberley White	$8.95
Across	Carol Payne	$12.95
After the Vows	Leslie Esdaile	$10.95
(Summer Anthology)	T.T. Henderson	
	Jacqueline Thomas	
Again My Love	Kayla Perrin	$10.95
Against the Wind	Gwynne Forster	$8.95
All I Ask	Barbara Keaton	$8.95
Ambrosia	T.T. Henderson	$8.95
An Unfinished Love Affair	Barbara Keaton	$8.95
And Then Came You	Dorothy Elizabeth Love	$8.95
Angel's Paradise	Janice Angelique	$9.95
At Last	Lisa G. Riley	$8.95
Best of Friends	Natalie Dunbar	$8.95
Beyond the Rapture	Beverly Clark	$9.95
Blaze	Barbara Keaton	$9.95
Blood Lust	J. M. Jeffries	$9.95
Bodyguard	Andrea Jackson	$9.95
Boss of Me	Diana Nyad	$8.95
Bound by Love	Beverly Clark	$8.95
Breeze	Robin Hampton Allen	$10.95

Other Genesis Press, Inc. Titles (continued)

Broken	Dar Tomlinson	$24.95
By Design	Barbara Keaton	$8.95
Cajun Heat	Charlene Berry	$8.95
Careless Whispers	Rochelle Alers	$8.95
Cats & Other Tales	Marilyn Wagner	$8.95
Caught in a Trap	Andre Michelle	$8.95
Caught Up In the Rapture	Lisa G. Riley	$9.95
Cautious Heart	Cheris F Hodges	$8.95
Chances	Pamela Leigh Starr	$8.95
Cherish the Flame	Beverly Clark	$8.95
Class Reunion	Irma Jenkins/John Brown	$12.95
Code Name: Diva	J.M. Jeffries	$9.95
Conquering Dr. Wexler's Heart	Kimberley White	$9.95
Crossing Paths, Tempting Memories	Dorothy Elizabeth Love	$9.95
Cypress Whisperings	Phyllis Hamilton	$8.95
Dark Embrace	Crystal Wilson Harris	$8.95
Dark Storm Rising	Chinelu Moore	$10.95
Daughter of the Wind	Joan Xian	$8.95
Deadly Sacrifice	Jack Kean	$22.95
Designer Passion	Dar Tomlinson	$8.95
Dreamtective	Liz Swados	$5.95
Ebony Butterfly II	Delilah Dawson	$14.95
Echoes of Yesterday	Beverly Clark	$9.95
Eden's Garden	Elizabeth Rose	$8.95
Everlastin' Love	Gay G. Gunn	$8.95
Everlasting Moments	Dorothy Elizabeth Love	$8.95
Everything and More	Sinclair Lebeau	$8.95
Everything but Love	Natalie Dunbar	$8.95
Eve's Prescription	Edwina Martin Arnold	$8.95
Falling	Natalie Dunbar	$9.95
Fate	Pamela Leigh Starr	$8.95
Finding Isabella	A.J. Garrotto	$8.95

Other Genesis Press, Inc. Titles (continued)

Forbidden Quest	Dar Tomlinson	$10.95
Forever Love	Wanda Thomas	$8.95
From the Ashes	Kathleen Suzanne	$8.95
	Jeanne Sumerix	
Gentle Yearning	Rochelle Alers	$10.95
Glory of Love	Sinclair LeBeau	$10.95
Go Gentle into that Good Night	Malcom Boyd	$12.95
Goldengroove	Mary Beth Craft	$16.95
Groove, Bang, and Jive	Steve Cannon	$8.99
Hand in Glove	Andrea Jackson	$9.95
Hard to Love	Kimberley White	$9.95
Hart & Soul	Angie Daniels	$8.95
Heartbeat	Stephanie Bedwell-Grime	$8.95
Hearts Remember	M. Loui Quezada	$8.95
Hidden Memories	Robin Allen	$10.95
Higher Ground	Leah Latimer	$19.95
Hitler, the War, and the Pope	Ronald Rychiak	$26.95
How to Write a Romance	Kathryn Falk	$18.95
I Married a Reclining Chair	Lisa M. Fuhs	$8.95
Indigo After Dark Vol. I	Nia Dixon/Angelique	$10.95
Indigo After Dark Vol. II	Dolores Bundy/Cole Riley	$10.95
Indigo After Dark Vol. III	Montana Blue/Coco Morena	$10.95
Indigo After Dark Vol. IV	Cassandra Colt/	$14.95
	Diana Richeaux	
Indigo After Dark Vol. V	Delilah Dawson	$14.95
Icie	Pamela Leigh Starr	$8.95
I'll Be Your Shelter	Giselle Carmichael	$8.95
I'll Paint a Sun	A.J. Garrotto	$9.95
Illusions	Pamela Leigh Starr	$8.95
Indiscretions	Donna Hill	$8.95
Intentional Mistakes	Michele Sudler	$9.95
Interlude	Donna Hill	$8.95
Intimate Intentions	Angie Daniels	$8.95

Other Genesis Press, Inc. Titles (continued)

Jolie's Surrender	Edwina Martin-Arnold	$8.95
Kiss or Keep	Debra Phillips	$8.95
Lace	Giselle Carmichael	$9.95
Last Train to Memphis	Elsa Cook	$12.95
Lasting Valor	Ken Olsen	$24.95
Let Us Prey	Hunter Lundy	$25.95
Life Is Never As It Seems	J.J. Michael	$12.95
Lighter Shade of Brown	Vicki Andrews	$8.95
Love Always	Mildred E. Riley	$10.95
Love Doesn't Come Easy	Charlyne Dickerson	$8.95
Love Unveiled	Gloria Greene	$10.95
Love's Deception	Charlene Berry	$10.95
Love's Destiny	M. Loui Quezada	$8.95
Mae's Promise	Melody Walcott	$8.95
Magnolia Sunset	Giselle Carmichael	$8.95
Matters of Life and Death	Lesego Malepe, Ph.D.	$15.95
Meant to Be	Jeanne Sumerix	$8.95
Midnight Clear	Leslie Esdaile	$10.95
(Anthology)	Gwynne Forster	
	Carmen Green	
	Monica Jackson	
Midnight Magic	Gwynne Forster	$8.95
Midnight Peril	Vicki Andrews	$10.95
Misconceptions	Pamela Leigh Starr	$9.95
Montgomery's Children	Richard Perry	$14.95
My Buffalo Soldier	Barbara B. K. Reeves	$8.95
Naked Soul	Gwynne Forster	$8.95
Next to Last Chance	Louisa Dixon	$24.95
No Apologies	Seressia Glass	$8.95
No Commitment Required	Seressia Glass	$8.95
No Regrets	Mildred E. Riley	$8.95
Nowhere to Run	Gay G. Gunn	$10.95
O Bed! O Breakfast!	Rob Kuehnle	$14.95

Other Genesis Press, Inc. Titles (continued)

Object of His Desire	A. C. Arthur	$8.95
Office Policy	A. C. Arthur	$9.95
Once in a Blue Moon	Dorianne Cole	$9.95
One Day at a Time	Bella McFarland	$8.95
Outside Chance	Louisa Dixon	$24.95
Passion	T.T. Henderson	$10.95
Passion's Blood	Cherif Fortin	$22.95
Passion's Journey	Wanda Thomas	$8.95
Past Promises	Jahmel West	$8.95
Path of Fire	T.T. Henderson	$8.95
Path of Thorns	Annetta P. Lee	$9.95
Peace Be Still	Colette Haywood	$12.95
Picture Perfect	Reon Carter	$8.95
Playing for Keeps	Stephanie Salinas	$8.95
Pride & Joi	Gay G. Gunn	$15.95
Pride & Joi	Gay G. Gunn	$8.95
Promises to Keep	Alicia Wiggins	$8.95
Quiet Storm	Donna Hill	$10.95
Reckless Surrender	Rochelle Alers	$6.95
Red Polka Dot in a World of Plaid	Varian Johnson	$12.95
Reluctant Captive	Joyce Jackson	$8.95
Rendezvous with Fate	Jeanne Sumerix	$8.95
Revelations	Cheris F. Hodges	$8.95
Rivers of the Soul	Leslie Esdaile	$8.95
Rocky Mountain Romance	Kathleen Suzanne	$8.95
Rooms of the Heart	Donna Hill	$8.95
Rough on Rats and Tough on Cats	Chris Parker	$12.95
Secret Library Vol. 1	Nina Sheridan	$18.95
Secret Library Vol. 2	Cassandra Colt	$8.95
Shades of Brown	Denise Becker	$8.95
Shades of Desire	Monica White	$8.95

Other Genesis Press, Inc. Titles (continued)

Shadows in the Moonlight	Jeanne Sumerix	$8.95
Sin	Crystal Rhodes	$8.95
So Amazing	Sinclair LeBeau	$8.95
Somebody's Someone	Sinclair LeBeau	$8.95
Someone to Love	Alicia Wiggins	$8.95
Song in the Park	Martin Brant	$15.95
Soul Eyes	Wayne L. Wilson	$12.95
Soul to Soul	Donna Hill	$8.95
Southern Comfort	J.M. Jeffries	$8.95
Still the Storm	Sharon Robinson	$8.95
Still Waters Run Deep	Leslie Esdaile	$8.95
Stories to Excite You	Anna Forrest/Divine	$14.95
Subtle Secrets	Wanda Y. Thomas	$8.95
Suddenly You	Crystal Hubbard	$9.95
Sweet Repercussions	Kimberley White	$9.95
Sweet Tomorrows	Kimberly White	$8.95
Taken by You	Dorothy Elizabeth Love	$9.95
Tattooed Tears	T. T. Henderson	$8.95
The Color Line	Lizzette Grayson Carter	$9.95
The Color of Trouble	Dyanne Davis	$8.95
The Disappearance of Allison Jones	Kayla Perrin	$5.95
The Honey Dipper's Legacy	Pannell-Allen	$14.95
The Joker's Love Tune	Sidney Rickman	$15.95
The Little Pretender	Barbara Cartland	$10.95
The Love We Had	Natalie Dunbar	$8.95
The Man Who Could Fly	Bob & Milana Beamon	$18.95
The Missing Link	Charlyne Dickerson	$8.95
The Price of Love	Sinclair LeBeau	$8.95
The Smoking Life	Ilene Barth	$29.95
The Words of the Pitcher	Kei Swanson	$8.95
Three Wishes	Seressia Glass	$8.95
Ties That Bind	Kathleen Suzanne	$8.95
Tiger Woods	Libby Hughes	$5.95

Other Genesis Press, Inc. Titles (continued)

Time is of the Essence	Angie Daniels	$9.95
Timeless Devotion	Bella McFarland	$9.95
Tomorrow's Promise	Leslie Esdaile	$8.95
Truly Inseparable	Wanda Y. Thomas	$8.95
Unbreak My Heart	Dar Tomlinson	$8.95
Uncommon Prayer	Kenneth Swanson	$9.95
Unconditional	A.C. Arthur	$9.95
Unconditional Love	Alicia Wiggins	$8.95
Until Death Do Us Part	Susan Paul	$8.95
Vows of Passion	Bella McFarland	$9.95
Wedding Gown	Dyanne Davis	$8.95
What's Under Benjamin's Bed	Sandra Schaffer	$8.95
When Dreams Float	Dorothy Elizabeth Love	$8.95
Whispers in the Night	Dorothy Elizabeth Love	$8.95
Whispers in the Sand	LaFlorya Gauthier	$10.95
Wild Ravens	Altonya Washington	$9.95
Yesterday Is Gone	Beverly Clark	$10.95
Yesterday's Dreams, Tomorrow's Promises	Reon Laudat	$8.95
Your Precious Love	Sinclair LeBeau	$8.95

Order Form

Mail to: Genesis Press, Inc.
P.O. Box 101
Columbus, MS 39703

Name _____
Address _____
City/State _____ Zip _____
Telephone _____

Ship to (if different from above)
Name _____
Address _____
City/State _____ Zip _____
Telephone _____

Credit Card Information
Credit Card # _____ ☐ Visa ☐ Mastercard
Expiration Date (mm/yy) _____ ☐ AmEx ☐ Discover

Qty.	Author	Title	Price	Total

Use this order form, or call 1-888-INDIGO-1	Total for books _____
	Shipping and handling: $5 first two books, $1 each additional book _____
	Total S & H _____
	Total amount enclosed _____
	Mississippi residents add 7% sales tax